Praise for Becky Harmon

Listen to Your Heart

Listen to Your Heart is filled with the off-again, never really on-again, allure of the two main characters' romance. Jemini is convinced she must return to her fulfilling career and unrewarding personal life because she feels Riverview holds nothing for her but unpleasant memories of rejection by her beloved grandmother. Stephanie's job as deputy sheriff makes for an interesting subplot as she pursues a peeping tom. Harmon's story has enough mischief and intrigue to keep readers interested. This tale of romance—with a little mystery thrown in for good measure—is an attention-grabbing read that will entertain readers to the end.

- Lambda Literary Review

Tangled Mark

I took pleasure in reading this book and it was exciting to see such sexiness written into an action book. If you are an action reader and looking for a book with engagement and some passionate loving, I'd recommend this book.

- The Lesbian Review

This is a refreshing combination of storyline. Despite the hot romance the action adventure keeps on coming. The plot is full of suspense and definitely creates an intriguing page turner. Excellent debut novel, look forward to reading more, whether it is a sequel/series or something completely different. Definitely one to watch.

- Lesbian Reading Room

This debut novel is an action-packed tale of security agents Nikki Mitchell and Mel Carter, who both work for the same private agency but on opposing sides. Both agents are strong women; they did not get the jobs they have by not being so. And yet what Harmon reveals as we learn more about them is that they each carry vulnerabilities when it comes to matters of the heart. A good debut, and I'm intrigued to see what Harmon will write next.

- *Rainbow Book Reviews*

GUARDIAN ANGEL

About the Author

Becky Harmon was born and raised just south of the Mason-Dixon Line. Though she considers herself to be a Northerner, she moved south in search of warmth. She shares her life with her partner, two cats, and Manny the dog. If you haven't seen Manny before, you can check out plenty of pictures on Becky's Facebook page.

Romance has always been Becky's first love and when she's not writing it, she's reading it. Her previous published works, *Tangled Mark*, *New Additions*, *Illegal Contact*, *Listen to Your Heart*, and *Brace for Impact* are available from Bella Books.

You can reach Becky at beckyharmon2015@yahoo.com.

Other Bella Books by Becky Harmon

Brace for Impact
Listen to Your Heart
Illegal Contact
New Additions
Tangled Mark

GUARDIAN ANGEL

BECKY HARMON

BELLA
B O O K S
2020

Bella Books, Inc.
P.O. Box 10543
Tallahassee, FL 32302

Printed in the United States of America on acid-free paper.

First Bella Books Edition 2020

Editor: Medora MacDougall
Cover Designer: Judith Fellows

ISBN: 978-1-64247-101-4

Acknowledgments

As always, I am extremely grateful to Linda and Jessica Hill for providing the opportunity for me to share another book. I am honored to have the Bella Books logo on all of my books and to be in the company of so many fantastic authors.

To my coworkers who put up with my ramblings about what I'm writing now and to Angela for anxiously pestering me for the next book to read. And, of course, to Kathy for her always ingenious title suggestions. Even this one that came before the idea of what to write.

Many thanks to those that work behind the scenes at Bella Books with their tireless ideas and enthusiasm. You make Bella the best!

Thank you, Medora MacDougall, for once again helping me craft a work of art.

I had a few ideas for this cover. Thank you, Judy, for combining them all into one.

As with everything I write, there is a lot of fiction. I tried to keep the relevant information pertaining to Mauritania as factual as possible. As for the US embassy in Mauritania, the general description is real, but everything else including the people were all modified to fit the story. Any errors are all mine.

To all the readers, thank you for taking another ride with me. I hope you enjoy this one as much as I did.

Lastly, to my DB, thank you for never growing bored with just one more read-through.

Dedication

To every American who has ever worked on foreign soil.
Thank you for your service.

CHAPTER ONE

Ambassador Elizabeth Turner paced her office, resisting the urge to duck as gunfire erupted once again on the street outside the embassy. She glanced through the four-pane window installed to protect her from physical hazards and tried to locate the gunman in the gathered crowd. Taking a deep breath, she repeated in her head the words that had become her mantra over the last week. *I will not be driven out of my embassy.*

"Madam Ambassador," her assistant called through the open door. "Mr. Flagler is on line one."

"Thank you, Chloe."

She picked up the headset and switched it on before placing it over her head so she could continue to pace. "Hey, Vince. How are you?"

"I was fine until the secretary of state called me."

"She did, huh? What did she have to say?"

"She said you needed protection, Ellie."

She frowned at the serious tone of his voice. She had expected his call but maybe not quite this soon. Her situation wasn't dire enough to make the six o'clock news back home yet. Apparently her earlier phone call with the secretary of state hadn't gone as well as she had thought.

"Tell me what's going on and I'll send whatever you need," he continued.

Vince had been her surrogate big brother from the day he had joined her father's embassy detail as a young Central Intelligence agent. At fifteen, she hadn't completely understood the dangers of living in Africa. Mauritania was simply her home. Vince had readily added her personal safety to his already heavy load of responsibilities.

Twenty years later when she left her position at the Central Intelligence Agency—a career inspired, in part, by his example— she had considered joining his private security company. Flagler Security worked for and with the US government as well as more clandestine operations around the world. She had seen enough of the secretive behind-the-scenes operations and had instead opted to run for the United States Senate.

"Ellie?"

"Madam Secretary may have exaggerated my situation. A crowd has gathered outside the embassy gates, but I'm completely safe behind my bulletproof glass."

"Your embassy security isn't able to engage offensively to protect you, but my agents can. I'll send Angel's team. That's forty agents, but I can easily send more."

"Hold on a minute, Vince. I don't want to escalate things. Except for a little unfocused gunfire, we haven't been threatened."

"Yet."

"Yet," she conceded. "If we increase security with trigger-happy—"

"I take offense to that, Madam Ambassador. My agents are well-trained, and they know how to hold their fire until the response is needed."

She struggled to keep her frustration out of her voice. "I'm sorry, Vince. I'm afraid more troops on display will heighten the resistance. I think it'll all blow over on its own."

"When did it start?"

"Just over a week ago. Groups started to appear randomly and within a few days they were staying through the night." She sighed. "Yesterday they began backing up their chanting with occasional bursts of gunfire into the air."

"Did you pull your staff in?"

"Yes, everyone has been advised to remain inside the embassy gates."

"Angel's my best negotiator. Maybe that's what you're missing."

"I'm listening," she said hesitantly.

"How about if I send ten, but keep another ten waiting in-country in case they're needed."

"I can live with that."

"That's all I want to accomplish, Madam Ambassador."

She chuckled. "You always were such a charmer."

"Too bad my efforts were wasted on you."

She could hear the smile in his voice as he said goodbye, promising to call her when Angel's itinerary had been planned. This wasn't the first time Vince had stepped in to rescue her from a difficult situation in Mauritania. That had happened several decades earlier when she had accompanied Ameera, the prettiest girl in school, to the local street market for pizza. She would never forget the look of surprise on his face when he had run into them in the Marche Capitale. Although she had been there many times with her father, she wasn't supposed to traverse the streets of Nouakchott by herself, let alone use public transportation to do so.

She and Ameera had been helping each other grasp their native languages. Ameera's father, a local hire at the embassy, had been encouraged to allow her to attend the American International School of Nouakchott, which was located on embassy grounds. English was the language of instruction, but students were expected to know French and the local dialect, Hassaniya Arabic, as well.

The school closed before noon on Fridays so the Mauritanian boys could attend prayer at the local mosque with their fathers.

Ameera had been told to return straight home after their tutoring session, but instead she suggested they go for pizza in the market. Few restaurants were open on Friday afternoons, but Ameera knew of one near her house.

Taking public transportation was a normal way of life for Ameera, and neither teenager realized it might not be safe for Ellie. Her pale skin stood out like a lighthouse beacon on a clear night and drew many curious and potentially threatening stares. Despite Ameera's attempts to put everyone at ease, the harsh comments were hurtful and frightening to Ellie. She had been scared and very relieved to see Vince, even if it meant she was in trouble.

Ellie pulled off her headset and stepped to the door of her office, abstractedly wondering what had happened to Ameera. She should try to find out but not today.

"Chloe."

Chloe Allen sat with her back to the wall and with a direct visual on the doors that led into and joined their offices. Opposite her desk was a sofa that was more for décor than comfort. The last night or so, though, she had seen some of Chloe's embassy friends lounging on it while they waited for Chloe to finish her work for the evening. It wasn't a normal occurrence and she understood being restricted to the embassy had changed everyone's way of life.

Chloe's blond hair was pulled away from her face with several decorative barrettes; her fingernails, though not long, were painted a vibrant blue to match her outfit. Ellie estimated that she wasn't more than an inch or so taller than her own five foot eight, but Chloe always wore heels which put her closer to six feet.

Chloe's neck was bent as she concentrated on the computer monitor on her desk. She was barely twenty-five and had a rosy morning-fresh complexion no matter the time of day. These factors combined to make Ellie feel much older than she really was whenever she was around her. Their conversations were superficial and they were still getting to know each other, but she had managed to get Chloe to talk long enough to know that her mom was a marine. Chloe had moved from base to base her entire life, some overseas and some in the States.

"Chloe," she said again, raising her voice only enough to gain the young woman's attention.

Chloe jumped to her feet. "Yes, ma'am."

Ellie motioned her back into the chair. She still wasn't accustomed to the way her staff responded to her. She had repeatedly asked her staff to call her Ellie, but they were still as formal as the day she had arrived at the embassy six months ago.

"Please call Sergeant Miller and ask him to come see me when he gets a chance. No rush. Whenever he's free is fine."

"Yes, ma'am. I'll call him right now."

She returned to her office as Chloe picked up her phone. Though most meeting rooms in the embassy contained pillows for seating to make their local guests feel more comfortable, she was pleased that her office here on the second floor had been outfitted with couches for her comfort.

She sank into her chair and spun to look out at the crowd beneath her window. Not for the first time, she wished she could pick up the phone and call her father. His knowledge of embassies and the challenges she faced would certainly be welcome. She felt the niggling thought that she had reacted to his death the same way he had reacted to her mother's passing— by running away to a country where she could re-create their happiest of memories. She pushed the thoughts aside. Now wasn't the time for her delve into the past or second-guess her decisions.

She would need to brief her staff on the changes that were coming. They probably wouldn't be surprised that she was increasing security. When the picketing had started, she had requested that all embassy employees consider relocating their families to inside the embassy rather than returning to their homes throughout the city. At the time, she thought it was a temporary precaution, but the sporadic gunfire had ended up transforming her request into an order.

The marines and the diplomatic security agents that protected them did an outstanding job, so she wasn't looking forward to her conversation with Sergeant Miller. She respected him and the job he did and didn't imagine he would be very happy with a private security agency sending in reinforcements.

Sergeant Shane Miller was on his second three-year tour as a member of the Marine Corps Embassy Security Group. As the highest-ranking marine on embassy staff, he handled all security-related communications with her. He was always formal during his contacts with her and she felt like she needed to always maintain a professional demeanor with him as well. She longed for someone she could discuss ideas with. Maybe the Flagler agent would be someone she could use as a sounding board. Maybe she could bring him into her inner fold and she wouldn't always have to be the ambassador.

* * *

The wind whipped through Angel McTaggart's hair as she stared through her binoculars. She didn't need her sniper rifle for today's simulation. Her voice was the only weapon she required.

"You're dead, Johnson," she said softly. The microphone running along her cheek relayed her message to both sides of the mock battlefield.

"Stiner, what are you laughing at?" She frowned as the tall, red-headed man quickly dove for cover. "Too late. You're dead too, Stiner."

She hated Friday afternoon maneuvers. It was hard for the agents to keep their heads in the game. They were anxious to start the weekend and she couldn't really blame them.

Taking a deep breath, she barked into the microphone. "Everyone freeze. Remain in your current position."

She glanced down at the forty agents below her. From the observation post high above the fake town Flagler had built for practice maneuvers, she could see almost all of them. She needed them to take every drill seriously. How they performed as they trained was how they would react in real situations. She let her binoculars dangle on the strap around her neck as she glanced at her watch. They had two more hours reserved at this site and she wanted to end their week on a positive note.

"Alpha Team, return to your rally point. Bravo Team, return to your original protected positions. We're going to start this exercise again. If I spot you, then you get to run it again. Those that meet their objective can head home for the weekend."

Her announcement was met with cheers. They now had motivation to complete the course properly.

"Move," she ordered.

She watched the agents scamper like ants below her as they all returned to their starting positions.

"Here we go again. The clock is ticking," she said, restarting the exercise.

Alpha Team moved slowly toward the first building they needed to clear, and she was pleased to see each agent carefully locating cover or concealment before moving to a new position.

Her phone rang and she grabbed it from her belt. Switching her headset microphone to mute, she held the phone to her ear.

"I'm busy."

"Too bad." Tamara Bowden's voice boomed in her ear. "I'm about to make you busier."

She held back a groan. Her teams wouldn't be headed home tonight after all. "I'll be there in thirty."

"That's fine."

She placed her phone back on her belt and turned her microphone back on. "Rally in the town square immediately."

She removed her headset but not before she heard the groans of her team. They knew a rally meant training had ended, but their day was only beginning.

CHAPTER TWO

Angel slid onto the hard, plastic classroom chair and focused her attention on the woman standing in front of her. At fifty-three, Tamara Bowden was tall and athletic with the ability to command a room with only a glance. At Vince's side Tamara had guided, praised, consoled, and instructed agents at Flagler Security for over twenty years.

As she had thousands of times, she watched Tamara remove the elastic hair tie holding her blond ponytail and carelessly secure it again. As a teenager, she once had grown her hair long to emulate her. After her parents had passed away, Tamara and Vince had become her role models. As she got older, Vince had changed from caregiver to mentor. Tamara was always around, but she maintained a working relationship with Angel, offering a strong female example of what Angel could do with her career and always reminding her that she could do anything her male counterparts did.

Working her way up through the ranks, Angel performed and then ran basic security and protection details as well as clandestine operations. She never used her relationship with Vince to gain favors or receive better assignments; she was willing to go anywhere and do anything that was asked of her. Now she led a team of forty men and women.

Tamara slapped an eight-by-ten glossy color photo on the desk in front of her. "Ambassador Elizabeth Turner."

It wasn't a close-up, but even so Angel found herself captivated by the mosaic pattern of the ambassador's eyes. In only a second, she was transported from the classroom to the nearby emerald waters of the Gulf of Mexico. There the bright sun, periodically covered by fluffy white clouds, illumined the algae hidden beneath the surface of the water. Dark green, light green, and a variety of shades of blue, their hues all swirled together to protect secrets hidden within them.

She mentally shook her head. Being distracted on occasion wasn't unusual, but giving in to random thoughts like these was unlike her. She sat back and studied the publicity shot in front of her, noting that Ambassador Turner wasn't wearing a power suit as most female politicians did. Dark blue pants and a creamy off-white blouse with only three buttons at the top gave her a casual, genuine appearance.

Angel was surprised to feel an interest stir in her that she hadn't felt in a long time. Women were a hindrance, something she preferred not to be bothered by. The ambassador was an attractive woman, but she was drawn more toward her turquoise and emerald eyes. There was a deep hollowness within them that she felt a strange longing to fill.

She could feel Tamara's eyes drilling into her and lifted her head. She saw the flash of a questioning look before Tamara began her briefing.

"Our embassy in Mauritania is at risk of being attacked. The crowd of protesters is growing every day and random gunfire has started to erupt. Vince believes a show of force would settle things down, but Ambassador Turner disagrees. They've met in the middle. You'll take a team of ten directly to the embassy to work with the marines. Leave twenty agents here for rotation in case the job lasts longer than expected. The remaining ten

members of your team will position north of Nouakchott."
Tamara pointed to a location on the map of Africa behind her.
"Exact coordinates are in the file."

"Their response time from that location?" she asked.

Tamara's hesitation was brief but obvious. "Approximately thirty minutes."

"That's not really an adequate response time."

She met Tamara's eyes, waiting to see if she would call her out for her criticism. What she saw surprised her—hesitancy with maybe a little sympathy, which Tamara didn't hide in her words.

"I voiced the same concern this morning. I was told to make it work."

Angel frowned. It was unlike Vince to put her team at such a disadvantage. "How large is the crowd?"

"It's irrelevant. Your team of ten will be the only response unless tensions escalate."

She nodded her acknowledgment of Tamara's instruction and moved on to her next concern. "Do I have control of the backup team?"

Tamara's silence answered her question.

Her gut clenched with foreboding. She didn't like any of this. If boots on the ground couldn't call in backup then what good was having them nearby? Not that she considered thirty minutes response time as nearby anyway. Getting permission through the chain of command would take even longer. She never hesitated to speak her mind, especially if the safety of her team was in jeopardy, but she also knew when to remain silent and accept her orders.

She nodded again and stood. "I'll prepare my team."

Tamara handed her the closed file as she passed.

Angel stepped into the empty hallway and leaned against the wall. Something felt funny about this mission. She had always been able to count on Vince to make sure every detail was properly covered and assigned to the best team. This wouldn't be her first venture into the political world on foreign soil, but this would be the first time working with a female ambassador.

Especially one as attractive as Ambassador Turner. Despite her concerns, there was a part of her that was looking forward to this mission.

* * *

"Madam Ambassador?"

"Yes, please come in, Shane." Ellie stood and motioned for Sergeant Shane Miller to take one of the seats in front of her desk. The call from Vince had just come in advising of the Flagler team's imminent arrival and now she searched for a tactical way to relay the information.

"What can I do for you, ma'am?" he asked politely.

She studied his lean face. He was the perfect marine. His uniform was pressed and clearly worn with pride. His hair was cut short in traditional military style. There wasn't enough on the top of his head to identify its color, but his eyebrows and the shadow on his chin showed the dark strands.

She knew from past conversations that he had two sons living with his wife in the States. Though US troops on embassy detail could bring their spouses and children, he had chosen not too. He had never been forthcoming with his reasons, and she had never felt the need to question him, knowing how hard it had been to convince her father to allow her to join him here after her mother's death. She had liked the boarding school in Switzerland and she loved to ski, but the shock of being shipped there by her father was too much to handle on top of learning to adapt to life without her mother. Her father had selected the post in Mauritania to help himself get over the loss, she knew. It was a country in endless need of assistance, a place where he could make a difference. Which was one of the many reasons she had volunteered to be here now.

She paced in front of her desk, struggling to find the proper words to inform Shane of the private security force on its way to join them. She didn't want to undermine his authority and she certainly wasn't questioning his or his marines' ability, but—

"Ma'am, just lay it out and we'll deal with it."

She smiled. She loved his clear-cut, we-can-handle-it attitude. She took a seat in the other chair in front of her desk and turned toward him. "The secretary of state is concerned for our safety."

"Well, your safety is the reason we're here. Is she sending FAST?"

Ellie shook her head. Active aggression was required before the Marine Fleet Anti-Terrorism Security Team was deployed and apparently the disturbance outside was considered only a small-scale irritation to most of the politicians in Washington.

"Right," he said, nodding his head. "Not considered a large-scale aggression yet. Does she want to send more troops?"

"She did, but she couldn't get approval for the funds."

He shrugged. "We're a small post and normally things are fairly quiet here."

As if on cue, gunfire erupted from the street outside.

She watched his face tense. "Do you need to go check on things?"

"No, ma'am. My men will call me if I'm needed. Please continue."

"Are you familiar with Flagler Security?"

"Sure. I've worked with a few of their staff on other details."

She sighed. Maybe this wouldn't be as hard as she had envisioned. "Great. Vince Flagler is sending us a team of ten to supplement your staff."

"Only ten? They couldn't spare more?"

She laughed. "I was afraid you would feel that I didn't have confidence in you or your team, so I lobbied for as few as possible."

Shane shook his head. "I'm happy to have the help. Do you know who they're sending?"

"I can't remember the last name, but Angel, I believe, was the first name."

"Oh, right. That makes sense. The Guardian Angel."

"Guardian Angel? Do you know him?"

"I know of *her*. She's an excellent sniper. Now she mostly deals with volatile groups, negotiating, and crowd control.

Never been lucky enough to work with her though." He stood. "When should we expect them?"

"They're scheduled to arrive in the morning. Bring this Angel person directly to my office and the three of us can make a plan."

"Yes, ma'am."

She watched him leave and then returned to her chair behind the desk. Turning it, she looked out the window. For the last week constantly appraising the situation and trying to anticipate what the future might bring had been her regular practice.

At first glance, the men gathered below didn't appear threatening, but somewhere in their midst was the rifle or rifles responsible for the sporadic gunfire. They stood in one massive group that stretched from sidewalk to crumbling sidewalk, parting slowly whenever it was necessary to allow a vehicle to pass. She couldn't see any difference in their demeanor from earlier in the week, but apparently Shane did. He seemed to readily accept the assistance being offered, and she wondered how worried he really was.

Her thoughts turned to the woman who would be leading the security detail and her curiosity grew. Guardian Angel. She picked up her secure line, bypassing Chloe, and dialed the direct number to the CIA office she had worked in for many years.

"Agent Cutter's office," a pleasant feminine voice announced. "Would you like to leave a message?"

"This is Ambassador Turner. I'd like to speak with Agent Cutter, please."

"Yes, ma'am. Please hold."

Several seconds passed while Ellie debated the logic in making this phone call. Though she trusted Micalah, she knew secrets weren't always kept and she didn't want to get off on a bad start with the woman Vince had chosen to head the protection detail. Before she could change her mind, her friend's voice came on the line.

"Ellie!"

"Thanks for taking my call. I know you have better things to do, but I have a personal favor."

"I thought you'd never ask. I'm ready and willing," Micalah teased.

"Do you ever take a break?"

"Lighten up, Ellie. You know I'm only joking." Her tone turned serious. "What do you need?"

"Any information you can find on a Flagler Security agent named Angel."

"Angel McTaggart?"

"I'm not sure. They call her the guardian angel?"

"Yep, that's McTaggart. Why do you want information on her?"

"Vince is sending her team to back up my security."

Micalah was silent for several seconds, and Ellie knew she had said too much. When Micalah spoke again, her voice was filled with concern.

"What's going on, Ellie?"

She released an audible sigh. Another friend hell-bent on protecting her. "A small crowd has gathered outside the embassy. Vince is reinforcing the boots on the ground. Everything is fine."

"It doesn't sound fine. Is there gunfire?"

"Occasionally."

"I don't like this. It sounds more like rioters to me. Why don't you leave for a while? Come back to the States for a visit."

"I refuse to be driven from my home," she easily spoke the words she had only said in her mind.

"That's ridiculous," Micalah chastised. "Will you be saying that when they overrun your marines and storm the embassy like they did in Benghazi?"

"If the threat intensifies, I'll leave, but I can't jump ship every time things get a little uncomfortable. I'm in a country that's not always friendly and I have to put a strong face forward to get anything accomplished."

"Maybe I should come for a visit."

"Please, no," she groaned. "I don't need you to babysit me. I have a staff of marines and Diplomatic Security, and the Flagler agents will arrive tomorrow."

"Okay, but if anything changes I'll be on the first plane."

"If you want to help, send me the information on Agent McTaggart."

"I'm sure we have a complete file. Do you want that or only background?"

She bit her tongue. She wanted the complete file, but her stomach knotted at the intrusiveness. She knew firsthand how deep the CIA could go. After she had announced her run for the US Senate, information from her many background checks had been leaked to multiple news outlets. From interviews with the grade school principal who had expelled her for fighting to the friend she had once smoked marijuana with in college. Fortunately for her, the attempt at a negative spin had provided the voters with a personal view of her that quite possibly had won her the election. Taking a deep breath, she vowed to let the Flagler agent speak for herself especially about anything not pertaining to her job qualifications. "Just the background is fine."

"I'm going to send it all. If it bothers your morals, you don't have to open anything but the background."

"Thanks, Micalah. I'll talk to you soon."

"You bet you will. I'm going to be checking on you."

She hung up quickly before Micalah could change her mind and decide she did need her protection. She looked out the window again at the crowd. They were chanting and waving their arms. She couldn't tell what they were saying, but it was probably something about death to America. She studied the men closest to the gates. Their clothing was simple, and they didn't look like radical extremists. She laughed at herself. What *did* radical extremists look like? Some of the protesters carried signs or banners, but she still couldn't see any weapons.

She knew there had been horrific events at US embassies over the last decade, and thanks to her years in the CIA she knew how quickly a peaceful protest could turn deadly. It wasn't always possible to see what was brewing. She was trained to recognize global hot spots and deep down she understood why everyone was concerned about her, but that didn't mean she was ready to tuck her tail and run. She had plans for this country. Plans to make it a better place for all of its citizens. A plan to end slavery and child abuse. A plan to save lives.

CHAPTER THREE

Angel stuffed her toiletry kit into her duffel and zipped it. Closing the window on the fall breeze blowing in from the Gulf Coast, she looked around her small two-room apartment. Vince had designed it and he had an identical one across the hall. After one too many back-to-back missions, he had found her sleeping on the wooden bench in the locker room. Two weeks later, they moved into their new apartments in the rear of the Flagler headquarters building.

Tucked into a wooded area on the panhandle of Florida, this huge one-story building was used by soldiers in the 1800s. The Spanish-style design provided a surrounding stucco wall that led to the tiled courtyard entrance. Dozens of native and imported palm trees were scattered around the grounds like silent sentries, greeting her each time she returned. On a windy day she could smell the salt in the air from Pensacola Beach. She was proud to call this building, with its arched windows and clay-tile roof, home.

One day she would have a place of her own, though. One with lots of horses. It had been her mother's dream and now it was hers. When she was little, before her mother had gotten sick, they had lived beside a horse farm. Evenings and weekends were spent riding and grooming the horses. She liked that horses didn't try to hide their moods and that they didn't ask a lot of questions. Unlike most of the women she had tried to date.

The social world outside of Flagler was something she chose to avoid. She wasn't antisocial, but if she was honest maybe she was a little asocial. She interacted when it was necessary and could be quite charming at times, at least that's what she had been told by more than one person in the past. But given the choice, she would stay away from dating and social events. Not because they made her nervous or uncomfortable, but because she preferred the peacefulness of being alone.

A solitary life on the horse farm was all in the future. A retirement plan. For now the few personal items she owned barely filled the apartment and she felt comfortable here. Vince took advantage of her being onsite and if she wasn't out on a mission he put her to work providing intelligence or coordination for other teams. He often hinted at her job becoming more administrative, but she loved what she did too much to think about a time when she wouldn't be doing it.

"Hey, Tag, you ready?" Eric Fleming, one of her team leaders, called as he knocked on her open door. He was an inch or two shorter than her six-foot frame, but his shoulders were broad and his arms bulged with huge biceps. He liked to work out and could be found in the gym at all hours.

He was single and, like her, he preferred the company of other Flagler agents to that of anyone in the outside world. His dark curly hair barely touched the collar of his uniform shirt. Its unruliness was a contrast to his starched tactical uniform and freshly polished black boots.

She picked up her duffel and backpack.

"Everyone's returned?" she asked as they walked toward the briefing room.

She had given the twenty men and woman who would be accompanying her a few hours to return home and visit with their families. The others had remained to prepare equipment since they would be able to return to their families later that evening.

Eric nodded. "Shroder was the last to arrive."

She couldn't help but smile. Jim Shroder was dependable and disciplined but always the last to arrive.

She stepped into the briefing room and dropped her bags by the door. She looked around the room at the men and woman in various stages of undress and relaxation. Like her and Eric, they each wore a variation of the Flagler official dark blue tactical uniform—cargo pants, a Flagler-embossed polo shirt with a button-down shirt to go over it as needed, and boots. Making eye contact with her team leaders, she headed for the front of the room. When she turned, she wasn't surprised that the chaos from moments ago had vanished and rows of eager faces awaited her instructions.

"We're headed to the Islamic Republic of Mauritania. For those that don't know, it's on the northwest coast of Africa. It's a country about the size of Egypt or six times the size of Florida." She pointed to the map on the wall behind her. "Eric's team will be team one and positioned with me at the US embassy in Nouakchott, the capital. Currently, there is a crowd of protesters on the street outside. Random gunfire has been heard, but it has not been deemed a threat yet."

She walked the length of the room while she talked. It was a habit she had developed to make sure each team member was listening. She watched their eyes follow her as she paced. "Our mission is to protect the ambassador and her staff. Mauritania borders Mali, where al-Qaida and the Islamic Maghreb are active, so the risk of terrorist activity is great." She held up her hand to stop any questions that might be coming. "At this point there is no reason to assume the gathered crowd is connected to any terrorist group. They have not made a public statement or given themselves a name."

She looked at the attentive faces around her. Terrorism was a part of everyone's life these days and even more so for this organization of men and women. They trusted her and for the moment she had curbed their concern for what they were going to face. She only hoped the information was accurate. She would make her own determinations once she was on the ground.

"Ninety percent of Mauritania is desert. The northern portion is part of the Sahara. The population is sparse in this area, roads are few and far between, and travel is limited. We will remain in the populated areas, but we'll need to keep in mind that there is a curfew for Westerners."

She turned to address the leader of her second team, Sarah Duncan. As usual, Sarah's shoulder-length hair was stuffed under a Boston Red Sox cap but a few curly, red strands stuck out. At five foot five, she was one of the shortest members of Angel's teams. Over the years, she had earned respect with a resilient vivaciousness. She was often referred to as Flagler's Energizer Bunny.

"Sarah, your team will be at a remote location approximately thirty minutes from the embassy, so setting up and maintaining communications will be a top priority."

She saw the questions in Sarah's eyes but continued, knowing Sarah wouldn't ask them unless they were alone. "Our plane departs in two hours. Travel will be courtesy of Flagler so you will be responsible for your own weapons." This news brought smiles to the faces around her. Not only was normal commercial travel slow, but special arrangements had to be made for weapons. "The two active teams will assemble in the parking lot in thirty minutes. Everyone else, stay prepared. Team leaders, stay behind for additional information. Everyone else is dismissed."

The room erupted as the agents grabbed their luggage and hurried into the hall. For the next twenty minutes, she laid out the specifics of their mission to the team leaders. She was clear and concise, leaving no room for questions. Then she sent them to prepare their teams.

She made her way to the weapons room and signed out her lightweight Five-seven pistol, along with a P90 automatic weapon and a metal case full of ammunition. To make things easier on the agents in the field, both weapons fired the same caliber of bullet and the ammunition was interchangeable. She secured both weapons and ammunition in her duffel bag. She had one more stop to make.

The halls were empty, and she easily made her way to the last office at the rear of the building. She nodded at Mandy, his secretary, as she crossed the room and rapped lightly on the interior door.

"Come in," Vince Flagler's husky voice commanded.

She pushed the door open but remained in the doorway. "We're heading out now."

Vince leaned back in his chair behind his huge mahogany desk and took a deep breath. He was a large man and the desk seemed to fit him rather than dwarf him. The gray hair at his temples didn't reach to the rest of his dark hair or the stubble on his chin.

She watched his eyes as he contemplated what to say. When he spoke his voice was firm and without hesitation. "I don't have to tell you that she's important to me?"

She nodded. It was a conclusion she had already reached. There was no other reason for Vince's accommodations to the ambassador.

"She's levelheaded, but very headstrong. You can push, but she'll push back. Just keep her safe, okay."

She nodded again and tapped the door in salute.

"And keep in touch," he called to her retreating back.

CHAPTER FOUR

Angel took a sip from the small glass of whiskey she held in her hand. It warmed her throat and she began to relax. She liked the fast-moving pace of her job, but she also knew when to let go. Taking a deep breath, she stretched her legs out in front of her. The luxurious leather chair seemed to wrap around her and for a brief second she thought about sleep.

The interior of the Flagler plane was mostly white and peach with chairs on the left and several couches on the right. It was plush and pristine, a stark contrast to the dark-clothed bodies spread around her. Some lay on the seats and some had made beds on the floor around others' feet. At home in any environment, her team members took advantage of the down time to sleep, clean their weapons, or play cards. She could even see a push-up contest going on in the rear of the plane.

All four of her team leaders were battle-tested and she trusted them with her life. In fact, she had on many occasions. She didn't play favorites when selecting teams for a mission, but her uncertainty earlier had played a part in her selection this time.

Sarah was logical and brilliant at seeing the big picture. She could be counted on to offer guidance without prejudice. Eric never let a situation influence his calm demeanor nor would he react without careful thought. With the two of them, she was free to focus her attention on negotiating or finding a peaceful ending to the disturbance. She always knew they were watching her back. As if on cue, Sarah slid into the seat beside her.

"Can't sleep?" she asked.

Sarah grinned. "It's the rattle of your ice cubes. Can't you drink any quieter?"

She shook her head and passed her the glass. Sarah took a huge gulp.

"Better now?" she teased back.

Sarah nodded, resting her head against the back of the seat and closing her eyes.

She took her glass from Sarah's hand and took another sip. Glancing at her watch, she calculated about six more hours in the air. That would put them in Nouakchott at about eight a.m. local time. She pulled the tray from beside her chair and dropped it in front of her. Setting her drink down, she opened the background file on Mauritania.

She wasn't surprised to see that it had become a hiding place for terrorists. She did find a little comfort in the fact that few actual attacks had taken place there. The biggest areas of trouble were in the eastern region where Mauritania shared a border with Algeria and Mali, but kidnapping was an active threat for Westerners throughout the country.

She turned the page to find a detailed report from the US State Department on human rights violations. It listed mistreatment of detainees and prisoners, lengthy pretrial detention, harsh prison conditions, and corruption. She had traveled to many places where these crimes were committed, but what made the alcohol in her stomach start to turn sour were the unforgivable crimes against female children. She quickly skimmed the pages detailing accounts of genital mutilation, arranged marriages, and the practice of force-feeding that went beyond obesity.

The last practice was one she found particularly barbaric. It took young girls from their homes and sent them to camps where they were forced, often violently, to consume large amounts of food in a short time. Rolls of fat were regarded as attractive, something that made the girls more desirable to their future husbands and flaunted a husband's ability to feed his wife generously even though others were starving in the drought-prone country.

There was also the lack of access to education, jobs, and health care for females. She took another sip of the whiskey, hoping to numb the queasiness. She held the liquid in her mouth for a second before letting it burn its way down her throat.

Sarah lifted her head. "Enough with the loud thinking. Want to talk about it?"

"Not really," she said, passing the Mauritania background file to her. "Read for yourself."

Sarah could draw her own conclusions about the country and the atrocities committed there, and there wasn't anything she wanted to say to her about the woman they were going to protect. Over the years, she had protected plenty of women in various governmental positions, but from the moment Tamara had produced the photo something about this assignment had felt different.

She leaned her head against the back of the seat. She couldn't understand why an educated woman like Elizabeth Turner would volunteer to serve in this country. Maybe she was a political appointee being repaid for something. A reward? Maybe, but in a place where women outnumbered men and were still discriminated against in every area of their lives, it sounded more like a punishment. She wanted to know more. Not for her job, but for her. She needed to know more. Much more.

She pulled the background file on Ambassador Turner out of her carry-on and started looking for the answers to her questions. Elizabeth Turner spent her formative years following her father from post to post around the world including two years in Mauritania when she was eight and then again when she was fourteen—after her mother died.

That was certainly a part of the ambassador that Angel could relate to. Losing a parent was hard at any age, but as a teenager, believing that you aren't alone in the world becomes a struggle. She had spent more than a little time wondering where she might have ended up if Vince hadn't been one of her father's closest friends and willing to take her in.

The ambassador, on the other hand, hadn't had a father who was fighting a war in an undisclosed desert halfway around the world. Turner's had been returning to Mauritania to start his second tour as US ambassador. After a few short months in a prestigious boarding school in Switzerland, the future ambassador had joined her father until she graduated from The American International School of Nouakchott.

Things were starting to make sense now. She knew Vince had been shuffled through many countries during his early years with the Central Intelligence Agency. He must have crossed paths in Nouakchott with a teenaged Elizabeth Turner. She drank the last swallow in the glass and set it down hard on the tray.

"What?" Sarah asked.

"Ambassador Turner's father was assigned to Mauritania at the same time as our fearless leader."

Sarah nodded. "That certainly helps explain why we aren't following normal protocol."

"Yep."

"Is that her background info?"

"It is."

"Anything good?" Sarah asked, leaning to read over her shoulder.

"She has a degree in political science from Harvard. This is her third time in Mauritania. She was there twice as a kid."

"Interesting. She must have really liked the country or the people. Or one particular person?"

She shook her head. "No indication of that here. Never has been married. She's fluent in standard Arabic and speaks several Arabic dialects as well as French, which is probably one of the reasons the CIA recruited her."

"Wasn't she in politics?"

"That was after twelve years with the agency and a masters in national security studies from the Naval War College."

"I was in Virginia seven years ago. I remember her senate campaign." Sarah rested her head against the back of the seat and closed her eyes again. "I'm pretty sure I voted for her. She won by a landslide."

"Impressive career," Angel said softly, closing the folder in front of her.

Elizabeth Turner did have an impressive career, but the information in the file had left her with more questions than answers. Why did she leave the CIA? Or politics for that matter? There was nothing, for instance, about why she had chosen to serve in this desolate country rather than one of the many beautiful locations she could have chosen. The years she had spent there should have been a reason not to go back. Maybe she had been too young to see the truth in the country. If the opportunity arose she would enjoy hearing all of these answers directly from the ambassador.

* * *

Ellie walked down the hall and entered the office of the embassy's deputy chief of mission. Sam Pantone was her second-in-command and the man she counted on for all diplomatic relations. As the son of a retired Foreign Service officer, Sam had grown up in various parts of Africa. He followed in his father's footsteps and remained mostly in Africa and Europe during his time in the Foreign Service. He had been assigned to Mauritania for three years as a public affairs officer before returning to Washington for the required political elbow-rubbing. He had returned to Mauritania about a year ago after spending the previous eight years moving through three different embassies in Africa.

He came quickly around the desk when she knocked on his open door. "What's up?" he asked. "You should have called. I'd have come to you."

She waved away his concern at finding her in his office. She had a regular scheduled meeting with him every morning and an informal one before he left at the end of the day, so she seldom had the need to search him out. For some reason it bothered Sam if she had to come to him.

"I need to fill you in on some security changes."

His eyebrows, like fuzzy white caterpillars, creased in concern.

"What's happened?" he asked, motioning to the couch opposite him and waiting for her to sit before he did.

His hair was cut short on the sides leaving a small amount of gray stubble above his ears. His lean build made him look younger than his sixty-four years. Today he was dressed in a black suit, a red shirt, and a blue-and-white-striped bow tie. His glasses rested on the end of his nose and he tilted his head down to look at her over them.

"Do you know Vince Flagler?" she asked.

"Flagler Security, right? I've heard of him."

"The secretary of state contacted him concerning our situation. Apparently she has exhausted all of her means to send us more troops so Vince is sending a detail."

Sam nodded. "I'm not against that. Our situation is a bit hairy at the moment. How many men is he sending?"

She didn't miss his reference to the Flagler agents being men, but she didn't take offense. Sam was old school in terminology but certainly not in his opinions. He never had seemed to mind that she was assigned the position of ambassador and from her first day on the job he had been her strongest supporter. His encouragement had gotten her through days even she wasn't sure she would survive.

"A team of ten will be assigned directly to the embassy. Ten more will be at a location nearby."

"Ten won't increase our visual effect much. Which I'm sure was your goal?"

"Correct," she said. "As Vince explained, his crew will be able to engage if needed without following marine or embassy protocol."

"Maybe, but we'll still be held responsible for their actions."

She took a deep breath. "I know. That's my concern. Have you talked with Minister Aboye today?"

Minister of the Interior Habib Aboye was responsible for the police force in Nouakchott as well as the surrounding area. He was one of the few remaining leaders in Mauritania that remembered her father. It was a connection that had helped her when she first arrived in the country, and he had been sympathetic when the crowd first appeared. They hadn't had much luck convincing him to disband the crowd completely, though, despite Sam's daily phone calls.

"I talked with him this morning," Sam said with a sigh. "Again. He's unable to provide any assistance other than the occasional response team."

"Okay. Let him know that we're bringing in a private security company that will have permission to engage, if needed."

"He won't like that," Sam said, shrugging. "But at least he'll be aware that we won't be following normal protocol. Want me to brief the staff too?"

"That would be great. Let me know if you feel like they need to hear from me as well. I don't mind talking to anyone who seems concerned. This should make them feel safer though."

"Maybe bringing in new faces will bring new ideas on how to move things along or to help figure out why they're out there," Sam suggested. "Do you think we should have someone attempt to speak with the crowd again?"

She and Sam had gone out the first morning after the crowd had stayed through the night. Sam had done most of the talking at her suggestion. She thought he might make more progress with the men than she would. His questions were met with silence even when they offered food and water.

"Let's wait for the Flagler agents to arrive. Our first attempt did nothing but increase their presence and bring gunfire."

CHAPTER FIVE

Angel scanned the tarmac as she stepped out of the plane. Nothing more than sand stretched as far as she could see beyond the airport. There were a few metal buildings that had been randomly placed on both ends of the runway, and a large glass-and-steel building that housed the main terminal behind her.

The constant coastal breeze reminded her of home, but it wasn't refreshing. It was hot. She estimated it was close to 100 degrees, which was normal for Mauritania in October. It was significantly less humid than Florida, though.

The Flagler plane had been directed to a small hangar away from commercial travelers. Eight black Toyota SUVs stood in a perfect line at the foot of the stairs. Her teams gathered at the rear of the plane to unload their bags and equipment.

She pulled Eric and Sarah to the side. "Sarah, call me with a status as soon as you arrive at the safe house. Remain at a Level One readiness unless you hear otherwise. You guys video call with each other this evening once you're settled in and get familiar with each other's location. I'll provide annotated copies of the embassy blueprints as soon as I put them together."

They both nodded and she could see the anticipation of a new assignment on their faces. She also felt the stirrings of something new in her future.

"Okay. Let's load up," she called to the group as she gathered her own equipment and placed it in the rear of the lead SUV.

Climbing into the front passenger seat, she waited for the rest of her team to get settled. If the driver was surprised to find a woman in the seat next to him he didn't show it. She greeted him in English and he responded in kind. Though his English was broken, she knew it would be better than her attempt to speak French or Arabic.

Eric knocked on her window and gave her a thumbs-up. She nodded to her driver and he pulled forward, accelerating slowly—something which she would learn shortly was not his normal driving method. He stopped at the security gate, where the SUVs immediately were surrounded by local customs and law enforcement officers. She passed them the Mauritania equivalent of a concealed weapons permit, her own temporary thirty-day visa, and passport. She didn't expect the vehicles to be searched, but she had a contact number to call at the embassy if they ran into any problems.

The officers moved quickly to each vehicle then waved them through the gate when they were all cleared. As they passed in front of the commercial airport entrance, she could see the shiny tile floors and huge round pillars inside. It looked like every other international airport she had flown through, rippling with the movement of people. Beautiful water fountains and palm trees lined the front along with two rows of flagpoles. Whipping in the wind at the top of each pole was the Mauritania flag, a yellow star with a half-moon scooped beneath it centered in a green background with broad stripes of red across the top and bottom.

Their driver accelerated hard as they turned south onto N2 or Nouadhibou Highway, the main north-south thoroughfare. Sarah's team split off, traveling the same road but heading north toward Nouadhibou instead. The multilane road was paved and easily traversed, and there was no apparent speed limit. They shared it with an occasional truck and a few camels.

It wasn't long before Angel could see Nouakchott in the distance. One- and two-story tan buildings made of stone or concrete surrounded the heart of the city. After passing through a third checkpoint, she understood why Tamara had given them multiple copies of what was being referred to as a fiche, a single-page identifying document for each of the travelers in their party. Despite the multitude of checkpoints, she didn't get the sense from the police they encountered that they had any real security concerns.

She gripped the armrest on the door as the street became crowded with people and animals. Their driver no longer held the pedal to the floor, but he also didn't apply the brakes. There were no traffic lights or signs indicating their route and she tried to identify landmarks. Two large pillars in the distance clearly identified a local mosque, undoubtedly one of many in the capital. An occasional restaurant sign in French advertised the available food options, *poisson*, *poulet*, and *viande*, which she mentally translated as fish, chicken, and meat. Contemplating the possible meanings of the third option of generic "meat" made her cringe.

Their driver tapped the brakes as several people and a few goats crossed in front of them. Squeezed between their SUV and the sidewalk, a donkey pulled a cart loaded with crates. An elderly man sat on top of the stack as it bobbed precariously from side to side. Cross traffic stopped in front of them and their driver swerved, narrowly missing the donkey and the red-and-white-striped curb, then picked up speed again. She checked the rearview mirror to make sure her other vehicles were keeping up.

She caught an occasional glimpse of people as they flew past, but mostly what she saw was a blur of vibrantly colored mulafas, long pieces of fabric wrapped around women's bodies and then around again to cover their heads. A few faces were completely covered; they were found mainly in the gaps between buildings where the sand blew without mercy.

Their vehicles slowed at the edge of a street market. Tent canopies and tarps covered the shops to block the sun more than to guard against any possibility of rain. The vendors were selling everything from home-grown vegetables to handmade jewelry and multicolored fabrics and sunglasses. Large bags of rice and grain covered the ground and slabs of meat hung in the air.

They slowed a small amount as they turned onto Avenue Moktar Ould Daddah and neared the embassy. Situated on ten and a half acres in the Tevragh Zeina district, it was surrounded by an almost blindingly white concrete wall. After years of constructing friendly and open embassies, since 9/11 the US government had attempted to strike a balance between beauty and security.

Angel knew from the material in her briefing packet that the lot held a four-story main office building, a barracks, and maintenance facilities along with a utility building, multiple access pavilions, and several community facilities. Finished in 2017, the new facility was a secure and modern environmentally sustainable workplace. The barracks could house over one hundred people and the first-floor café could feed double that amount. The State Department's first major wind-powered turbine for an American embassy was housed within the walls as well as an onsite water treatment plant for irrigation reuse.

As they approached, the crowd outside the embassy became visible. The men parted following minimal yelling from her driver and she tried to look at each of them. Thankful for the tinted windows, she studied their eyes as they passed within inches of the glass. Their faces were filled more with curiosity than with anger, and they stopped chanting to watch the four vehicles.

"They've been hired," Max Pollock said from the backseat. Max was a twenty-year veteran with the US Army Military Intelligence branch and had seen firsthand violence in all parts of the world.

She nodded. These men didn't cause her any concern. Men with a cause didn't lose their anger to curiosity in the blink of an eye. They were being paid to do a job. A job that currently required them to stand and chant. The nagging thought in the back of her mind was how far would they go if asked and who had been firing the rifle?

She lowered her window as the marine guard approached. Passing her Flagler identification for him to review, she kept her eyes on the rearview mirror and the safety of her team.

"The other three vehicles with you, ma'am?" the soldier asked.

"Yes."

"Welcome to Nouakchott." He motioned for them to pull inside.

At the base of the four-story white stone building were two roll-up doors. As her vehicle pulled forward, the door on the right opened to reveal the embassy motor pool. Inside were tool benches, a vehicle lift, and several black sedans.

She assessed the man in a tan marine uniform approaching her with his hand stretched out.

"Sergeant Shane Miller," he said.

She guessed his age to be late twenties. In today's military that meant he had seen at least one if not more conflicts somewhere in the world. She stepped from the vehicle and shook his hand.

"Angel McTaggart."

He nodded to her and moved to greet each of her team members. His height matched hers and that of most of the men on her team. In or out of uniform, Angel had no doubt she would recognize him as a marine. The way he moved and handled himself was not only representative of a soldier but also of a soldier who spent his days under public scrutiny.

"Let's get you guys unpacked and settled in. Then we can talk," he said as he returned to Angel's side.

She nodded and quickly grabbed her gear. Within seconds her team was standing behind her ready to move. They left the underground parking garage and climbed up a flight of stairs. Following Miller, they detoured around the metal detectors and turned away from the large café covering the right half of the first floor. They passed several passport offices and a large community meeting room before exiting out the rear glass doors.

When they entered the three-story barracks building, Miller stopped. "My men and Diplomatic Security are on the first floor. The embassy staff is on the top floor. The middle is a hodgepodge of local embassy staff and any overflow. You guys will be housed there." He motioned to the elevators. "Second floor. Doors are tagged with occupants so chose any open room."

He waited until her agents had moved into the elevator foyer before speaking to Angel. "I put you in the main building a floor below the ambassador's suite. That's where I am too. I like to be near the Communications Center."

She nodded.

"This is a gathering spot," he said, motioning to a long table with folding chairs around it. "Everyone that has been here for any amount of time has a television in their room, but there's one here if your agents want to use it. Not a lot in English, but we have a DVD player and some DVDs."

He unlocked a closet near the lounge and placed her bags inside it before leading her back the way they had come.

"First stop is the ambassador's office," he informed her. "She wants to meet with us before anything else."

He scanned his badge at the rear entrance to the main building before continuing. "Probably the most important thing to know is that there are alert buttons throughout all of the buildings, including the ambassador's office. The alert tone rings in the Communications Center and they'll dispatch units to the location. Does your cell phone have reception?"

She pulled her phone out of her pocket. "Yep, full strength."

"Good, then I won't have to give you a new one. When your team gets settled give me their room numbers and I'll pass everything to the Communications Center."

CHAPTER SIX

"That was Sergeant Miller. The Guardian Angels have arrived," Chloe informed her. A huge grin covered her face as she hung up the phone.

Word about Agent McTaggart's nickname had blazed through the embassy like a wildfire even though Ellie had tried to discourage it. Her staff had been confined to the embassy for several days now and visitors were a welcome distraction. Not to mention a visitor who had saved countless lives and single-handedly stopped major riots, if the scuttlebutt could be trusted.

"Let's stop using that name, okay?" Ellie suggested. "I don't want to disrespect her or her team."

Chloe nodded, although her smile didn't disappear.

Ellie wondered if she needed to be firmer. Before she had a chance to say more, she heard boots coming down the hall. She quickly retreated to her office and closed the CIA file on her desk, shoving it into a drawer. Micalah had sent the information she requested, but she had barely had a chance to begin reading through it. She had thus far resisted taking even a peek at the personal information.

What little she had read informed her that Angel McTaggart had joined Flagler straight out of high school. Vince had taken her under his wing and trained her to be a sniper. She didn't get a chance to think about this any longer as Chloe announced her visitors and she looked up at the figure filling her doorway.

The woman Vince had sent to protect her was more attractive and more imposing in person than her file photograph had suggested. She matched Shane's height and her shoulders were broad. Or maybe they only appeared that way because of her rigid posture. Her stance was wide, occupying all the open space around her. She wore dark blue multipocketed cargo pants and a black three-button polo shirt embossed over her left breast with the Flagler emblem.

There was no pistol strapped to the belt that rode low on her hips and that surprised Ellie. She had expected a show of force even though she and Vince had discussed her concerns. Maybe he had heard what she said and passed it along to his team. The woman wasn't diminished without a weapon even when standing beside Shane who was never without one.

"Madam Ambassador," Angel addressed her before stepping into the office.

Ellie crossed the room and reached out her hand. "Thank you for coming, Agent McTaggart."

The agent enfolded her hand in a firm but warm grip. Ellie was surprised at the sense of comfort and security the handshake occasioned and the flutter that filled her stomach. She glanced at the corded muscle in the woman's forearm and at their hands, which were still clasped together. Shifting her gaze to her face, she was surprised to see a slight lift at the corners of the agent's mouth. Had they already shared a secret?

Shane cleared his throat as he entered, and the new arrival released her hand, pulling Ellie from her daze. She motioned to the chairs in front of her desk.

Once they had each taken a seat, she rolled her chair from behind her desk to join them. She wanted this conversation to be informal so the two of them would feel comfortable enough to speak freely. Shane was used to her approach, but Angel didn't seem surprised by her actions either. She pushed aside the irritation that maybe Vince had shared more about her than he had shared with her about McTaggart.

She hadn't asked for information about the agent he was sending but he hadn't offered any either. Not even that she was a female. She met the dark eyes of Vince's protége. They were intense and left her feeling slightly vulnerable and exposed. Maybe the pebble in her shoe was more from how off balance she felt in contrast to the coolness emanating from the agent sitting across from her. She quickly focused on Shane before she became flustered and unable to talk.

"Have your marines worked with private security before?" she asked.

"Yes, ma'am. My men will accept and work with Tag's team as if they were their own."

Tag? She liked it.

She studied the man and woman in front of her. Their appearances were alike in many ways and yet so different in others. Both held their backs stiff against their chairs, allowing only their eyes to follow her. The agent's dark shoulder-length hair framed her face in contrast to Shane's almost bald head. And her eyes...

For a second she was lost in the depths of Angel's dark eyes again. Up close she could see that they were actually brown with flecks of black that seemed to grow at times, taking over the entire eye. She broke contact with them and searched for the words she had prepared.

"Sergeant Miller can tell you I'm not a dictator, especially when it comes to security. You guys know best. I'm sure both of you have a plan on how you would like things to work. I would prefer if you discussed it here so I can be kept in the loop."

Shane nodded at his new colleague, and she could see that some discussion had already taken place between them.

Angel McTaggart's voice was deep and commanding and her words concise. "I only have ten agents, ma'am. Judging from what I saw coming in, I strongly recommend that we bring in my response team immediately."

She shook her head. "I don't want to increase tensions by looking like we're bracing for a storm." She grimaced as she realized she was contradicting her previous comment. Okay, so sometimes she was a dictator. She stood and began to pace.

"Let me be honest here...I can be honest, right?" She faced them and waited until they each nodded before continuing. "It's not easy being a woman in this country and I can't afford to appear scared. Increasing the number of troops outside will make it appear I'm jumping at shadows."

"Isn't it better to jump than to let them storm inside?" McTaggart asked.

Ellie studied her face again. The tone of her voice was dispassionate, but the firm set of her jaw was easy to interpret, and she didn't appreciate the implicit criticism. She tried to keep the rising anger out of her voice.

"Maybe, but keeping them from storming inside is what you're here to do."

The Flagler agent raised her eyebrows before giving Ellie a slight nod.

"Then allow me to make some suggestions," she said, turning to Shane. "How many snipers do you have on the roof?"

"One. He's mobile, watching all sides."

McTaggart suppressed a grimace before responding.

"Let's add three of my agents and keep a constant visual in all directions, moving them to whichever building gives the best view of their direction."

"It'll take six of your agents to cover both shifts," he reminded her.

"I know, but if we use those same eight bodies every day they'll be familiar enough with the conditions of the protest to notice when something changes on the ground."

He nodded. "I see your point."

"Let's put the other four members of my team, which will include my team leader, Eric, into your shift rotation at the front gate. One extra body there shouldn't draw too much attention."

When Shane nodded his agreement, Ellie stopped pacing and leaned against her desk to look at them. "Great. We have a plan. Now, what about when I leave the embassy?"

The Flagler agent's eyes narrowed. "Why would you leave the embassy?"

"There are people I have to visit and meetings to attend. It's why I'm here."

"I think for now you need to remain inside where we can keep you safe."

Ellie shook her head. Didn't she just explain her situation? She glanced at Shane, but he remained silent. "Not attending previously scheduled meetings also will be viewed as a sign of fear. As well as being disrespectful to the host."

"Can you ask them to move the meetings here instead?"

Apparently the agent was prepared to keep plugging away on this subject until at least something went her way.

"I will ask."

McTaggart nodded. Clearly to her the issue was resolved. *If only it was*, Ellie thought. She certainly hoped it would be when the day came for her inspection of the new solar panel farm being built in the desert about five hours northeast of Nouakchott. She had pushed hard for that inspection and she certainly wasn't going to cancel it. It was still two weeks away, though, so it was a battle for another day.

Shane stood. "Let's introduce the teams and get everyone settled. Then I suggest you guys get some sleep before going on duty."

"What time does the rooftop shift change?"

"Noon."

"Let's get the extra coverage up there now. We slept on the plane so they can hang for a couple of hours."

"The gate guards work on a six-hour shift rotation."

"My team will be fine until their scheduled down time." McTaggart turned and addressed Ellie. "Madam Ambassador, I won't be far from your side throughout the day. Call if you need anything."

"Her cell number will be on the alert list shortly," Shane informed Ellie.

She watched them leave. A part of her felt safer with the added security, but another part felt like she was now being held captive.

She looked up in surprise as the agent's head appeared in her doorway, bangs falling slightly across her left eye. "Would you like a briefing every morning, night, or both?"

She resisted the insane urge to say she wanted her here all the time. She liked the way she commanded a room. Her office had felt empty after she'd departed. "Let's start with both and we'll see how it works out."

"Eight and eight work for you?"

She nodded.

"I'll see you then."

CHAPTER SEVEN

Angel walked around the edge of the roof. On one side, far in the distance, was the deep blue water of the Atlantic Ocean. Low-level structures closer to the coast blocked the shoreline and port from view. An occasional hotel stood a little higher than the rest, showing the Western influence in architecture. The views from the remaining sides of the embassy were identical to each other—crumbling buildings and walls in varying shades, ranging from sun-bleached white to terra-cotta.

She kept walking until she could see the crowd below. A large stretch of grass and palm trees supported by bracing bars was between the building she stood on and the six-foot-high stone wall that surrounded the compound. Steel bar gates allowed access in the front and the rear. The front of the embassy, where the crowded was gathered, was heavily secured and guarded by marines at the entrance.

She turned her attention to the protesters. She had noticed when they arrived that the group didn't seem organized the way dissidents with a common goal might be. That had eased her mind but not enough to keep her from requesting the ambassador's approval for additional support. Not that she had expected her to agree to the request.

From this height, she could see a man standing alone behind the crowd. A white robe covered most of his body, leaving only a black head of hair and not-from-the-sun brown skin exposed. He wasn't moving around like the others, and he didn't raise his voice to join in the protesters' shouts. It was obvious to her that he was the one calling the plays.

She dropped to a knee as he took a seat on the low stone wall that bordered the business across the street. His posture was relaxed and his gaze scanned the crowd, never looking up though she was sure he knew she was there. A member of the group approached him and they spoke for a few minutes. He pointed to an empty area around the fence of the embassy and protesters were quickly repositioned to fill it.

"What do you see?" Miller asked as he took a knee beside her.

She shifted her position to give him a view of the man. "The man across the street. He seems to be giving instructions. Let's find out who he is, shall we?"

Miller pulled his cell phone from his pocket and snapped a few pictures. "I'll email this to the Communications Center. It shouldn't take them long to put a name to a face."

She continued to watch the ringleader while Miller explained basic embassy protocols. He handed her an access identification badge. "You should have access to every door in the embassy with this. Eric's badge will as well, but your other agents will have the same access as my marines. There are some areas they don't need to be in and for their own safety they're better not having access."

She nodded.

"Would you like a tour now?" he asked.

"I'd prefer to explore on my own first."

They exchanged cell phone numbers, and she dropped her phone into her pocket as Miller walked away. She scrutinized the crowd below. A quick count told her there were about thirty men. She took a deep breath and pulled her phone out again, dialing from memory. She was surprised when Vince answered on the first ring.

"Angel? How are things?"

"The crowd is calm, but if that changes they're too big for us to control. I need more boots. I'll keep them out of view unless they're needed."

Vince was silent, and she wondered if he was considering her request or trying to figure out how to persuade the ambassador.

"Vince?"

"You know I value your opinion, but I can't go against her wishes…yet."

She heard his pause so she pushed again. "She's being unreasonable."

"Maybe, but it's her call. Focus on keeping her safe."

"I will."

"Great. Call me if anything changes."

She sighed as she pocketed her phone again. She could tell Vince agreed with her, and yet he wasn't willing to fight the ambassador. This wasn't the Vince she knew. She wasn't comfortable letting someone outside her chain of command make decisions for her agents, even an ambassador.

She gave instructions to her snipers on the roof, drawing their attention to the man she had observed earlier. The rest of her team had been dispatched to their appropriate positions, either to the barracks for rest or to a duty position. She was now free to get familiar with their terrain. Miller had given her a map of the embassy, but a map didn't tell you where staff was positioned or cameras were placed, though, details that were of operational importance. She'd pencil those in and then send pictures along to Eric and Sarah.

She made her first stop the second floor of the main building and the location of the ambassador's office. Cubicles filled half of the floor space; four offices filled the rest. She spent a few minutes making small talk with Chloe before moving on.

In need of caffeine, she returned to the barracks and retrieved her personal bag from the locked closet in the first-floor lounge.

After filling her black travel mug with slightly scorched coffee from the coffeemaker there, she scouted all three floors of the barracks. She marked cameras on the map and made a detailed audio record regarding the layout before taking her bag to the main building and the third-floor room Miller had assigned her.

Tossing her bag on the bed, she secured her weapons in the lockbox provided in the room. She liked to keep her pistol with her generally, but it seemed unnecessary inside the embassy. Over the next couple of days she would observe the behavior of the crowd and the lone man on the wall and make a plan. Even if she decided to attempt to speak with them, a weapon might not be required.

The only thing on the third floor other than a few hotel-style rooms was the Communications Center. She would wait for Miller to provide that tour. She took the stairs down to the first floor. Most of the rooms there were in use so she stuck to the hallways, making a quick pass through the café before heading outside. It was at least twenty degrees warmer there than on the rooftop. There was an occasional breeze with a hint of salt from the ocean, but it wasn't enough to cool the air.

As she passed in front of the main building, she studied the window to the ambassador's office. It appeared dark with the afternoon sun shining onto it, but she felt the ambassador's presence. She kept walking in case she was being watched from the window. She was still processing their first meeting, but she had seen firsthand evidence of Vince's assessment. She really felt that "headstrong" might be an understatement when it came to Ambassador Turner.

She was pleased that her initial perceptions of the ambassador were correct. She was open and friendly, not exploiting her position to belittle those around her. Her staff seemed to like and respect her, though time would show the truth of that observation. It was hard not to admire her determination and persistence in the face of Angel's suggestions about embassy security. It was always easier to work with people who yielded to her every suggestion, but Angel didn't find them nearly as interesting as she was finding Elizabeth Turner.

When she finished surveying the supply and maintenance areas, she returned to the main building. Continuing to dictate her observations into her phone, she entered through the parking garage and was surprised to find the motor pool area empty of people.

"Three black sedans, and the four SUVs we arrived in are to the left. A lift rack and tool benches on the right. A small office in the rear. A metal fireproof door leading to the main parking garage is at the end of the row of vehicles."

Passing sun-faded vehicles belonging to embassy staff, she walked its length, recording on her map where cameras were located.

The last area on her map was the fourth floor. Across from the stairwell and elevators was a glass door leading to a gym. It held all the typical equipment you would find in a hotel gym. It was an open room with one camera in the front and one in the back. A second door in the hallway was equipped with a security access lock. This was the ambassador's private living quarters. She hesitantly swiped her badge, her body tingling with anticipation. She forced herself to concentrate, making a mental note to see who else had access to this floor.

She heard a soft click as the door closed behind her. Pictures lined the hall on both sides and she walked down it slowly, turning back and forth to study them. Many showed the ambassador at play or shaking hands with notable people, including several US presidents. Although she had read all the background information that Vince had provided, the woman she had met earlier was still largely a mystery to her and she found herself wanting to know more.

Angel stopped in front of a picture of the ambassador in shorts and a tank top. There was a number pinned to the front of her shirt and the running shorts accentuated her long tanned legs. The spandex shirt hinted at what lay beneath, small firm breasts, and she felt her mouth grow dry.

"That was taken at the Marine Corps Marathon in DC."

Her body stiffened in surprise and she swallowed hard, attempting to find her voice before she turned to face the ambassador. Why hadn't she heard the click of the door?

"Ambassador," she said as she turned and met the blue-green eyes.

"I didn't mean to startle you, Agent McTaggart."

"You didn't…Okay, yes, you did." She smiled. No need to deny the obvious. She cleared her throat. "Please, Angel or Tag is fine."

The ambassador stuck out her hand as if they were meeting for the first time. "Ellie."

She took the offered hand and, unlike the first time they touched, allowed herself to appreciate the soft skin of Ellie's hand and the firmness of her grip.

Realizing Ellie was studying her equally as hard, she dropped her hand and turned back to the photo on the wall. "You ran the Marine Corps Marathon."

"Yes, and finished."

She could hear the laughter in Ellie's voice, but she refused to meet her eyes again. The first glance had rocked her and she was still trying to regain her composure.

Her admiration for the woman was growing. The Marine Corps Marathon was not just a normal 26.2-mile event. The real challenge was to "beat the bridge," the race inside the race. Even if they ran the full course, runners had to maintain a fourteen-minute-per-mile pace and cross the Fourteenth Street Bridge at Mile Twenty within four and a half hours. If they didn't, then they weren't considered an official finisher.

"That was really your question, right?" Ellie teased.

She had to look at her then. The grin on Ellie's face wrinkled the edge of her eyes, and her shoulder-length blond hair fell around her face, causing her to continually tuck it behind her ear. The repetitive motion was mesmerizing.

"Well, that is what's important," she countered. Her heart raced as the threat of losing her composure pulled at her. She had crossed an invisible line by entering this hallway and now she was allowing herself to be drawn in by the woman she was sent to protect. "I'm sorry I'm in your personal space."

"Sorry you're in it? Or sorry I caught you?"

She shook her head but couldn't stop the grin on her face. "You don't pull any punches, do you?"

"Nope." Ellie motioned down the hallway. "Can I give you a tour?"

"I would appreciate that." She held up her map. "I'm trying to get familiar with the entire building."

"So I heard."

She frowned.

"Something you'll learn very quickly, Angel, is that word travels fast in this building."

"And everyone knows something."

Ellie pointed up at the camera in the corner. "Someone knows everything."

She waited while Ellie pushed open the door to their left and then stepped aside. "Welcome to my home away from home. Feel free to explore. I'll wait here."

She gave her a wry smile. "Thanks. I'll only be a second."

* * *

When Ellie heard that the Flagler agent was covering every corner of the building, she had set out to find her. She didn't think the woman would venture into her living space without permission, and she wanted to be there to offer it, knowing it was an important aspect of her security duties. She hadn't planned on catching her studying her photo, though.

She watched McTaggart—Angel, she corrected herself—move through her bedroom, remaining by the door on purpose. The lack of composure that Angel had exhibited when she approached had made her ego swell; it was nice to think that even at forty-five she still had some attractiveness left. Being in such an intimate space with her, however, was not a good idea, she had decided. Though her libido appeared to disagree.

Angel stepped out of her bedroom, her face tense in concentration as she drew a sketch on the paper in her hand.

"Are you marking where I keep my toothbrush?" she teased.

Angel looked up from her map and gave her a sideways grin. Her long bangs fell across one eye in the most irresistible look Ellie had ever seen.

"I can if you fear for its safety."

CHAPTER EIGHT

Angel pulled out a chair and sat down at the rectangular table in the lounge outside the marine barracks. The posters on the wall reminded everyone of the hazards related to living outside the US as well as the rules to be followed and the responsibilities they carried as US citizens in a foreign country. A television held the place of honor high on the wall in the far corner with an extra-long couch and two armchairs placed in front of it.

The coffeemaker was an older model but still seemed to handle the demands placed on it. After her first slightly scorched serving, she had consumed more than one acceptable steaming cup. She had briefed her agents here earlier before they went on shift, and now she prepared her notes for an information exchange with Miller before she met with the ambassador for her first briefing.

The day had passed quickly and she already felt confident about her surroundings. She was not, however, confident about where she stood with the ambassador. *With Ellie.* It was easy to forget the position the woman held within the building. Her relaxed personality seemed to put everyone in a pleasant mood, though her staff remained courteous and professional. Angel knew blurring the line between her responsibilities and her desires was dangerous. She liked Ellie and wished she could get to know her better, but she needed to maintain a professional distance to be able to offer her the protection she required.

"Hey, Tag. How was Day One?"

She smiled as Miller pulled up a chair beside her.

"I think my team has settled in. Are you seeing anything that needs to be tweaked?"

"Not from my end."

She turned her tablet so Miller could see the screen too. "I ask Rodriquez to send me a video from the rooftop at least three times a day. Just a scan of the crowd and anything else going on around the building. The man we observed this morning was replaced with this guy a few minutes before our shift change."

"Right," Miller said. "We'll check him too, but I'm guessing he won't have any kind of criminal record or be on our watch list. Same as the first guy, Imad Abadi."

"I had my remote team work on him as well. Duncan, my tech guy, is identifying the men in the crowd. I'll have him work on this guy too. I'll send you this photo and everything he finds."

She zoomed in on the new man-in-charge, captured his face in a snapshot, and emailed it to Miller and to Duncan.

She continued to speak while they watched the rest of the video. "The crowd seems to be mostly dockworkers and we haven't seen any weapons all day. Haven't uncovered any mysterious loyalties or family connections to terrorist organizations either. They don't appear to have a game plan other than doing what they're directed to do by the man on the wall. I think someone else is behind this and he's being careful to avoid players that would send up a red flag."

"That makes me even more suspicious," Miller said.

"Me too. Has anyone from the embassy reached out to them?"

"The ambassador and Deputy Pantone made an attempt early on. No one had anything to say to them though."

She nodded, closing her tablet as the video ended. "Can you send me the duty schedule?"

Miller pulled out his phone. "Just for the marines or everyone?"

"Everyone." Her agenda for tomorrow was to begin connecting names with faces, starting with the marines and Diplomatic Security and going all the way to the Mauritanian housekeeping staff. She wanted to know everyone that was inside the embassy.

Miller stood. "If you have a few minutes, I can introduce you to the head of the Diplomatic Security, Agent Connor, and give you a tour of the Communications Center."

"Now is good." She still had more than twenty minutes before her meeting with the ambassador.

She followed him back to the main building and up the stairs to the second floor.

"Danielle Connor is the regional security officer for the Diplomatic Security Service and, as such, the senior law enforcement civilian within the embassy. I'm not sure if you've worked with DSS before, but they handle a broad range of security operations. Since we are currently without an assigned CIA analyst, here in Mauritania they're basically stuck conducting counterintelligence operations and all investigations."

"Will she still be in her office this late?"

"I spoke with her about an hour ago and asked her to hang around."

They rounded the corner and Angel could see an office light glowing beyond the rows of empty cubicles.

"Agent Connor and I arrived at the embassy on the same day," Miller continued. "This was her first post as RSO and with a staff of only two she was quickly overwhelmed with the workload. It was easy for us to decide for my marines to handle physical security. Some embassies allow the host country to help out, but neither of us was comfortable with that." He slowed their pace as they neared her office. Turning toward her, he spoke softly. "She's pretty straightforward so don't take offense at what she might say."

Angel nodded.

He knocked and then stepped inside the office.

"Agent Connor, this is Flagler Agent McTaggart."

The dark-haired woman behind the desk stood and reached out her hand. Her suit was wrinkle-free and stretched tight where it buttoned at her waist. A line of freckles dotted the area beneath her eyes, softening her polished appearance. Angel guessed her to be in her mid-thirties, but the stress of her job was showing in the smattering of gray hair at her temples.

"It's nice to meet you," Angel said as she shook her hand.

"So, your boss thinks you can do a better job than Miller here, huh?" Agent Connor asked, looking Angel up and down.

Angel glanced at Miller and then met the woman's stare. "I don't believe that was the assumption. I'm here to work with both of you, not by myself."

Agent Connor nodded as if Angel had said exactly what she wanted to hear.

"Let me know if there is anything I can help with while you're here." Agent Connor dropped back into her chair, returning her attention to the computer screen in front of her.

Clearly dismissed, Angel followed Miller into the hallway. She thought she saw the hint of a smile on his face, but she didn't know him well enough to make a sarcastic comment about Connor's brusque style.

"She seems nice enough."

Miller nodded. "Like I said. She's direct."

They climbed one flight of stairs to the communications room.

"Is the gym open access?" she asked, remembering the facility located on the fourth floor outside the ambassador's suite.

"For the marines and Diplomatic Security agents. Embassy staff can request access, which has to be approved by me and the ambassador. It doesn't get a lot of use. Everyone works long hours and up until the lockdown even I preferred to get my exercise outside the embassy gates."

Miller scanned his badge to enter the Communications Center.

"Who has access to this area?" she asked.

"You, me, Eric, the ambassador, and the marines that work here. There are two marines on duty at all times, working six-hour shifts. Six soldiers are assigned permanently and there are two alternates that rotate through."

Angel pulled up the list of marines on her tablet and marked the six Miller identified. She momentarily closed her eyes as they stepped inside the room, hoping to speed up their adjustment to the dim lighting. There were three fluorescent lights across the ceiling, but they weren't on. Two floor lamps sat in each corner and lit the room with a soft glow.

She studied the two marines sitting in front of a computer and monitor console that circled almost all of the room. Their chairs had wheels and they moved up and down the console, verbally relaying to each other what they were observing on the screens. She quickly counted two computers and ten camera monitors on each side.

"The audio in this room is recorded and backed up weekly. For everyone's protection," Miller mentioned as they stepped to the center of the room.

Angel nodded. She knew of plenty situations where the boots on the ground had informed the proper people of a situation, but the right decisions hadn't been made. The fallback always landed on the low man, and she appreciated that Miller was doing what he could to protect his troops.

"How many cameras are placed inside the embassy?" she asked, wanting to make sure her earlier findings were correct.

"There are twenty-five on each of the first three floors, ma'am," the female marine in front of the console responded. "Only ten on the fourth floor because of the ambassador's suite. The first floor has an officer on patrol and two at the public entrance. Elevators, stairwells, and the rear exit doors require an access badge."

Angel glanced at Miller. "And the ambassador's quarters?"

"Just the ones in the hallway."

She nodded again. That was what she had observed as well. "What about outside?"

"Both gates and every corner of the perimeter. Facing in and out," the female marine answered again.

She watched the monitors flip from camera to camera.

"There are five monitors for each floor. One is always on the elevator and the rest flip through the other cameras," the marine continued.

"Are the cameras movable?"

"Yes, ma'am, but they each have a set stationary position. If you move it to view something else you have to lock it in place or after thirty seconds it will return to the set position."

"Thank you, corporal." In the dim lighting, Angel couldn't read the woman's name tag, but she could see the rank displayed on her uniform.

She joined Miller in the rear of the room. "How are the backups handled?"

"It's all digital. You can view any footage from the last two years from here. Anything older than that has been sent to the vault in Washington and has to be requested."

She glanced at her watch. She only had a few minutes until her briefing. "I should go."

"One more thing." Miller moved to an end console, displaying a diagram of the embassy. "You can log into this map from any device."

She looked at the digital display in front of her. Tiny lights appeared all over the building. Some were moving and some were stationary. She leaned closer. "What is this?"

"Everyone wears a GPS tracking device. It's removable so it's not foolproof, but we're still working on the system. My marines and the DSS are red, the staff is blue, and the Mauritanian staff is yellow. You can run the cursor across each dot and the display will give you the name assigned to the band." He demonstrated. "The ambassador is purple and her band blinks every five seconds as long as it's on her wrist. She only removes it to shower." Miller shrugged. "Like I said, not foolproof."

She nodded. "It works." She watched Ellie's purple light flash inside her office. "Do you have enough for my team?"

"We didn't have much warning that you guys were coming, so for now the ambassador only has one for you. We should have enough for the rest of your team by the end of the week."

"Excellent." She handed her tablet to Miller. "Can you set it up for me?"

He downloaded the application and handed it back to her.

"Thanks. I'll catch up with you later."

* * *

Ellie stared at the paperwork on her desk. Her eyes were on the words, but her mind was on Angel McTaggart. The banter they had shared when she found Angel in her quarters was comfortable, and she found herself craving that companionship. She knew she shouldn't be anxiously awaiting her arrival. Angel was here to do a job. As ambassador, she needed to make sure that it was done appropriately and well. Something in Angel's stoic manner called to her, though, and she longed to see more of the softer side that she had caught a glimpse of earlier.

She put on her glasses and, pulling open her desk drawer, stared down at Angel's brown eyes. She hadn't meant for the photo to be on top of the file, but when it had ended up that way she didn't change it. Throughout the day she had found herself opening the drawer for no reason. Angel's face was serious, not unlike the way it had been when it appeared in Ellie's door that morning. The picture had been taken several years earlier; she liked the older, more mature look of today.

"Ambassador?" Angel spoke softly from the doorway.

Angel's voice brought goose bumps to her arms and she fought back a shiver. The gentleness of her voice was unexpected, and she wondered what might prompt Angel to raise her voice.

She took off her glasses and narrowed her eyes at Angel.

"Ellie?" Angel quickly corrected.

She smiled and pointed to the chairs in front of her desk. Instead of sitting, Angel stepped between them and remained at a modified position of attention. Her legs were spread slightly and her hands rested casually at her sides.

"You should know that I have attempted once again to convince Mr. Flagler to send backup but my request has been denied."

She hid her smile. Clearly she had made her point with Vince. Now she needed to work on this agent.

"My team is settling into their security assignments and I have nothing more to report at this time. Is there anything you require of me?"

She was puzzled at Angel's brusqueness. She had thought they would discuss the security measures already in place around the embassy. Was it possible that Angel was only going to go through the motions at each briefing? She certainly hoped that wasn't her plan.

She could see the bags under Angel's tired eyes and knew it had probably been a long time since she had slept. Asking her to stay longer would be selfish and could possibly hinder the rapport she hoped would develop between them. Her carefully crafted speech to remind Angel that ultimately all embassy decisions belonged to the ambassador would have to wait until morning.

"I have nothing for tonight, but I look forward to hearing tomorrow your observations from your earlier tour of the embassy."

Angel gave her a slight nod and then glanced at the GPS band laying on the desk.

"Oh, right. Except for this." She held the band out to Angel. "Did Sergeant Miller explain how these work?"

"Yes." Angel took the band and buckled it to her right wrist. "If that's all then, I'm going to retire for the night. Please call me if you need anything."

Ellie nodded, wondering again at Angel's brusqueness. She shrugged off her irritation as she watched Angel leave the office at a quick pace.

She logged into the GPS display on her computer and watched Angel move around the embassy. When her path took her out the front doors, she turned to the window and watched her stride down the sidewalk to the gatehouse, walking with a purpose. Ellie's thoughts jumped from one hypothetical idea to another. If they weren't in this country and being confronted by a group of protesters, would they be able to be friends? Or maybe more? She laughed at herself. She didn't know if Angel preferred men or women; had had to bite her tongue, in fact, to keep from asking Vince. It didn't matter to the job, but to her annoyance, she realized, it was coming to matter to her. A lot.

The deep background dossier called to her from the closed desk drawer. If she opened it, she would know the answer to all of her questions. There was a time and a place for having the information contained within it, but she wasn't at that point yet. Angel had been short with her tonight but she would blame it on the long day and give her a chance to start fresh tomorrow.

Her eyes narrowed as she tried to see the crowd outside the gate. There was only one streetlight on this block and the wattage was very low. It also flickered on and off often due to the power situation in Nouakchott. Several embassy floodlights covered the area around the main gate, but the crowd seemed to hang outside the coverage area.

After a few minutes, movement from the gatehouse caught her eye and she watched Angel returning to the main building. Directly beneath her window, Angel hesitated for a second before glancing up. Ellie forced herself to remain still. Angel's intense gaze penetrated the bulletproof glass, driving straight into her. She was fairly certain Angel couldn't see her, but she met her gaze anyway, watching as the breeze blew strands of dark brown hair across her face and Angel quickly tucked them behind an ear.

Dropping her gaze, Angel stepped into the building and out of Ellie's view. She turned back to the display on her computer screen and watched Angel climb the stairs to her new quarters. The red light become stationary and she wondered if Angel had fallen into bed or removed the band to take a shower. Hitting the button to close the display, she quickly stood. She couldn't let her mind continue down this path. Angel had a job to do, and she needed to stay out of her way.

* * *

Angel dropped into bed, lying with her arms behind her head. She knew sleep wasn't going to come fast. She often had that trouble when a mission was starting, but tonight it was more than work. Tantalizing visions of the ambassador were dancing in her mind. It was hard to see into the windows of the embassy even when they were lit up at night, but she had felt Ellie's eyes watching from her office. She rolled over and grabbed her tablet. Flipping on the GPS display, she located the purple light inside the ambassador's suite on the fourth floor. She flipped off the tablet and tossed it on the bed beside her.

As her eyes adjusted to the darkness around her, she dialed Sarah's number.

"Hey, boss. How do things look from your angle?"

"Unsettling."

Sarah chuckled. "That about sums up Eric's observation too. What's the ambassador like?"

Sarah would be more surprised to hear about her earlier banter with Ellie than to hear about her curt handling of this evening's briefing.

"She seems to have a handle on her job, but her single-mindedness will make our mission a lot harder. I'm preparing myself for a daily fight to keep her in check."

"Well, if anyone can handle her, it's definitely you."

Angel wished she felt as confident. She quickly changed the subject before she voiced her concerns. "How are your accommodations?"

"Good. The house has two floors and plenty of space to set up equipment. Keep sending the video footage and we'll eventually make sense of it."

Angel listened for several minutes as Sarah hypothesized on the gathering of the crowd outside the embassy and then told her to get some sleep. Truth was, her mind was going to the same places. Why had the crowd gathered? What were their goals? What would they do next?

She took a deep breath and let it out slowly. The ambassador's background and knowledge of this country made her a huge asset even if being near her elicited feelings Angel hadn't expected. She knew that the way she had handled this evening's briefing was not the solution. She couldn't speed through all of their contacts. She needed to use this resource, complete the mission, and return home. Just like every other assignment.

Feeling that she had reached a conclusion on how she would proceed, she closed her eyes and tried her usual breathing techniques for sleep. *Inhale. Hold. Exhale. Ellie. Inhale. Hold. Exhale. More Ellie.*

Her life wasn't really conducive to relationships. Between missions she looked for companionship when she needed it and then left before they asked too many questions. Usually that was before the next morning.

She didn't need a woman in her life permanently. Too many complications. Tamara went home every night to her wife and they had found a way to make it work, but Vince, like her, had never shown an interest in dating. Thankfully, she had never had to have the coming-out talk with him. Tamara was a lesbian, but she had never talked to her about it either. She grew up, she liked women, and that's the way it was. She couldn't remember ever struggling with her sexuality. She had always felt free to be who she was.

Her mind conjured up the photo of the ambassador at the Marine Corps Marathon. The tight running clothes that left little to the imagination. The strength and the resilience that completing the grueling course attested to were traits that the ambassador would need as she faced whatever this country threw at her.

She took another deep breath. The easy teasing between them was a luxury she wished she could enjoy. But the truth was nothing had occurred between them that would make her think Ellie might be interested in her. Or in any woman, for that matter. The background file on the ambassador hadn't mentioned any marriages or even a long-term relationship. Whatever that meant, now wasn't the time for anything that didn't pertain to the mission. She would file all these thoughts in the back of her mind and focus on her job.

Inhale. Hold. Exhale. Ellie.

CHAPTER NINE

Sunday morning arrived faster than Angel expected, and she groaned as the alarm on her watch vibrated. She climbed into the shower and took a moment to wake up under the cold spray before spinning the dial for warmer water.

Still naked, she quickly unpacked and hung her uniforms in the closet. She had brought one blue matching cargo shirt in addition to six sets of identical blue cargo pants and black polos. She preferred the dressier black shirt in this type of environment, but the cargo shirt was good for blending in with her team, if needed.

Dressed in a clean uniform, she stared at herself in the mirror. She wasn't prone to analyzing her own looks or even comparing herself to others. Vince had told her once that she had a strong chin. Whatever that meant. To her it sounded like something you would say to a man, but she knew Vince meant it as a compliment. Her face and arms held a light tan, a benefit of living in the Sunshine State. She was fit and trim too. She worked out whenever possible, keeping her body strong and able to do what she required of it.

She guessed that some women might call her attractive, but it wasn't a requirement in her work and that was what mattered to her most. That said, it wasn't hard for her to find some faults. It seemed like her hair always needed cut. The longer strands were starting to fall across her face more often. Six hours of sleep had cleared the bags from under her eyes. The stiffness in her muscles as she headed out reminded her, however, that she would need to make time to visit the gym today.

She located Eric at the gatehouse as he was arriving for his shift. He looked rested and his dark eyes were clear. She leaned in the doorway and listened as the off-going shift relayed the details of their quiet night. Eric stood between the two marines he would be spending the day with. Though they each had several inches in height on him, his muscular biceps and wide chest made them look almost scrawny. Angel consulted her tablet and studied the names of the off-going shift and Eric's two companions. When they had finished reviewing their agenda for their shift, Eric stepped outside with her.

"Everything seem okay so far?" she asked.

"Sure." He gazed at the crowd outside the gate. "I wish our backup was closer."

"Yeah, me too." She didn't have to explain why they still didn't have what they both believed they needed.

"Sarah's good with the layout of the embassy," he said. "I watched the surveillance you sent from Rodriquez."

"Good. I'll keep sending you the footage. Call if you need something."

She glanced quickly at Ellie's window as she passed underneath it, recalling the way the ambassador had looked yesterday as she leaned casually against the wall while she waited for Angel to peruse her bedroom. Comparing Ellie's calm demeanor to the nervous energy she was feeling inside, Angel hoped she would have time to hit the gym sooner rather than later.

* * *

Ellie watched the red GPS light move across her computer screen, tracking Angel's trek from the gatehouse to the roof. She had promised herself she was not going to spend the day watching her move around the embassy, but as soon as she had seen her outside the window this morning that plan had evaporated. When Angel's light turned toward her office a few minutes later, she quickly closed her laptop and pulled out a few files that she should have reviewed and signed off on the previous day. Her private line rang and she was relieved at the distraction.

"Ambassador Turner."

"How's things going?" Micalah asked.

"Everything's fine." Ellie strained to hear Angel's voice as Chloe explained she was on the phone. Angel's voice was too low for her to hear the response, but whatever she said made Chloe giggle. Ellie fought back a grimace, jealous, she realized, that Chloe was able to show her admiration of Angel so openly.

"Ellie?" Micalah said, demanding her complete attention.

"What?"

"I asked if the crowd had dissipated."

"No." Irritation flooded through her when Chloe giggled again. She wanted to get off the phone. "I have a briefing."

"With Angel McTaggart?"

"Why do you ask that?"

"I'm only making an assumption since you haven't heard a word I've said this entire phone call."

"I have a security briefing. Okay?"

"Okay. Okay. Call me later?"

"Yes." Ellie hung up without waiting for Micalah to say goodbye.

She walked to the door of her office and appraised the friendly way Angel leaned one hip against the side of Chloe's desk. She tried to remove all emotion from her face as she interrupted their conversation. "Chloe."

Chloe glanced at her and the smile dropped from her face. "Yes, ma'am." She motioned at Angel. "*The* Angel is here for your briefing." She giggled again before finding something on her desk that needed her immediate focus.

Ellie shook her head and motioned for Angel to follow her inside. She waited until Angel entered and then closed the door. As the click of the door latching into place resonated through her office, she wished she could open it again. She seldom closed her office door even during meetings, and she knew it would be noticed by her staff. She wasn't even sure why she had done it, only that she wanted Angel to herself for a few minutes. Shaking her head again, she walked behind her desk. She was already out of sorts and the day had barely started.

Taking a seat in her chair, she finally glanced at Angel. There was a hint of a grin playing in her eyes and she almost expected her to wink. As anxious as she had been for Angel to arrive, now she wanted her gone. This was her terrain and Angel was an intruder. She struggled to regain control.

She removed her glasses, laying them on the desk in front of her. "I apologize for Chloe's behavior, but something tells me this will be an ongoing thing. She seems to be quite taken with you."

Angel shrugged.

Ellie watched her face. What did the shrug mean? She didn't care or it didn't matter? Or was she used to that kind of attention? Of course she was. She was beautiful. The smooth lines of her face gave way to the muscular cords of her neck. Her six-foot height gave her a strong, protective appearance.

Ellie swallowed hard, pulling her gaze away and trying to focus her thoughts on security issues and not on Angel's hair. The wind on the rooftop had given it an adorable tousled look that Angel apparently found annoying. It was just long enough to continually drop into her face and she was constantly pushing it back with one fluid motion. A movement that Ellie was beginning to find extremely sexy.

She barely heard Angel's briefing as she battled to keep her face unreadable. Each time she raised her eyes they connected with Angel's, and though Angel continued to talk, she had a quizzical look on her face.

When Angel finished, Ellie dismissed her with barely a nod, returning to the paperwork in front of her—and cursing her libido. To say she was displeased with her lack of professionalism would be an understatement. It had been a long time, admittedly, but this definitely was not the time or the place to be reminded of the frustrations that were an almost inescapable component of the work she had chosen.

She took a deep breath, stood, and stretched. She mentally hit reset on her day as she walked to the coffeemaker beside Chloe's desk.

"I would have brought you a cup," Chloe said softly.

She turned as she stirred cream into her coffee.

"I know and I appreciate it. Next time."

She gave Chloe a sincere smile, hoping to convey that everything was okay now that she had her head on straight. Resisting the urge to check on Angel's whereabouts, she paced and sipped her coffee. Maybe now would be a good time to visit the gym.

* * *

Angel located Miller and went over a few issues with him before returning to her room. The flight yesterday and the tension from Ellie were hitting her in waves, and she desperately needed a workout. She changed into gray cotton gym shorts and a light blue tank top. She was pleased to see she was the only one interested in working out in the middle of the day. She chose a treadmill in the corner where she had a view of the room and began a moderate walk that soon moved into a slow run.

As she settled into a comfortable pace, she thought about the look on Ellie's face when she had interrupted Angel's conversation with Chloe. She had seen what—possessiveness? The surprise on Ellie's face after she closed the door had almost made Angel laugh. Maybe she wasn't the only one battling feelings she wasn't used to.

She had taken advantage of Ellie's distraction by mentioning the lone man on the wall. She hadn't made a conscious decision not to tell her, but she had planned to wait until she knew if he was the man responsible for everything or only someone hired to do a job. She hoped she would have all the answers if Ellie decided to question her later.

As she ran, she regularly glanced at the tablet propped beside her, keeping an eye on Ellie's GPS signal. It was easy to tell herself that she was only watching to make sure Ellie remained safe. Now if she could only make the flutter in her stomach go away, she might be able to believe her intentions were pure.

She held her breath as Ellie's light came close to the gym and then turned toward her own suite. Forty minutes would have to be enough for today. She needed to clear the floor before Ellie came back out of her room, and a nice cold shower was in her future.

* * *

Ellie pulled open the door to the gym and entered, taking in the familiar scent of sweat and cleanser. Before she could take another step, she collided with an unmovable object. Strong hands grasped her shoulders, stopping her mid-fall. And leaving her staring directly at Angel's chest. She quickly moved her gaze from the supple mounds there to meet Angel's eyes.

"I'm sorry. I didn't see you," she said quickly, watching the darkness in Angel's eyes deepen.

"No problem. Have a nice workout."

She watched Angel disappear into the stairwell, her clothing soaked with sweat and clinging to her in a way that accentuated her wide shoulders, narrow waist, and the slight curve of her tight butt. Ellie groaned as she realized her reasons for working out had just multiplied.

She took a seat on the stationary bike. Of all the equipment in the room this was her least favorite, but she really needed to sit for a few minutes. Her attraction to Angel was influencing her ability to perform her everyday functions. She needed to get her feelings under control. She tried to block the image of Angel's sweat-soaked body from her mind and concentrate on the work she should be focusing on today, starting with security issues.

There had been no gunfire yesterday or today. Did it stop because of the arrival of Angel's team? The crowd didn't seem to be changing their demeanor or growing in size. Why were they there? She thought about her conversation with Sam. Someone needed to try again to find out if they had demands. She would ask Angel at their evening briefing. She was fairly sure she wouldn't agree to let her outside the gate, but maybe Angel or someone from her team would have better luck negotiating on the embassy's behalf.

* * *

Angel felt refreshed after her cold shower, but unfortunately it had done nothing to stop the image of the taut body covered by Ellie's tight red workout shirt and black shorts from popping repeatedly into her mind. Forcing her mind to clear, she climbed the stairs to the roof. The transfer of leadership by the men on the wall seemed to be taking place at designated times each day and this time she wanted to see it in person.

She pushed open the rooftop door and braced herself for the pressure of the wind. It was another near-100-degree day.

She pushed her hair out of her face as she walked the perimeter of the roof before joining Rodriquez near the front. She took a seat beside him out of sight of the crowd below but close enough to the edge that they could view the man who stayed away from the embassy gates. Rodriquez wasn't on duty, but his curiosity was as strong as hers.

"Organized enough to have a leader. What does that say to you?" he asked.

She contemplated the question that she had been asking herself too. "The crowd is not as random as it appears. Maybe they do have an agenda."

"Someone does." He focused his camera to catch an approaching black sedan on video.

She watched two men get out of the car. The first one started walking through the crowd, talking and shaking hands.

The second one went straight to the low stone wall, taking a seat beside the man who was already there. At this point she knew he probably wouldn't appear on any terror alert watch lists, but she wanted a record of each man that appeared anyway.

"Make sure you zoom in on both of them. It makes Duncan's job a lot easier," she reminded him.

"I know. Sarah already yelled at me."

The first man returned to the car and leaned against it, waiting for the two men on the wall to finish talking. "I know the window is tinted but get the driver the best you can. Hey, wait…Shouldn't there be a license plate on the front of the car?"

Rodriquez grunted and she took that to mean yes.

When the two at the wall had finished their discussion, they stood and shook hands. The man who had been there for the day walked to the car and climbed in. The car backed a good distance away before turning and disappearing down the street.

"From now on I want pictures of the driver and the man sent into the crowd too," she advised Rodriquez.

He nodded to let her know he had heard her but continued to video.

She left the rooftop and went in search of Eric. She found him lying on the couch outside the barracks and dropped down beside him.

"Why is this room always empty?" she asked curiously. When she had seen the couch and television she had assumed this would be the hangout for off-duty marines.

"There's a small room in between the male and female barracks where the marines hang out. Too much scrutiny out here." He glanced at the camera mounted on the wall in the corner across from them.

"You were looking for solitude?" she asked.

"I was waiting for you."

She smiled. They didn't have an arranged meeting, but Eric knew her well enough to know she would come looking for him.

"You have an idea." His tone made it clear this was a statement and not a question.

"I'd like to send someone into the crowd when the leadership is switching. I want to know what they're saying."

"I can make that happen."

"Good. Do it."

Angel left him to work out the details. She would fill Miller in when Eric got back with her. She was only gathering information and had no intention of telling the ambassador yet. Ellie. The two names battled inside her mind for dominance. One formal and one friendly. She wanted to think of her as Ellie and she did. Most of the time. But the professional inside her needed to keep the ambassador at arm's length to be able to do her job.

She was growing weary with the push and pull of each interaction with Ellie. She would arrive prepared to exchange information and instead found herself providing minimal details before bolting from the room. She was giving Ellie plenty of opportunity to form the wrong opinion of her, she knew, but questioning her about what they were facing would not instill confidence either. She needed to get on solid footing with this investigation. Then she could share details with the ambassador.

CHAPTER TEN

Ellie motioned to the chair in front of her desk, but Angel remained standing. As Ellie knew she would. She was starting to feel suspicious about Angel's short briefings. She hadn't mentioned her idea to talk with the crowd to Angel last night at her briefing because Angel barely stayed long enough to say there was nothing to brief. This morning she was determined to get her to talk.

She walked around her desk and positioned herself between Angel and the door. She saw a flash of confusion on Angel's face before she covered it. Good, she had the upper hand. She motioned Angel to begin as she leaned against the back of the couch.

"There's nothing new at this time."

"Good. Then I have something."

Angel's eyes narrowed as they met hers.

"I want to talk to the crowd."

"No."

"I don't mean me necessarily. You or someone from your team."

"No."

"Maybe you could put an end to all of this by talking with them."

"No."

Her frustration erupted. "Aren't you a negotiator? Do your job."

A flash of something crossed Angel's face, but her demeanor did not change.

"No embassy personnel is talking to the crowd until we can figure out what they're up to," Angel said firmly.

"Maybe they just want to be heard."

"I understand an unsuccessful attempt was already made." Angel's tone didn't criticize but merely stated a fact.

"It was, but unlike you, we're not trained to negotiate with radicals."

Again, she read something in Angel's face. There *was* a plan. One that she wasn't going to be included in.

So that was the way things were going to be. Crossing her arms over her chest, she hid her disappointment and anger.

"We're done here," she stated with finality, making her dismissal of Angel clear.

She walked back to her desk and did not turn until Angel was gone. There wasn't anything she hated more than being kept in the dark. She considered calling Vince, but it felt too much like tattling. Besides, forcing Angel to reveal her plan would surely backfire in the end. She would figure out what to do this afternoon after her meeting with Minister Ganim. If she had to, she would talk with the crowd herself. She wanted all of this to be over so she could get on with her work.

* * *

Angel stood near the rear doors of the conference room on the first floor. She watched the ambassador pace as she briefed her staff on the agenda she planned to cover in this morning's meeting with a representative from the Mauritanian Ministry of Economic Affairs and Development.

Despite her clear disappointment with their morning briefing, the ambassador was focused on the task at hand and her voice was strong and passionate.

"Mauritania's coastal waters are among the world's richest fishing grounds making exporting fish one of their main sources of foreign revenue. However, fishing agreements with the European Union, China, and Spain have brought overexploitation and an increased number of large fishing boats into areas restricted for local fisherman."

Angel knew what was coming next. The large boats, referred to as trollers or trawlers, pulled huge nets through the water following the schools of fish, without any concern to their location or surroundings.

"Even minor collisions destroy local boats and often lead to the loss of life. In addition, a troller can gather more fish in a day than fifty local fishermen can gather in a year. We have to put pressure on the government officials to enforce the restricted zones instead of accepting money from the violators. We cannot leave the local fishermen without food for their families or the means of making an income."

A DSS agent appeared in the doorway to signal the arrival of their visitor. Angel had tracked Agent Connor down earlier and advised her on the new developments on the crowd outside the embassy. Connor didn't want to pull any of her agents from their assigned tasks but was willing to provide an agent for any meeting with the ambassador that brought in someone from the outside.

Assistant Minister Omar Ganim strolled confidently into the conference room and greeted the ambassador. He made no attempt to acknowledge the others in the room. He was a short man with a long, white beard that disappeared into the layers of white cloth that covered his chest. His robe stretched the length of his body, leaving only his sandaled feet exposed.

Once everyone was settled in the conference room, Angel moved into the hallway. She had considered staying in the room, but her presence seemed to be a distraction to Ellie. Or maybe she stepped out because there was an unhappy look on Ellie's face each time their eyes met. Ellie clearly had been dissatisfied with her briefing that morning, so much so that she had briefly considered returning to fill her in on what she and Eric were planning.

To her surprise it bothered her to keep things from Ellie. That was something she often had to do to prevent the subject being protected from getting too involved with the situation. The truth was that Ellie probably did need to know that the crowd was organized and that there might be a larger threat, but she wasn't willing to stand in front of her without having all the answers to the questions she would ask.

With only a small lean to the right, she could see Ellie inside the room without being seen. She probably should be watching the visitor, but she had learned sometimes you learned more by watching the person you knew. Ellie's reactions to his words and actions would tell her if she felt threatened or in need of assistance.

Ellie sat on a large maroon floor cushion with her legs crossed in front of her. A small table with teacups and pots of hot water sat between her and her guest. Ellie's staff was to her left and two additional visitors that had accompanied the advisor sat on her right side.

Although Ellie was dressed in a tailored suit, she looked comfortable with her jacket unbuttoned. She didn't seem worried about wrinkling her clothes and her laid-back posture set the tone of the meeting. She watched Ellie's fingers resting lightly on the ankle buckles of her shoes. They were black with a two-inch heel and Angel would never be caught dead in them.

After an hour, she was relieved when Ellie made the first signs that the meeting was coming to an end. From her position she hadn't been able to hear the conversation, but she knew they weren't speaking English. She could see Ellie pause periodically in her speech to search for the translation of a specific word.

Her guests seemed interested in the conversation and there were only a few times that the smile left Ellie's face. She didn't seem to labor at the negotiations or to be weighed down by the political consequences of her words or actions. It was clear that

Ellie believed in what she was saying. She gave and demanded respect from the man sitting across from her, a balance that she seemed to have perfected.

She grudgingly pulled her eyes from Ellie and glanced at her watch. Eric would be texting her soon and she wanted to be available to back her team up. He was prepping Joseph Toma, a member of the Flagler team, to wander through the crowd. Joe's Israeli heritage and ability to speak many languages made him the best candidate to infiltrate the crowd. She wished she were the one leaving the gates, not only because of the risk to her team member but also because she liked to be the one doing the talking. This time, though, she recognized that Toma might have more success not only as a man but as an Arabic speaker, and she pushed aside her reservations.

She watched the visitors exit the secured area and followed Ellie's entourage into the elevator. As they approached the ambassador's office she felt her phone vibrate. Discreetly checking the display, she confirmed it was a text from Eric. Disappointed that she wouldn't get to hear Ellie and her staff critique how the meeting had went, she gave a nod to the DSS agent and left him to escort the ambassador back to her office.

* * *

Ellie turned to speak with a staff member and saw Angel pull her phone from her pocket. She was surprised to see her disappear into the stairwell. Something was definitely going on. She quickly scheduled a time later to debrief with her staff and sent them back to their offices.

At her office door, she realized the DSS agent was still following her. She dismissed him with a nod. After a slight hesitation, he left. Angel must have told him to watch her. In her own office, no less. She pulled off her jacket and tossed it over the back of her chair.

When she walked to the window, trying to pace away her frustration, she was surprised to see Angel emerging from the building—and to see a pistol strapped to her waist. While all of the marines and the DSS agents always wore their weapons in plain sight, she hadn't seen Angel with a weapon.

Anger flared in her. She pulled her jacket back on and buttoned it. She was the ambassador. Everything that happened here was her responsibility. Holding her head high, she left her office and took the elevator to the first floor. She wouldn't stand for being kept out of the loop. She had expected more from Angel, frankly. She was supposed to be a negotiator, and Ellie had expected her to negotiate. Not threaten the crowd with a show of force. The first thing she would do when she returned to her office was call Vince and ask him to remove Angel and her team.

She followed the sidewalk across the yard toward the gate, her heels sounding crisp on the concrete. The crowd didn't seem hostile. The random gunfire was only that and it had been several days since she had even heard any. The men weren't hurting anyone. Maybe she didn't try hard enough the first time she and Sam had approached them. If she could give their concerns an ear, maybe that would make them happy enough to go away. How stupid would she feel if that was all it took?

"What the hell are you doing?"

She heard Angel's low gravelly voice before she appeared on the path in front of her.

"If no one else is willing to attempt to defuse this situation, then I will."

"You'll do no such thing. Turn around and go back in the building."

"I am the ambassador. You do *not* tell me what to do."

Angel's eyes narrowed. "Ellie." She stressed each syllable in her name. "Please go back in the building. I *will* brief you as soon as we finish here."

Ellie looked around. She couldn't see that Angel was doing anything but making a show of force.

"You're armed. It doesn't look to me like you're trying to accomplish anything peacefully."

"I promise you I'm not trying to stir anything up." She lowered her voice. "I have an agent in the crowd gathering information. This is only a safety precaution in case something goes wrong."

"And I would know this how?"

"As soon as he's safe, I'll come straight to your office."

She hated to back down, but if a Flagler agent was outside the gates then the top priority was getting him back in safely. The best way she could help was by removing herself. She took a few steps backward, watching Angel's dark eyes. They still held many mysteries, but she couldn't see any deception in them, not at the moment at least. She turned and walked back into the building.

Still fuming, she watched Angel and her team from her office window. She recognized that it was her fault that Angel didn't inform her in advance of this. She had been soft with her treatment of the agent. Why? Oh, she knew why. She liked the woman. Now she needed to make it abundantly clear that Agent McTaggart needed to keep her informed going forward. It wasn't a choice. It was essential if Angel wanted to continue her job.

* * *

"Dammit," Angel said under her breath. She had really screwed up. She had known instinctively that Ellie wouldn't stand for being left in the dark and still she had baited her by trying to do so. As soon as Toma was safe she needed to do her best to fix things with her.

She tried to wipe Ellie's displeasure from her mind and joined Eric inside the gatehouse. Miller and two marines waited beside him.

"Tag, this is Corporal Shelby. He'll be our translator." Miller introduced the taller of the two marines. "Private First Class Baker will operate the recording equipment."

Angel shook their hands and glanced at Eric. "Where's he at?"

"He should be reaching the crowd anytime now. He went out the rear gate about ten minutes ago. He'll circle around so that it appears he came from downtown."

It made her nervous that she couldn't identify him in the mass of people in front of her, but she knew Rodriquez would be watching him closely from the roof. Her assistance on the ground would only be critical if things went wrong. Toma's voice came through the laptop speakers clearly.

They all turned to Shelby.

"So, how much are you getting paid?" Shelby translated Toma's question. "He answered that he'd rather not say," he relayed the response.

"At least he got him to admit they're being paid," Eric mumbled.

"Yeah, I understand." Toma's words were again translated. "I thought we were all making the same amount, but I just found out I'm making less than that guy over there."

"We all are. He's the supervisor." Shelby translated a different voice from the crowd. She could hear the disdain in the man's voice even without the translation. Toma was unknown and the men were hesitant to speak freely with him. A different man spoke and Shelby relayed his words. "Stop complaining or you won't be making anything at all."

She hoped Toma wouldn't push too hard, but she had to trust his instincts.

Toma spoke quickly, his tone apologetic. "Right, right. I'm sorry. I really need the money." He waited a few beats before asking. "How long do you think we'll be needed here?"

She held her breath at Shelby's translation. Learning if there was a time period that the men were hired for would be big information.

"I was told it would be a month or so," Shelby translated when a different voice finally answered Toma.

"Yeah, that's what I heard too." Another pause and then Toma's voice again. "Do you know why we're here?"

She strained to hear an answer, but the chanting of the crowd was all that came through the speaker. She glanced at Shelby and he shook his head.

"Guess I reached my question limit," Toma said softly. "Working my way toward the greeter."

After a few seconds the chanting faded and a deep male voice could be heard.

Shelby began relaying the words. "Morning greetings. He's asking how their families are. Oh, wait…" He paused, listening intently. "The men are grumbling and want to return to their jobs so he's handing out cash. This isn't their regular paycheck." He glanced at Angel. "He says it'll all be over in less than two weeks. They've agreed to stay until then."

She keyed the microphone attached to Toma's earpiece. "Come in."

The gatehouse was silent while they waited for Toma to advise that he was back inside. Then she turned to Eric. "I'll meet you guys outside the barracks in thirty minutes."

She headed to the second floor to face the ambassador. Climbing the stairs slowly, she thought about what they had heard and what she should disclose. She knew Ellie wanted the truth, but disclosing suspicions without details wasn't a good idea. Something was going to happen within two weeks and she had no idea what.

She was usually good at skirting the real issues, but for some reason everything seemed different with Ellie. Ellie's background made her more knowledgeable than others she had protected, but it was still Angel's job to keep her safe. Not to run to her for help in analyzing every piece of evidence or telling her she suspected everything was going to get worse before it got better. That wouldn't ease Ellie's mind. Admitting she didn't have all the answers wasn't an option either.

Chloe waved her through without any conversation, and she knew there were some serious ruffled feathers. That was reinforced when Ellie removed her black-rimmed glasses and pierced Angel with her green lasers.

"So, here's what we've learned so far," she began quickly. "The man supervising the crowd is replaced once a day. They come and go in a black car with another man who moves through the crowd. Agent Toma was able to get close enough for us to hear what he was saying. The men want to return to their jobs at the docks, but he gave out money and persuaded them to stay."

"The men in the crowd are from the docks but aren't upset with us? They're being paid to stand out there?" Ellie asked.

"Correct. Do you know about anything happening in the next couple of weeks that they might be trying to influence?"

It was brief but she noticed Ellie's hesitation before she answered.

"No."

"Okay. I'll try to talk with the men tomorrow and see if we can convince them to go back to their regular jobs."

Ellie nodded. "Please let me know when you do."

"I don't want you anywhere near the front gate." Seeing quickly that demanding something from Ellie wouldn't work, Angel hastily changed her tone. "I'll do it in the morning and then I'll come straight here for our morning briefing."

"I'll wait for you here."

When Ellie returned her attention to the paperwork in front of her, Angel knew she had been dismissed. She turned and left the office. Unfortunately, it seemed that everything wasn't being forgiven.

* * *

Ellie rubbed her face as she turned her chair to the window. Knowing that the crowd was hired didn't really make her feel better. If anything it made her feel worse because now she knew there was something bigger behind all of this. Even if Angel wasn't saying so. She was disappointed that Angel didn't confide in her. All her talk in the beginning of briefing twice a day and keeping her informed had been a lie. She was exactly like everyone else.

"Ellie?"

"Come in, Sam."

He glanced around the room as if he expected to see someone else. "I thought you were being briefed."

"No. It appears I'm not," Ellie said harshly.

He dropped into the chair in front of her. "What's going on?"

"Why do you think something's going on?"

He smiled. "McTaggart is wearing a gun." He shrugged. "Word travels fast."

Ellie shook her head. "Everything is fine. She sent a man into the crowd to gather information. She was there for backup."

"Did she find out anything worthwhile?"

"The men in the crowd have been hired to stand out there and chant."

He frowned. "So they aren't just disgruntled citizens. Someone has an agenda."

"It seems that way. Was there something you needed?"

"I wanted to let you know that I'm still getting complaints from the fishermen in the coastal villages. The commercial fishing boats are coming way too close to the shoreline."

"I'd almost forgotten that we promised them a visit. I doubt our new protectors will allow that now. See if any of the fishermen are willing to come here. I'm sure money is changing hands at the government level and that's why the laws are not being enforced. Although I couldn't get Minister Ganim to admit to anything this morning."

"I'm afraid you're right, and I'm hearing a lot of the same thing from the Mauritanian customs agents at the docks too."

Ellie rubbed her face again. "See if you can find us a bargaining chip."

"Something we can provide in return for them doing their jobs?"

"I know it's not ideal, but we have nothing to back up any threats with. Call Inspector Asker and see if he'll come here for a meeting. He's proven to be trustworthy in the past. Maybe he can help us come up with a plan."

Police Inspector Faizan Asker wouldn't be happy being summoned to the US embassy, but she needed his support if she was going to stop the bribery that was working against them.

"I'll get right on it."

He stood to leave but hesitated at the door. "Are you still planning to visit the solar panel farm?"

She nodded.

"I wondered. I saw it was still on your schedule. What's your protection detail say about it?"

"Nothing yet. I'm hoping it won't be an issue by then."

"It's coming up soon."

She shrugged, but his words registered as she remembered Angel's question. Was this trip what the crowd was trying to influence? That didn't make sense. A hostile crowd could delay her visit, preventing the much-needed solar panel farm from providing electricity to the community. That included the men standing outside. The two things couldn't be related.

"We'll figure it out when the time comes," Sam said, nodding his understanding.

"Yes, when the time comes."

CHAPTER ELEVEN

On Tuesday morning, Angel made her rounds to check on her agents and then strode across the lawn toward the gatehouse. She spoke briefly to Eric, Miller, and the two marines before moving to the walking gate. Using the key Miller had given her, she unlocked the deadbolt and stepped outside the embassy gates, carefully securing the lock behind her.

The crowd had grown quiet as she approached, and now they gazed at her intently. She wasn't surprised that they had pushed back giving her plenty of space. Most Mauritanian men wouldn't take a chance of touching her even by accident. It was possible they wouldn't speak to her either.

"Is there anyone willing to talk with me?" She spoke loudly in English to the crowd. She would try French if she had to, but her repertoire was sparse. She could have brought Toma or someone from the embassy staff as a translator, but she was interested to see what would happen if she didn't present that option.

After a few minutes, she heard Rodriquez's voice in her ear as he watched from the rooftop. She wasn't armed so she was counting on his watchful eye. "The man on the wall is approaching."

She waited, studying the men around her. Some wouldn't meet her eyes, but she boldly responded in kind to the ones that did, memorizing their appearance. Most of the men wore shorter pants beneath their robes, but there was an occasional pair of jeans or long pants. Sandals were the only foot attire if there was any at all.

Finally working his way through the crowd, Imad Abadi approached. He was dressed roughly the same as the men from the crowd, but his black dress shoes stood out on the sand-covered road.

He studied Angel as he approached.

"Can you speak for the crowd?" she asked when he stopped in front of her.

"I can."

"The ambassador would like to know how we can resolve this situation. What can she do to help you?"

She watched his eyes as they checked out the area behind her as well as the rooftop.

"We want her to leave our country," he said firmly. His voice was strong, his eyes dark and unreadable. The beard covering his face moved as he spoke but hid any expression.

Her jaw tightened at the hostility in his words.

"She's here on behalf of the United States government as well as the Mauritanian government. Why do you want her to leave?"

"She forces her way into places she doesn't belong. She's not wanted here."

"If there's something you need, the ambassador would be happy to meet with you and discuss how she can help." Even as she said the words she knew she would never allow this man near Ellie. She had broken one of the most important rules of negotiation. She had lied.

He knew the truth as well because he turned and began walking away. His parting words barely reached her as the chanting began again.

"We don't want her help."

She watched his retreating figure until it was swallowed up by the crowd.

Rodriquez's voice sounded in her ear again. "Unlock the gate. I've got your back."

She turned and let herself back through the gate. There was no question in her mind that the man's words had been rehearsed. It was a script he had been told to say, but his words would still hurt Ellie. Clearing her face of emotion, she started the long walk to Ellie's office.

Miller fell into step beside her as she reached the stairs. He was silent as they climbed. When they reached the second floor, he placed a hand on her arm and she turned to face him.

"Maybe the ambassador shouldn't hear the recording," he suggested.

She was glad the people closest to Ellie cared about more than her physical protection.

"I feel the same way."

"Glad to hear it," Miller said, heading back down the stairs.

She was surprised to see Sam in Ellie's office. He was settled into one of the chairs in front of her desk, and it was clear he had no intention of leaving. She approached Ellie's desk and remained standing.

Choosing her words carefully, she spoke gently, "The crowd isn't speaking for themselves. They're repeating someone else's agenda."

"What did they ask for?" Ellie asked, her voice soft but clear and strong.

Angel glanced at Sam before looking back at her. "Nothing."

"Then why are they out there?" Sam demanded in frustration.

"I believe their goal is to drive the ambassador away." She watched the hurt flash across Ellie's face as she spoke. "As for why, they didn't say. They did say they don't want anything from you."

Ellie turned her back to them, facing the window.

"Well, we're not going away," Sam said, standing. "I'll review everything that has happened in the last couple of weeks. Maybe we stepped on the wrong person's toes."

"Go back a month or two," she suggested.

Sam nodded and left the office.

She studied Ellie's back as she stared out the window. She was dressed in a white silk shirt that hung loosely from her shoulders. It was tucked into black dress pants with a narrow black belt that circled her waist. The matching black jacket hung across the back of her chair. Her body was still, without any of the nervous energy she normally displayed. Angel wasn't even sure she knew she was still in the room until she spoke.

"I've worked hard to make things better for everyone, but especially the dockworkers. I've pushed for fair and increased wages, and they even have a form of health care now. Why are they fighting against me?"

"It's not them. This is someone else's agenda. Sam's right. You did or said something that upset the control someone thought they had and that individual is orchestrating this whole ordeal. We'll figure out who's behind it, but until we do just keep doing what you're doing."

Ellie turned to face her. The hurt she had displayed moments ago had transformed into anger. "How are you going to do that?" she demanded.

"I have a few ideas."

"Ideas that you're not going to share with me."

She didn't miss that Ellie's words were more a statement than a question. The words tugged at her. "Once I work out the details, I'll fill you in, okay?"

Ellie nodded and turned back to the window.

She wasn't sure Ellie believed her. That thought unsettled her more than her lack of ideas on how to actually deal with the crowd.

* * *

Ellie struggled to push her frustration with Angel and the men outside from her mind as she focused on the presentation she was about to hear, a background review by a staffer of Mauritania's northern border.

She took her seat at the end of the conference room table and smiled at Chloe as she set a cup of black tea in front of her. "It's a calming blend with a caffeine kick," she whispered as she took the seat beside her.

She chuckled softly. Chloe never ceased to amaze her. An adult barely out of her teen years, she could be so intuitive at times.

Sam slid into the seat on her other side as the young man at the podium began his presentation, pointing to the map on display behind him.

"Morocco, our northern neighbor, has sent troops to their most southern village. They claim they are there to fight against drug trafficking and to prevent all types of smuggling. The Western Sahara, which separates Mauritania and Morocco, is controlled by the Polisario, an Algerian-backed movement. The Western Sahara has abided by the 1991 ceasefire agreement because it held the promise of their independence. This move by Morocco has increased tension in the area despite their claim that the gendarmerie has been charged with police duties and not for war. The Polisario consider their movement a violation of the agreement."

This information wasn't new to Ellie. If the Polisario and Morocco began open warfare, she was fairly sure Mauritania would join as well. Mauritania's economy could not fund or survive a war. Would she remain if Mauritania went to war? Could she ask Vince to keep Angel here for extra protection? Speaking of whom…

She glanced to the rear of the room and felt a weight lift at seeing Angel leaning against the wall. When she and Chloe had left their office, there had been no sign of her. Though she didn't like to admit it, Angel's presence made her feel safe.

She had never before felt afraid while performing her duties as ambassador. Shane's attention to detail always gave her a level of comfort in and out of the embassy. She didn't need this tall, strong, beautiful woman to protect her and, yet, she liked the feeling that she could. She couldn't help imagining what it would feel like to be wrapped in Angel's arms.

Sam's elbow dug into her side.

She gave him a quick frown as she became aware that the others around the table were all looking at her too. Realizing she had missed a question directed at her, she smiled at the staffer giving the presentation.

"I'm sorry, Cody. Could you repeat the question?"

Behind her, she could feel Angel's laughter.

* * *

Angel felt some responsibility for Ellie's lack of attention, but it still brought a smile to her face. She stepped out of the conference room, softly closing the door behind her. Ellie didn't need her hanging over her shoulder. She pulled her phone from her pocket and dialed Sarah.

"Hey, boss. How's embassy life?"

She laughed. "Things are okay here. How's things on your end?"

"Shroder and Blake brought back lunch when they went out earlier. A local rice dish with unidentifiable meat. Once I picked out the meat it was delicious."

"I know what you mean. Even the word *viande* gives me chills."

"Eric said you tried to negotiate earlier. How'd that go?"

"That's actually why I called. To fill you in. Although I should have known Eric would too."

"He's my best source of information."

She laughed again. "What's that supposed to mean? I tell you everything."

"No, you tell me what you want me to know. Eric tells me everything else."

"Okay. How about you tell me what Eric told you then?"

"Where's the fun in that? Besides you already know that the beautiful ambassador has a temper."

Remembering the look on Ellie's face as she crossed the yard yesterday made her shake her head. "That she does."

"It's a shame it was focused on you, though," Sarah said, laughing.

"I'm here to keep her safe, not make her happy." She knew as the words left her lips that they weren't true. She wanted Ellie to be happy as well as safe.

"Harrumph."

"What?"

"How could you not be attracted to her? She's beautiful, successful, and has a dark CIA past."

She lowered her voice even though there was no one nearby. "Even if I was attracted to her, you're assuming she likes the fairer sex."

"She does."

She normally liked Sarah's ability to gather intelligence, but something told her this wouldn't necessarily be mission-relevant information. She bit her lip as the words fell out anyway. "Spill it."

"There was a bit of a scandal in Cambridge concerning a Harvard theater arts student and an ambitious poli-sci major who would become an ambassador. I'm waiting for a callback. I think I found a firsthand accounting."

"That was over twenty years ago and it's gossip."

"It's not gossip. It's intel."

"That's a debate for another time." She could still hear Sarah's laughter as she disconnected the call.

CHAPTER TWELVE

Inside a first-floor conference room, Ellie stood behind the podium in front of her staff. The three-quarter sleeves on the dark blue sweater she was wearing over a blue and white open collar shirt seemed to be irritating her; she continually pushed them above her elbows.

"As most of you are aware, President Aziz has announced he will not change the constitution to allow himself to run for president again. If he holds to this statement, this will be a significant step forward for Mauritanian democracy. It also means that we need to work fast to make the changes we know President Aziz will approve."

The mesmerizing sound of Ellie's voice dragged Angel through the events of the last week. After Monday's fiasco, she had shared her plans to go into the crowd. She had even briefed Ellie immediately after. Through the rest of the week, she had continued to be as forthcoming as possible. Nothing had changed outside, and she didn't have a plan yet, though she sensed that each day was bringing them closer to whatever event was going to be the catalyst to ending the protest outside and she was getting frustrated playing defense.

Worst of all was the way Ellie's behavior had changed toward her. The quick easy smile didn't reach her eyes anymore, and their interactions were tense. Angel continued to be present when Ellie had scheduled events or visitors from outside the embassy, but she no longer eagerly anticipated their private briefings. She could only think about reviewing analysis of the crowd, blocking out any thoughts of what might have been growing between them.

Her disappointment at the loss and Ellie's lack of confidence in her didn't change her thinking. She still believed that Ellie didn't need to know what she truly thought about the men on the stone wall. Her job wasn't only to protect Ellie from physical threats; she needed to keep the worry of potential threats away from her as well. Okay, maybe that wasn't in her job description, but it allowed her to feel like she was at least accomplishing something.

She knew the need was irrational. And Sarah had confirmed it, laughing at her when she had mentioned it the previous night.

"What?" Sarah said. "You don't really feel responsible for the ambassador's level of anxiety, do you?"

"Maybe not directly, but I am responsible for what I tell her."

"I don't know, boss, but I'm pretty sure you don't want to decide what you tell her based on that philosophy."

Sarah was the only one that called her "boss" and the only one who could get away with chastising her. Not liking the direction the conversation had started to spin, she quickly ended the call.

Of course, that wasn't her only reason for not sharing everything with Ellie. She hated to admit it, but her ego was in there too. She felt like they were digging in the wrong sand pile. How much more time would pass before she had answers to all of her questions?

Sam hadn't been able to recall any specific embassy action that could be linked to the days before the crowd had appeared, but he was still looking. She had asked Sarah's team to search through the records too to see if they could spot anything that might have a significant negative impact on any group or person. Ellie's administration had been hard at work, so Sarah had a lot of material to research.

She was fairly confident that the men on the wall were being paid to do a job the same as the crowd. Were they responsible for the gunfire? There had not been any since her arrival. Were they only there to keep tabs on the crowd and make sure the men were doing what they were paid to do? If one of their jobs was to speak when someone from the embassy approached, would they also be the ones to give the order for the crowd to become more violent?

All of her free time now was spent reviewing videos of the men or standing on the rooftop watching them. Her mind played with ways she could lure the men away from the crowd to see what would happen, but she had yet to come up with something solid. They never ate or slept and barely talked to anyone while they sat on the stone wall. The only time they deviated from this was when they were called to prayer by the mosque. Five times a day the men would get in a single line with their backs to the embassy and lay down their prayer rugs.

Duncan had been able to identify the constantly rotating faces in the crowd, as well as the men on the wall, as dockworkers, but they came from a variety of employers. She had asked Duncan to dig deeper into each company that had employed the men, trying to find a connection between them.

The lack of information was starting to wear on her. She wanted to brief Ellie quickly and return to her review of the perimeter videos. Maybe tonight would be the night she would find what she needed to make the pieces fit together.

* * *

Ellie could feel her emotions bubbling to the surface though she was doing her best to hide them. Each day she forced aside the thought that everything was her fault, but she couldn't help but wonder if everything would return to normal if she left today. It was getting harder to remain calm and be patient.

It was also getting harder to work with Angel. She wanted to believe that she would come to her with any information they found and they would be able to discuss it, but for several days, Angel's briefings had been short and lacked any substance. Angel stood at attention in front of her each morning and night divulging only the smallest amount of material. Ellie could see she was holding back. Tonight she was going to try and break through Angel's façade.

Her office door stood open and Angel was scheduled to arrive any minute. Although the embassy had closed at noon as it did every Friday, some staff still hung around to wrap up any unfinished work from the week. She had forced Chloe out an hour ago despite her protests. The younger crowd gathered in the café in the evenings after dinner. To make the confinement more bearable, Ellie had asked the café staff to leave snacks and beverages out for them.

So far everything within the embassy walls was going smoothly, but she wasn't sure how much longer her staff would manage before everyone went stir crazy. That was one of the reasons she herself was looking forward to her trip to the solar panel farm despite the fight it would take to get Angel to agree to it. She didn't believe the risk would be too great, and she wasn't sure how much longer she could avoid the issue.

She poured steaming tea into two cups sitting on the coffee table, glancing up when movement in the doorway caught her attention. Angel stood outlined by the light coming from the outer office. She hadn't realized how dark it had gotten inside her office, and she had a fleeting thought about how it must look to Angel. Realizing she didn't care, she motioned to the seat across from her. Tonight, she would make Angel sit.

She watched Angel's gaze take in the drinks on the coffee table before she slowly crossed the room, taking a seat on the couch across from her. Angel's back was stiff and she sat with her knees together and both feet flat on the floor.

"Would you like cream or sugar?" she asked.

Angel shook her head.

"I know you normally drink coffee." She didn't finish her sentence. She would have said that she was hoping the tea would be relaxing, but telling her that would certainly provoke the opposite reaction.

"Vince prefers tea," Angel said softly.

Surprised at the personal disclosure, she sensed a crack developing in the wall between them.

"Yes, I have enjoyed a few cups of late-night tea with him." She extended a cup toward her. "As you have, I imagine?"

Angel nodded, taking the cup. "He never offers. He assumes. Seems you learned something from him."

She smiled. Thankfully, Angel wasn't running from the room.

"Is there a purpose to this or are you hoping I'll divulge company secrets?" Angel's voice held the hint of a smile.

"I was hoping we could talk."

"Okay. I'm listening."

"Fine. I'll go first. When I found out you were coming and even before I knew you were a woman, I'd hoped that you and I might be able to develop a friendship. I have a lot of staff around me, but no one I can really talk with."

Angel's eyes studied her, and she hesitated only a second before continuing.

"You have a job to do, as do I, but there isn't any reason we can't be friends, right?"

Angel took a sip of tea before speaking. "My first priority is my job to protect you, but as long as a friendship doesn't interfere with that, then, no, there isn't any reason we can't."

"Good. We've found a common ground." She slid her heels off and dropped them to the floor before tucking her feet under her. "How did you end up working for Vince?"

"Starting with the hard questions?"

She grimaced. "I thought I was starting easy."

Angel's head bent as her gaze settled on her cup of tea. Her voice was soft again when she finally spoke.

"Vince took me in and trained me. He gave me a home."

"I figured as much. Your use of his first name told me that he was more than an employer."

"As did my file."

She took a sip of her tea while she contemplated her answer, thankful for the darkness that hid the blush she could feel on her face.

Angel saved her from answering. "I wouldn't have expected anything less from someone in your position. You need to know who's working for you. Besides…I read your file too."

There wasn't enough light to read her face, but she could hear the teasing in Angel's voice. It reminded her of the day she had arrived. She didn't realize how much she had longed for this easiness between them again. She reached behind her head and turned on the lamp. "Just so it was only my file and you didn't get any of Vince's insight."

Angel smiled. "No. Only the professional file."

She felt the heat on her face again. She hadn't read the personal file that Micalah had sent, but it was still in her desk drawer. Having met Angel, it felt like a betrayal to read the file now. She hadn't been able to bring herself to shred it as she had planned, though, in case she changed her mind.

"So if we're asking the hard questions—why did you leave the Senate?" Angel asked.

She couldn't count the number of times she had been asked that in the last year. She had several carefully prepared phrases that she used to avoid the topic, but she didn't want to use any of them on Angel. She took a deep breath. "I needed a change when my father passed away. I didn't feel like I was making a difference. It felt like I was being swallowed by the political lion, and soon I would be just another mouthpiece in Washington. I couldn't stand the thought of that."

Was that a flash of admiration that crossed Angel's face or only a shadow from the lamp? She wasn't sure, but she hoped she hadn't made a mistake by speaking from her heart. To avoid saying more, she quickly asked her own question. "Your career seemed to have a solid path. Why did you switch to negotiation?"

Angel set her empty mug on the coffee table and sat back on the couch. Her posture was a lot less rigid than when she had arrived. She almost looked relaxed.

"I wanted a chance to fix situations before the snipers had to act." Angel paused as if considering her next statement. "Snipers spend a lot of time waiting, and then they have to run like hell. I was sick of running."

Ellie chuckled. She liked Angel's sense of humor even if it came out of avoidance of the real answer. Angel's file had not listed a specific number of kills, as was to be expected by a private organization, but there were over a hundred cases marked as "mission complete." She wouldn't speculate on how many of them included Angel following through with her assignment as a sniper. She wished Angel would keep talking. She could sit here for hours and listen to her. Or just look at her.

Angel stood. "I guess I should get back to work."

She wanted to say no. She wanted to encourage her to stay longer, but she knew she had gotten all she was going to get from Angel tonight.

"Thank you for the tea," Angel said as she left.

She stared at the empty spot on the couch across from her. She had been right in her initial evaluation. Angel was exactly what she wanted in a confidante. Someone who would let her speak her mind but not pull any punches in her responses. She wanted to spend more time with this woman.

She realized, too, that Angel had managed to escape once again without giving her a briefing of any sort.

* * *

Angel paced the hallway outside her room. She had considered going to the gym, but Ellie's tea had relaxed her body and she didn't think she had the energy. Her mind was still racing, however. She had been keyed up with all the surveillance, but she hadn't expected Ellie to be the one that grounded her again. The way she had curled her feet under her on the couch had been endearing. She tried to push those thoughts from her mind.

She was here to protect this woman and to make sure the embassy was not overrun. Drinking tea and chatting was not in her job description, though she had to admit she had enjoyed that almost more than anything she had done since she had arrived. Ellie was a fascinating woman, and her mind was only too happy to flash images of Ellie taking charge of an embassy meeting or pacing as she persuaded others to see her viewpoint.

She needed to focus on work and not on the many sides of the woman she was tracking on her tablet. She swiped her badge into the communications room and randomly flipped through all the cameras. The marines had gotten used to her late night appearances, and they allowed her free rein. She settled on the camera outside the embassy that covered the front guard post. The men on the street moved around, talking with each other. They weren't chanting or waving their arms like they did during the day.

She moved the toggle at the base of the monitor, sliding the camera toward the man on the stone wall. She took a deep breath, unable to shake a feeling of apprehension. There he was, doing the same thing the men on the wall always did, sitting and staring. As she watched him doing nothing, her apprehension continued to grow.

She stood and patted the PFC on the shoulder. "Thanks." Returning her chair to its spot, she left the room and walked to the rooftop.

Her agents and the marine there were all stationary, their gazes scrutinizing the world beneath them. She walked to the agent with a view of the man on the stone wall. Forrest Arden, the guy who regularly handled early shifts during their assignments, lay on his stomach watching him through the scope on his rifle. She patted his shoulder as she lay down beside him.

"Has he done anything since he arrived?"

Arden shook his head. "Same as always. Why?"

She was silent for so long he finally glanced at her. "Tag?"

"Just a feeling."

"What? Something's going to change?"

"They've been doing the same thing long enough to make us relax. Now maybe they'll show their hand. Remain vigilant. Call me if he does anything. Anything at all."

Arden nodded, his gaze returning to the ground below.

She stood and walked slowly back to her room. Inside, she lay down on top of the covers. Something was going to happen soon. She could feel it. She hoped she would be able to stop it before it threatened the embassy or the ambassador.

CHAPTER THIRTEEN

Angel leaned against the doorframe and stared into the café. She had been in Nouakchott for a week now, and normally she would be knee-deep in negotiations by now. Something was throwing her off balance. She couldn't decide if it was the situation outside or the woman inside. Ellie had been distant, almost standoffish in their morning briefing. She was starting to realize that too much or too little Ellie was equally distracting. Maybe it was time to find a little balance.

She watched as Ellie moved along in front of the food selections, her tray resting on the metal track in front of her. She stopped occasionally to talk with the café workers behind the plastic barrier, smiling at each of them. Her hair fell around her face as she moved down the line, and she casually brushed it behind an ear. She wore tan dress pants with a dark blue shirt open at the collar. A matching jacket was folded over one arm. Angel wasn't surprised. In the week that she had known Ellie, she knew she wouldn't be caught outside her office without her jacket. Always the professional, even at lunch on a Saturday.

Her gaze stopped when it reached Ellie's shoes—blue open-toe heels with crossing straps at the ankle. The narrow heel had to be at least three or maybe even four inches high. She had to admit that they looked good on Ellie, but she still wondered how she kept them on her feet or even walked in them. She had been told once that the trick was to stay on your toes, but she wasn't going to try it to see if it was true.

She took a few steps into the café, appreciating her own footwear. Black tactical boots that were good for walking, standing, or even running. She was prepared for whatever situation might arise. She glanced up and caught Ellie's gaze on her. The edge of her mouth was slightly turned up as if she knew exactly what Angel was thinking.

Fighting down the blush that threatened, she concentrated on the food selection in front of her. She chose a bowl of chicken noodle soup and filled her tray with onion-flavored crackers. The crackers were light and buttery and added much needed flavor to the soup. After the first time she had tried them, she discovered that the onion smell didn't linger on her breath like real onions and this had become her favorite selection.

"Can I join you for lunch?" she asked softly as she moved beside Ellie at the beverage counter.

"I'd like that." Ellie gave her a wink. "You aren't afraid people will talk?"

"No fear here. Being seen with you is good for my image."

Enjoying the sound of Ellie's chuckle, she followed her to a beige laminate table in the middle of the room. It was held together with metal legs and surrounded by multicolored plastic chairs. Sitting across from Ellie, she crushed a pack of crackers before opening the cellophane and dropping the crumbs into her bowl. After several packs, she glanced up to find Ellie watching her.

"Like those crackers, do you?" Ellie choked back a laugh.

She took the spoon from Ellie's tray and dipped it into her bowl, offering the bite to Ellie.

Ellie leaned forward to accept, but then quickly took the spoon from Angel's hand. She slid the bite into her mouth. Her eyes never left Angel's as she savored it.

"Okay. I'm sorry I teased you. That's good. I haven't eaten the soup in months. It's always been a little bland."

"Just a little?"

Ellie chuckled. "I try hard not to complain about the food they make. It's hard to please so many people seven days a week." Ellie took a bite of her sandwich.

Last night's conversation had dissipated the uncomfortable tension that had been growing between them. She was happy to have the playful banter back. It didn't escape her attention that she had almost fed the ambassador a bite of her soup in the middle of the café.

"That's very true," she said. "I try never to complain when anyone else is providing me with food. I tend to eat the same thing day after day even when I'm cooking."

"So, it's more about convenience than quality?"

She raised her eyebrows. "I guess so. I never thought about it. I like to keep things simple. If a food requires a bunch of extras then it's not worth it."

"That's funny. Where do you draw the line? Salt and pepper is okay, but cheese and sour cream goes too far?" Ellie teased.

"You're awfully harsh today. Not enough sleep?"

"I'm just trying to figure you out."

She felt the heat flood her face again as Ellie studied her. It wasn't her practice to let any woman get under her skin, and yet, without any effort Ellie was already there.

She narrowed her eyes. "What's to figure out?"

"When did you become the Guardian Angel?"

She groaned, shaking her head. "Vince started it. I guess I should have expected it with a name like Angel."

"And yet it bothers you."

She washed her bite of soup down with a drink of water as she struggled to contain her emotions. She could let the question pass like she did with everyone else, but she liked being the focus of Ellie's attention. It was intoxicating and she wanted to give her more. "Everyone assumes it's because of my sniper days."

"It's not?"

She had never talked about her mother with anyone but Vince. Surely, Ellie already knew all of this. It was in her file. She could still change the subject. Or she could take a chance and keep going. She took deep breath.

"Vince said my mom told him I was always nearby waiting to help her, even when I was really little. She was sick from the time I was born. I can remember thinking if I could always watch over her she might be okay."

"But she wasn't?" Ellie asked softly.

"She died when I was thirteen."

"We have that in common. And your dad?"

"Active duty Special Forces. He was killed about a year after Mom died."

"And then Vince took you in?"

"He was just starting Flagler so he took me with him when he could." She pushed back from the table. "Now you know all there is to know."

"I highly doubt that."

She stood, ignoring Ellie's words as she gathered her trash onto her tray. Her heart hurt. She wasn't sorry she had shared, but she couldn't stand to see pity in Ellie's eyes. She walked to the trash bin, stacked her dishes, and dumped the rest. She knew Ellie was behind her, and she slowed her pace when she reached the empty hallway, giving Ellie a chance to catch up if she wanted to.

She turned when Ellie touched her arm. Ellie's eyes were moist, and they radiated warmth and compassion. She felt like a piece of chocolate that had been left in the car on a hot day. She touched Ellie's cheek. She had wanted to do it, but she was shocked when she felt Ellie's soft skin beneath her fingers. Ellie seemed surprised as well, but she tilted her head into Angel's palm. Sliding her hand under the hair at the base of Ellie's neck, she gently pulled their bodies together. Her gaze lingered on Ellie's lips.

The scrape of a chair sliding across the floor echoed from the café through the hallway, breaking the connection between them. She quickly dropped her hand as Ellie took a step backward. Ellie's neck was flushed, and Angel knew she should apologize. More for what she had almost done than for what she did. Or maybe for what she wanted to do. She met Ellie's green eyes, and the words caught in her throat. She had never seen such open desire.

She had to reestablish the professional distance between them. Even if she didn't want to. "I'm sorry."

Ellie guided them down the hall toward the elevator. "I'm not."

Angel's head swam. The pressure of Ellie's fingers wrapped around her arm was making her want to pick up where they had left off. She needed distance, but she couldn't pull away. The elevator doors opened and they stepped in. Ellie let go of her arm temporarily as they turned their backs to the wall, and then she slid her fingers around Angel's bicep. She tried not to flex her muscle, but each time Ellie's fingers tightened her body responded.

When the doors opened on the second floor, she walked with Ellie down the hall. She hadn't planned to follow Ellie back to her office, but she couldn't think of anywhere else she needed to be. Their pace was slow and she felt Ellie's hand slide down her arm. She grasped it, sliding her fingers between Ellie's for barely a second before releasing it.

Through the open door, she could see Chloe at her desk. She slowed to let Ellie enter first and to put some much needed space between them.

"How do you walk in those shoes?" she asked, making Ellie laugh and breaking the electrical current that connected them.

"You get used to it," Ellie said, stopping at Chloe's desk. "Any messages?"

"Just one. It's on your desk."

Ellie nodded. "Okay. Thanks. Why are you here on a Saturday anyway?"

Chloe shrugged. "I knew you would be."

"I'm always here, but you don't need to be."

As if waiting for permission, Chloe stood. "Great. I'll see you Monday."

Ellie paused in the doorway, waiting for Angel to enter. The last thing Angel needed was to be alone behind a closed door with Ellie, but she stepped inside anyway. Her body tingled as she heard the click of the door closing behind them. She stood in front of Ellie's desk as she watched her read the note Chloe had left. When their eyes met, she could still see the remnants of desire.

"Something for Sam to handle," Ellie said, tossing the note on her desk and walking around it.

She held her breath as Ellie approached. She was a soldier and she could withstand any pressure put on her, but the desire she felt for Ellie was not something she was used to. How had things escalated so quickly? She held her position, her feet frozen to the floor, her posture rigid and tense. She found comfort in standing at attention. This she knew how to do.

At the last minute, Ellie turned away from her and took a seat on the couch. Releasing her breath, she watched Ellie drop her shoes to the floor and curl her feet under her.

"Join me?" Ellie asked.

She moved slowly to the couch, her heart racing. She had been braced—prepared almost—for Ellie's touch. She was in forbidden territory. She sat, placing both hands on her knees and wishing she had the strength to leave but praying she wouldn't. Ellie was beautiful. Her green eyes were smoldering.

"Is this your first time in Mauritania?" Ellie asked, handing her a cup of tea.

She nodded, hoping her voice wouldn't come out in a croak. "Yes, but I've been in countries like this before."

"What does that mean?"

Ellie's defensive tone snapped Angel from her lingering haze of arousal, and she answered without thinking.

"Countries that restrict and violate their people's rights."

"That's not how I would define Mauritania."

She was puzzled. How had their morning taken such a terrible turn? She wasn't trying to pick a fight, but she wasn't going to let Ellie deny the truth either. There was no way Ellie moved around this country without seeing the reality of it. "How long have you been here?" she asked.

"Almost six months."

"But you were here as a kid? Twice?"

Ellie's fingers ran circles around the rim of her cup, a sign that she was contemplating her answer or their conversation. The tenseness of the muscles in her neck was also a sign that Angel was treading on thin ice.

"Yes, this was my father's first assignment, and then he came back when I was a teenager," Ellie answered.

"You were young the first time, but when you were older surely you could see how bad things were. Why would you want to come back now?" She wanted to bite her tongue, but she knew it was too late. She had asked the question that kept nagging at her, but she knew now wasn't the right time.

"This is a beautiful country with a lot of great people. Why wouldn't I want to come back?"

"The government is corrupt and treats women like they're property. Your being here gives them approval to keep doing what they're doing."

Ellie's face flushed with anger. Angel knew she had gone too far to stop now. It wasn't any of her business why Ellie had made the choices she had, but she wanted to know.

Ellie's voice quivered with emotion. "I draw attention to the corruption and stand up to anything that's not right. I don't cover it up or make excuses."

"They take young women and force them to binge eat to make them fat and then sell them into marriage with men four times their age." There were even worse acts performed on young women, but she couldn't bring herself to put them into words. "And what about the twenty percent of the population that's still in slavery."

Ellie shook her head. "This country was built on tradition and it takes time to teach new ideas."

"And in the meantime, children are being traumatized, not to mention the innocent people who are being held in prisons and starved to death."

"Things aren't always simply right or wrong," Ellie said vehemently.

"Yes, they are." She stood. "And the truth is you're not safe here."

Ellie stood too. "Your world is only black and white, but mine is gray. I can't walk away when there are still things here that I can accomplish."

Angel shook her head. "You're risking your life to stay in a country that would kill you without a thought. Why?"

"Because I can make a difference."

"I will never understand that."

"Then maybe I should ask you to leave. Permanently."

She was too angry to smooth Ellie's ruffled feathers this time. She should leave before this conversation got her fired. If it wasn't too late already. Her job was not to pass judgment on the country or on the job the ambassador was doing. Vince would not be happy with her.

They both froze at a knock on the door. Was this protocol? Shouldn't Chloe have buzzed the phone line before someone approached the door? Then she remember Chloe had left for the day.

"Yes. Come in." Ellie turned toward the door.

She quickly stepped in front of Ellie, placing her body between Ellie and the door.

The door opened and a Mauritanian embassy employee stuck his head through the opening and began talking immediately. "Madam Ambassador, I need to talk with you urgently."

"What is it, Farook?"

His gaze froze on Angel. "I should speak only with you."

Angel studied the man's face, placing him as responsible for the embassy vehicles. She wanted to hear what he had to say and she was prepared for a fight. Ellie was ready to have her removed from this detail, and she was confident she was about to be asked to leave the room.

"This is Agent McTaggart, my head of security. She should be present for any discussions concerning the security of our vehicles."

She quickly hid her surprise, sticking her hand out to help ease some of the harshness in Ellie's words.

He shook her hand and then turned his back to her, pulling on his jacket sleeves nervously. "Madam Ambassador, two of the vehicles are in need of repairs and must be taken out of the embassy."

"That's fine. Please secure two replacement vehicles for us to use until they're repaired."

He nodded and hurried out the door. She watched him leave and then turned to Ellie.

"What was so confidential about that?"

Ellie shrugged. "Nothing. It was a hierarchy struggle play."

"What would he have gained by making me leave the room?"

"Again, probably nothing."

Ellie walked around her desk and took a seat in her chair.

"I expected you to ask me to leave," she said hesitantly.

"Because of our conversation?"

"Yes."

"Well, I wanted to, but I couldn't let him gain the upper hand."

She nodded and turned to go. Ellie was still upset and saying the wrong thing now might make things worse. They both needed time to cool off and the best thing she could do was leave. So she did.

CHAPTER FOURTEEN

Ellie dropped her head in her hands. It was Monday morning and she was still agonizing over pushing Angel into a controversial discussion. She had wanted to know her thoughts, but how could she expect an outsider to understand what she saw in this beautiful country? She was aware of the truth underlying the statistics, but instead of agreeing with Angel she had become defensive. She didn't want Angel to look down on a nation with so much potential. Yes, things were still being done wrong, but she had to believe there were others besides her that wanted to make things better.

She had taken Angel's attack personally. Was Angel implying that the country wasn't worth saving or that Ellie couldn't save it? She felt nauseous. She didn't need Angel to believe she could do this job, she reminded herself. Others believed in her ability and supported her work.

As if on cue, Sam stepped through her open door. Ellie gave him a big smile.

"What did I do?" he asked.

"You believe in the work we're doing here, right?"

"I do." Sam narrowed his eyes. "What's wrong?"

"Nothing. Nothing at all." She picked up the note Chloe had left on her desk on Saturday. "Inspector Asker returned your call. He's willing to come for a meeting. Schedule it and I can sit in or not, whichever you think would be best."

Sam nodded and took the note from her hand as he stood. "I'll call him right now."

At the door he turned back. "I see the solar panel visit is still on your schedule for next Monday. Have you set that up with your new security? Maybe I should go instead."

"No. We fought hard for that visit and you've been there twice. I want to see it."

"And your security?"

"They'll have to deal with it."

Sam's chuckle echoed through her office. She turned her chair to the window. The crowd was still out there. She always hoped each time she looked that maybe they wouldn't be there. Sam was right. Angel was not going to be happy with her. She would need to check with Farook and make sure he had vehicles for the trip.

As it had all day yesterday, her mind was still spinning on Saturday's lunch conversation and what had happened afterward. The way it felt to be held in Angel's arms and the almost-kiss had left her wanting so much more. She spun back to her desk. What had started as something very pleasant had turned sour and left her unsettled. Focusing on work would carry her through another day. If only she could concentrate.

* * *

Angel fought the urge to return to her room, but hiding was not her way of dealing with disasters. The after-lunch conversation on Saturday had been exactly that. A disaster. Once again, Ellie was upset with her. She had spent most of Sunday hidden away in the Communications Center and here she was again. This had become her new home. She liked the quiet, and maybe the subdued lighting, more than she wanted to admit. The marines assigned to this room were used to her coming and going and they only spoke if she prompted them first. Otherwise they left her to her own thoughts.

She pulled up the tracking app on her tablet and watched Ellie's light blink in her office a floor below. She liked to think she was only doing her job, but after the almost-kiss on Saturday it felt a little like stalking so she pushed the tablet to the side and concentrated on the cameras. She flipped through each one, studying the faces that were displayed and putting a name and whatever other details she could remember with each face.

She tried to review Ellie's upcoming schedule too, but all she could see was Ellie's angry face. She had never before let her personal feelings interfere with an assignment, and she couldn't now. She would make peace with her tonight at the briefing. No matter what she thought about the human rights violations in this country, it wasn't Ellie's fault and she didn't deserve to be criticized.

Ellie was intelligent and she wanted to know more about her. Arguing was not the way to gain that information, though. If she wanted to figure out why Ellie would come to a country where she was not considered an equal, she had to listen to the words she wasn't saying. Angel had traveled all over the Middle East and through many countries in Africa. She had earned the respect of men who considered women inferior, but most times it was through a form of violence—firing a weapon or hand-to-hand combat.

Ellie was anything but violent. She had a strong but generous demeanor. One more thing about her that Angel found intriguing. Understanding what made her tick was going to be harder than she had thought. During her time here, she had watched Ellie meet with Mauritanian men and never once had she seen her back down. She spoke her mind with a quiet strength that clearly had earned her respect. Maybe Ellie *could* make a difference in this country.

* * *

Angel emerged from the communications room in time to grab a quick sandwich before the café closed for the night. Her body was stiff from sitting all day, and she worked out the kinks while she made her rounds, checking in with her agents on duty. When she arrived in Ellie's office, she was relieved and disappointed when she didn't see the teapot on the coffee table. It was clear that, the same as yesterday, there would be no invitation to sit.

She offered a short briefing as not much had changed since the morning. She remained silent, standing in front of Ellie's desk when she finished. Ellie's attention returned to the paperwork in front of her.

She should leave. Just turn around and walk out. She took a deep breath instead. "I'm sorry about my comments on Saturday."

"Did you speak your true feelings?"

"I did."

"Then you shouldn't be sorry." Ellie finally met her eyes. "I'm sorry I threatened your job. I was out of line."

She nodded and turned to leave. The tension was still there between them, but at least she had apologized.

"One more thing." Ellie's voice was soft.

Angel stopped at the door and turned back to face her.

"I *will* show you what I see in Mauritania before you leave."

She *did* like this woman.

* * *

Ellie watched on her tablet as Angel made her nightly rounds. Occasionally she would run the cursor over Angel's light only to see her name displayed there. Agent McTaggart. When Angel left the main gate and headed back inside, she stepped to the window. As she had every night, Angel paused and glanced up.

She had been surprised at how easily Angel's words had made her lose her cool. She prided herself on being able to listen and not get angry. For some reason, the words had hurt more coming from Angel. She still felt a niggling of annoyance that Angel could condemn the entire country. Outsiders were quick to make assumptions, but she knew there were a lot of good people here. She worked with them every day.

She wasn't blind to the injustices, but she could already see the progress she had made in only a short time. There were two Mauritania government-approved organizations now in place that were working to stop child slavery and abuse. Each month, she met with several women's groups, and last month a few husbands had attended. She was opening up dialogue between the government and several southern-based ethnic groups. Changing traditional views about slavery and providing work opportunities for former slaves would make the country stronger. She was nowhere near ready to admit defeat.

CHAPTER FIFTEEN

Ellie paced the length of her office. She now had three days to convince Angel that the solar panel farm visit was something she couldn't postpone. Sam had made a point of reminding her about it every morning for the last week. It wasn't that she had forgotten. Her mind had been continually playing the ways she could approach the topic with Angel, but in all of them Angel's response wasn't in agreement with her. She was surprised Angel hadn't brought it up yet, but most likely she assumed that it would be postponed like every other excursion on Ellie's schedule had been.

"That's your third cup of coffee today," Chloe announced as Ellie passed her desk.

Everyone close to her knew she was insistent about her one-cup rule. Tea was okay in the afternoon, but she stayed away from the coffeepot.

"I didn't know you were counting?" She smiled to soften her words. It wasn't Chloe's fault that she was stressed. She honestly hadn't realized that she was on her third cup.

"Anything I can help you with?" Chloe asked.

She leaned against the doorframe and cradled her cup in her hands. "I'm looking for the words that will convince Agent McTaggart that the solar panel visit is essential."

"Oh, that's Monday, right?"

She nodded.

"I assumed that would be changed," Chloe said with chagrin. "I almost scheduled something over it."

"Please don't. I'm still hoping to make the trip."

"So, let's hear your argument. Convince me."

"Okay." She took a seat on the couch across from Chloe's desk. "The private company doing the construction is US-based so it's vital that we monitor them. Lately they've been very secretive. None of the recent updates they've provided include an estimated date of completion. According to the initial documents, it should have been finished already."

"Can't someone from the Mauritanian government do the site inspection?" Chloe asked.

"Not really. Under the contract their involvement is limited until after completion. Then the entire farm is turned over to their electric company."

"Hasn't Deputy Pantone already visited the site?"

She raised an eyebrow and Chloe laughed.

"I'm channeling your new security angel. That's what she'd ask right?"

"Okay, yes, he has been there. Twice, in fact. Once before I was assigned here and then a month into my tour. But I'm the ambassador and Mauritania needs this plant. It would power at least half of Nouakchott and all of the surrounding villages. It's only a couple hours' drive—"

"Really?"

Ellie chuckled. "Okay, it's about a five-hour drive. Akjoujt is about three and the plant is an hour or so beyond that. Almost to Atar. However, it's right along a developed road, so travel would be quick and easy."

Chloe laughed again. "You think she'll buy that?"

"Thanks for your encouragement." She stood. "I think I'll walk and rehearse the words in my head."

Chloe's laughter followed her down the hall and into the stairwell. She knew this wasn't going to be easy, but it was worth the effort. This solar plant would be the largest in Africa. It would allow the country to be more self-sufficient. Rather than being dependent on fishing, the locals would have the ability to support livestock and agriculture outside the city.

Dealing with Angel had not been her only concern. Farook had not been back with an update since he had advised her a week ago that two of the cars needed repairs. She could ask Sam to check in with him, but her legs needed a stretch and she wanted to know now.

The sound of her heels clicking on the concrete stairs made her think of Angel's comment on her shoes. She realized, sadly, that was the last time they had shared a comfortable banter. Angel was back to her rigid posture for briefings again, and part of her was relieved. The almost-kiss in the hallway was not something she could forget, but remembering the heated conversation that followed did dampen some of the thrill.

Pulling open the fire door to the garage, she stepped inside. The smell of oil and gasoline hit her hard, and she paused to let her senses acclimate to the odor. Farook, she saw, was standing behind one of the embassy sedans with the trunk open. He was listening intently as a man she didn't recognize spoke. The man's skin was light and his Arabic was broken. American? She could tell Farook was angry, and she strained to hear their conversation. As the fire door banged shut behind her, both men turned in surprise.

"Madam Ambassador?" Farook walked toward her as the other man quickly left through the door into the employee parking area at the back of the motor pool.

"Who was that?" she asked.

"No one. He was going to do some of the repairs on the broken vehicles. His prices are too high. I will find someone else to do the work. What can I do for you?" He moved them toward the stairs as he talked.

"Will we have vehicles ready by Monday?"

"Oh, yes."

Ellie frowned. Farook was always anxious to please, but today his brow was furrowed in displeasure. He was clearly upset at her for interrupting. His change in moods made her curious, and she wanted to question him further.

* * *

Angel's gaze strayed from the camera monitor to the tablet. Ellie's light was on the move, and she frowned as it continued to travel down the stairs toward the parking garage. When it reached the motor pool, she stood and grabbed her tablet. Where was Ellie going? She walked quickly to the stairs, struggling not to run. Ellie was safe within the building and she was confident she wouldn't leave. Wasn't she?

She had been trying to keep her distance from Ellie to avoid any more confrontations or awkward moments. Other than her briefings, which she was keeping short, she had purposely avoided being alone with her. She had isolated herself and now she was paying the price. Ellie was handling things on her own and it was her fault.

She pushed through the fire door, pausing to observe the scene in front of her. An angry scowl covered Farook's face as he turned to glare at her. He wasn't happy to see her. It shook her a little to see that he may not have been completely happy with the conversation he had been having with Ellie either. She saw a glimpse of relief on Ellie's face before she concealed it and was glad she had not hesitated to join them.

"Your appointment has arrived, Madam Ambassador," she said firmly.

Ellie looked confused and then nodded. "I'm coming." Turning to Farook, she smiled. "So, we're all good then."

He nodded.

Ellie turned and walked into the stairwell. Angel's gaze drifted between Farook and Ellie. Then she followed Ellie through the door.

"What the hell are you doing?" Ellie whispered angrily.

"Watching your back."

"I'm not a child. It's bad enough that we're all locked inside this building, but now you want to tell me there are places inside I can't go?"

"Farook didn't look happy."

Ellie shrugged, walking ahead of Angel. "I can make it back to my office without an escort."

She stopped and let Ellie continue to climb the stairs alone. She wasn't trying to upset her, and yet somehow she always managed to. She wasn't sorry that she had tracked her down, though. Farook's behavior made her apprehensive. She sent a text to Sarah to dig deeper into his background.

* * *

Ellie slowed her pace once she realized Angel was no longer following her. She wasn't sure why her temper had flared again. She had wanted to tell Angel about the conversation, but she didn't want to admit that something might be going on under her nose. She was still too angry to confide in her.

Chloe looked up as she entered the office.

"Can you ask Sergeant Miller to stop by?"

The surprise on Chloe's face was obvious. She realized she hadn't met with Shane since the day Angel had arrived.

Chloe didn't ask any questions, though, and immediately picked up her phone.

She sat at her desk and thought about the conversation she had overheard. The other man had looked and sounded like an American. She was sure he had said that the Conex was ready and that they were waiting for Farook to provide what he had promised. What would Farook have to do with a shipping container or anything being exported?

Shane tapped lightly on her door before stepping inside.

"Come in." She motioned him to a chair. "Thank you for coming so quickly. I need you to check on something for me."

She ignored the concerned look on his face.

"Sam's busy and Angel's too new in the country." She knew her excuses were lame. "You still have some customs contacts at the docks, right?"

"I have a few friends that work there," he answered hesitantly.

"It's nothing important, so I'd rather you not mention it to anyone here. Can you ask around the docks about what shipments are ready to depart?" She shrugged. "I overheard a conversation between Farook and another man, possibly an American. It piqued my interest."

If Shane was surprised by what she was telling him, his face didn't show it. She made a quick decision to tell him everything that she had heard.

He stood when she finished. "I can ask around. Do you want me to question Farook?"

"No, not until we know more. I appreciate your checking this out. Let me know what you find out." She hoped her last statement didn't betray her anxiety about the request. She knew she could trust Shane, but she didn't doubt that he would share everything with Angel if he thought he should.

CHAPTER SIXTEEN

Ellie towel dried her hair as she dressed. She had delayed the conversation with Angel about the trip on Monday long enough. It was now two days away, and Angel would be even angrier if she wasn't given enough time to prepare. This wasn't going to be a debate anyway. She had made her decision.

The solar panel farm was too important to the people of Mauritania. The current system was powered mostly by diesel generators, which resulted in severe energy shortages. If people had the ability to move outside the city for farming and to have livestock, it would decrease the overwhelming demand on the already strained Nouakchott electrical grid. Not to mention how much carbon dioxide output it would reduce.

She had no doubt that Angel would be able to understand the importance of this, but whether it would be enough to override her views regarding her security obligations would remain to be seen. If that didn't work she was resigned to calling Vince. Force wasn't the path she wanted to take. She wanted cooperation and maybe even agreement. She had considered asking Sam to sit in on the meeting. It would feel good to have someone on her side as she fought this battle, but she didn't want to back Angel into a corner.

She skipped breakfast and headed straight to her office. Her stomach was in turmoil as her mind played and replayed the words she would say. Chloe wasn't at her desk yet so Ellie started the coffeemaker and waited while it brewed. Taking her steaming cup, she walked to the window overlooking the front of the embassy. Lately she had been watching Angel's blinking GPS tracker far more than she had the crowd below.

She counted about thirty men moving among each other and chatting like it was a social gathering. Since Angel's arrival their numbers had not grown and there had not been any gunfire. Had she been wrong to resist a show of additional security? She watched the men as the city was called to prayer by the local mosque. They knelt in the direction of Mecca, the direction where the sun would eventually appear, but for now the sky held barely a hint of light. The words echoing throughout the city were muffled by the building surrounding her, but she had heard the beginning of the prayer enough times to know the words. *Allahu akbar* or "God is great."

She turned as Angel knocked lightly on her doorframe. She wasn't the only one starting her day early.

"Come in," she said, turning back to watch the men below.

Angel crossed the room and joined her at the window. Silently they watched the men stand and return to their previous conversations. Ellie could feel Angel's body lightly touching against her own. She leaned slightly against her, and Angel wrapped an arm around her waist. She savored the moment for a few seconds, drawing strength from their connection. Taking a deep breath, she stepped away from the warmth of Angel's body and met her eyes.

"What?" Angel asked.

"We need to talk."

She dropped into her chair and waited while Angel took up her regular position in front of her desk. The questioning look on Angel's face forced her to drive forward.

"I need to confirm something on my schedule with you."

She almost faltered as Angel's eyes narrowed.

"I have a trip scheduled for Monday to see the new solar panel farm."

"I saw it, but I thought we had an understanding. It's not safe for you to leave the embassy right now."

She stood, shoving her chair back, and began to pace. "This plant is costing over thirty million dollars. Sam has been out there twice, but the last two progress reports have been vague and provided no date of completion. A private company is doing the construction and they are being secretive about their production and imports. I fought hard to get this visit. Since it's a US-based company, I consider it more of an inspection than a visit. If I don't show, it will say that we don't care if they screw the Mauritanian government and its people."

She stopped in front of Angel and leaned against her desk. "Can you see how important this to me and for the United States?"

Angel's eyes pierced into her and she could feel every breath Angel took. She hadn't realized how close they were standing. Angel's gaze was intense, and she realized she wasn't sure if she was waiting for Angel to grant her approval or kiss her. When Angel finally spoke her voice was deeper than she had ever heard it.

"I understand," Angel said hoarsely.

She started to speak and Angel held up her hand.

"For your safety, though, I cannot allow you to leave the embassy. We don't know what's happening out there. What if this is the opportunity they've been waiting for? What if the plan is to kidnap you?"

"I don't ca—"

She squeezed her eyes shut as Angel's fingers touched her lips before sliding across her cheek and into her hair.

"I do," Angel said softly.

Angel gently guided their faces closer and Ellie stared into her dark eyes. Any thought of her office and the anticipated site visit disappeared as she leaned into Angel's touch. She wanted nothing except to feel Angel's lips on hers.

Angel didn't disappoint her. Their first touch was soft and gentle. She pulled Angel even closer, encouraging her to deepen the kiss. With permission given, Angel responded immediately. She eagerly met Angel's tongue as it traced her lips before exploring her mouth. Relief at finally giving in to the desire coursing through her made her head swim.

The intercom on her desk buzzed. She froze, breaking the kiss, but Angel did not release her. She rested her forehead against Angel's chest while she worked to find her voice.

"Yes, Chloe?" Angel answered for her.

She felt the vibration of Angel's husky voice surge through her body.

"I'm sorry to disturb you, but Sam's on his way over. He says it's urgent," Chloe answered.

She lifted her head and used all of her strength to step away from Angel. Her office door stood open, but Chloe had chosen to use the intercom instead. Her face flushed as she realized what Chloe might have observed. She gathered all of her dignity and crossed to her office door.

"Send him right in."

"Yes, ma'am," Chloe responded as she studied the computer screen in front of her.

She returned to her desk and forced herself to remain standing. She picked up her coffee cup and shakily set it back down. She placed her hands on the desk and leaned on them, giving her head a shake. When she finally looked up into Angel's eyes, she was instantly lost again. The dark swirling depths called to her and she longed to forget everything around them.

"Should I apologize?" Angel asked.

"Do you want to?"

"No."

She shook her head again. "Then don't."

Angel's mouth quirked in a mischievous grin. Ellie pulled away from the dark depths of Angel's eyes as Sam burst through the door.

"Ellie, we need to send someone to the fish market."

"What happened?"

"Another fishing boat was rammed. There's still one man missing."

"Okay. Get Gina."

Sam spun on his heel and was gone.

She avoided looking at Angel, but from the corner of her eye she could see the curiosity on her face. She pulled up her log to brush up on the exact date of the last "mishap," as the Chinese government was calling it.

"Want to fill me in?" Angel finally spoke.

She looked up. "A pirogue, that's a—"

"Small boat, I know."

"Well, when a troller rams a pirogue, it slices it in half and dumps the crew in the water. This is the second time in less than a month and someone is missing. We've been fighting to get the government to enforce the zone restrictions."

"Right. I was in the meeting you had the other day."

"Then you know that above and beyond trying to do something to help the man who's missing, this is important to our relations with the locals."

"You can't leave the embassy."

"I know." She sighed.

Angel paced the length of the room and then back before speaking. "What if this is a ploy to get you or someone else on the staff to the docks? We've already confirmed that these are dockworkers outside."

"It's two different things, Angel. Fishermen are not dockworkers and they don't bring their boats into the docks. The deep water port is where the dockworkers are from. The fishermen move in and out from the beaches or the marketplace." She took a deep breath. "This is a country that struggles to feed its own people. They can't afford to lose fishing boats or lives. We have to show our support."

"Gina's ready." Sam confirmed as he entered, glancing at Angel. "I should have asked first. Are you going to let her go?"

She could see the struggle taking place inside Angel. She met Sam's eyes as Angel pulled her phone from her pocket. After shooting an inquiring glance at Ellie, she said, "Gina Stewart?" Ellie nodded, and Angel tapped two buttons on the phone.

"Eric, can you do an escort? Meet Gina Stewart from the public relations office on the first floor and she'll give you the details…Take Falls or Staples with you. Call me when you arrive and before you return."

"Thank you," she said softly as Angel pocketed her phone. "I know that doesn't make you happy, but it's important to us and the work we're doing here."

Angel nodded. "I'm going to go meet with Eric before he leaves, but when I come back I want to hear *all* the details for this excursion you want to take."

"I'll be ready," she said, trying not to sound too excited. She couldn't believe Angel was agreeing to the solar panel visit so easily.

She met Sam's eyes as Angel left the room. He lifted his eyebrows. "It sounds like you've talked her into it."

"I'm working on it. Though security is her first thought, I think she's beginning to understand our challenges."

"I guess we'll see when she comes back."

* * *

Angel watched the two agents leave with an embassy driver and Gina. She wasn't comfortable with any of this. She knew she would feel better if she was the one going. Which was why she planned to accompany Ellie on her trip to the solar panel farm. There was no way she was letting her out of her sight outside the embassy. She didn't really want to let her out of her sight at all.

Their kiss was burned into her memory and would take more than a lifetime to forget. Ellie's lips had been as soft as she had imagined and the way she had responded had pushed her far beyond any measure of control. If they hadn't been interrupted by Chloe, she wasn't sure if she would have stopped. The thought was a bit frightening considering she had spent the last week working hard to keep their relationship on a professional level. One kiss and her job was all but forgotten.

She climbed the stairs and returned to Ellie's office. She was surprised to find Ellie alone, drinking tea on the couch. She took a seat across from her and opened her tablet.

"Where is the solar panel site? And what time do you need to be there?" she asked.

"It's between Akjoujt and Atar. About a five-hour drive. I don't plan on staying long and we can arrive anytime. The entire day has been reserved for us."

"If we left by seven and you spent less than an hour there we could be back by dark."

"I can make that work," Ellie said agreeably. "I wouldn't want to be out after dark anyway."

"I'd like to be back in Nouakchott as close to five as possible. You won't have much time to play with." She typed a few notes to help her remember later when she drew out the plan with Miller.

"I really appreciate this."

She looked up from her tablet and gave Ellie a reluctant smile. "I can see how important it is to you."

"Do we need to talk about what happened earlier?" Ellie asked quietly, leaning forward to place her cup on the coffee table.

Angel was in no way ready to talk about the disconcerting kiss. Even now she could feel the invisible tether pulling her closer to Ellie. She needed time to process what she felt, but most of all she needed time to figure out how she could keep it from happening again. She couldn't allow any distractions especially now with this upcoming trip. Her heart sank as she realized the distance she needed to put between them.

"I won't call it a mistake because that would be wrong, but I will say it can't happen again."

Ellie nodded, but her disappointment was obvious.

"I'd like to have marine drivers and maybe a few for security if Miller can spare them. Three cars with you in the middle." She was already planning a call to Vince to see if she could pull members from Sarah's team. Reducing the security at the embassy wasn't a good idea, and neither was traveling through the countryside without enough protection.

"It's best to use local drivers especially when leaving the city."

"Normally that would make sense, but with the current situation I want all the extra protection we can get for you."

"If we use local drivers, then the marines can focus on security."

She sighed. Everything was a negotiation with Ellie. She stood. "We can go over more specifics tomorrow after I have a chance to talk with Miller."

"Okay." Ellie said, pausing for a second as she studied Angel. A flirtatious grin spread across her face that made Angel's blood rush through her veins.

She glanced away, bracing for Ellie's words.

"And there's no wiggle room to negotiate for that next kiss?" Ellie teased.

It would be easier to give in to Ellie's request than to fight it, but she pushed back anyway. Fighting against what would inevitably bring a conflict of conscience. "You're living in a country that would sentence you to death for that type of action."

"Not a Western diplomat. Besides, change is why I'm here. The LGBT group we started is recognized by the government and has already met with them several times. This is one of those issues that I can help make a difference with."

"I certainly give you credit for your desire to make things better here, but it's a long way from being a reality," she said.

"Are we back to everything's black and white again? I don't see things the way you do. I see the possibility of a better future."

"The task seems daunting, but your ambition is admirable." She couldn't stop the words of honesty, but she hoped she softened the blow with her praise.

Ellie smiled and she returned it before quickly leaving the room. They were back on good terms again, and she didn't want another debate to force them apart again. Her words might be unwavering, but it was getting easier to believe in Ellie's ability to make change.

* * *

Ellie took a sip of her tea and rested her head against the back of the couch. Angel was a tempting distraction. The kiss between them had not only been demanding, but held a promise of something more. She wanted that something more, even though Angel was partially correct in her assessment of Ellie's current situation. Being a diplomat wouldn't protect her from a public scandal if the truth of her feelings were revealed. But the lure of Angel's kiss, she realized, was not something she could resist, or even wanted to.

She was surprised that Angel had agreed to her trip as well as allowing Gina to go to the fish market. Though her words were still the same, she was seeing a change in Angel. She hoped Angel was starting to see a country filled with potential like she did. She found it appealing to see that Angel had a much deeper, softer side. She did wonder, though, if their kiss had any influence on Angel's change of decision.

* * *

Angel answered her cell phone and listened as Eric relayed the details of what they were facing. She was pleased to hear that only the family and other fishermen were there. The missing fisherman had been found and rescued from the water. Eric felt that they would be able to return shortly. She told him to call on his way back so she could meet him at the gate.

She considered hitting the gym, but she didn't want to be in the middle of a workout when Eric called. She had texted Miller about the site visit, and he suggested they meet tomorrow. He would be stuck in teleconferences with his superiors for the rest of the day. She climbed the stairs to the roof and lay down on her stomach beside Rodriquez.

"Afternoon, Tag," he mumbled without moving his eye from the scope of his rifle.

She pulled a pair of compact binoculars from her side cargo pocket and zoomed in on the man across the street. He was looking up at her with an icy stare, and she felt the cold reach all the way to her toes. "This is a new guy. How long has he been there?"

"Arden said he came in about eight this morning. Didn't he send you a pic?"

She rolled on her side and slid her phone from her front pocket. Two messages. Both had arrived while she was distracted with Ellie. As she remembered Ellie's touch warmth flushed through her, thawing the ice from seconds before. Giving in to the thoughts for only an instant before pushing them aside, she brought her attention back to the issue in front of her.

She tapped on the e-mail icon. The first was from Arden. She stared at the photo he'd taken of the man who was sitting on the wall across the street. The second was background details from Sarah, and she read out loud for Rodriquez to hear.

"New guy is identified as an American. Craig Shepherd. He's lived in Nouakchott for the last three years on a temporary work visa. Last year, he married a Mauritanian woman. No, a child. Thirteen years old. No record of where he works." Angel frowned at the disconnection.

Rodriquez voiced her concern. "How can he be here on a work visa with no record of where he works?"

"Imad Abadi has been on the dayshift since we arrived almost two weeks ago. Why a new guy now?"

"Maybe he was busy today."

Why today? Why were they switching things up on the day she had given in to Ellie and was distracted by their kiss? Her phone vibrated with a text.

"Eric's on his way back. Let me know if Shepherd leaves or does anything different than Abadi."

Rodriquez grunted, and she took that as acknowledgment. She detoured past her room and strapped on her pistol before making her way to the entrance gate. Things were changing. She could feel it. She didn't expect any problems at the gate, but it eased her anxiety to be prepared. She was glad to know Rodriquez would be watching too.

She watched the crowd part as Eric's Toyota maneuvered up to the gate held open by one of the marine guards. She breathed a sigh of relief when it was closed without any problems.

"It was all smooth," Eric said as he climbed out to meet her.

The vehicle continued into the garage. They followed it as Eric continued his summary.

"She greeted people and wrote down their information to file a formal complaint with the government. She said none of it has helped yet, but they'll keep doing it. She has a couple of grants that she hopes to pull from to help the fisherman replace his boat. We were all relieved when they spotted him in the water. I'm gonna catch a few hours of sleep before my shift. Need anything?"

Angel shook her head. "Thanks for making the trip."

"I noticed an email from Sarah. Was she able to identify the new man on the wall?"

"Yes, I'm on it. We have more to talk about too. I'll be escorting the ambassador outside the embassy on Monday."

Eric frowned, and she held up her hand to stop his questions.

"Get some sleep and I'll fill you in tomorrow."

Eric headed for his room in the barracks, and Angel climbed the stairs to her room. She removed her weapon and cleaned it before storing it again. Changing into workout clothes, she headed for the gym. Running helped her clear her head and today that was exactly what she needed.

With her tablet propped up beside her, she occasionally glanced at Ellie's blinking light. It gave her comfort to know Ellie was two floors below and safe in her office. She forced her mind to focus on their upcoming trip instead of the silkiness of Ellie's skin or the demanding way her tongue had teased the edges of her mouth. After an hour on the treadmill, she worked her way through a few of the weightlifting machines. Her muscles were sore and aching, but her mind still raced with sketchy details on a risky trip and a whole lot of questions.

What would happen when the ambassador left the embassy? Would the embassy be more or less at risk? Would the crowd follow them? She knew the security team would do their best to keep the departure of the ambassador quiet, but word would spread. She returned to the treadmill, setting it on a slow pace as she dialed Vince.

"Any changes?" Vince asked without a greeting.

"We have an American in the mix now. Craig Shepherd. Did Sarah copy you on the email?"

"She did. What's your take?"

"I think they're preparing for something." She hesitated before continuing. Vince would never question her decisions, but she felt guilty for giving in to Ellie. "I've approved the ambassador to take a trip outside the embassy on Monday."

Vince was silent, and she wasn't sure if he was upset or only concerned. She quickly continued.

"She has a visit to the solar panel plant that's under construction that she feels is extremely important. It's only a day trip, but I'd like to pull in Sarah's team to assist. Either to accompany me or to cover for the marines I'll be taking."

"And Ellie agrees?"

"We haven't discussed it."

"Get her approval and then do it."

"And if she won't approve?"

The silence seemed to stretch forever before Vince finally spoke. "Do whatever you feel is necessary."

"Got it."

CHAPTER SEVENTEEN

Angel bit into the greasy cheeseburger as she waited for Sarah to answer.

"What's up, boss?" Sarah asked.

"It's time. Begin preparations to come in."

"The ambassador agrees?"

Angel dropped the burger back on her plate. The short-order burger had been the only option in the café. On a good day this would be a hard meal for her to consume, but today her stomach churned with uncertainty. She wasn't looking forward to another debate with Ellie.

"Tag?"

"Vince says do what needs to be done."

"I'm on it. Oh, and we couldn't find anything on Farook. He's been working at the embassy for almost ten years."

"Okay, thanks. Focus on packing up."

She tossed her phone on the table and glanced around the dining room. The area was empty except for a few of the younger crowd that had already drifted in for their Friday night gathering. She knew she had taken liberties with the translation of what Vince had said, but her mind was made up. She would discuss it with Ellie in a few minutes at their evening briefing, but her response didn't really matter. It was a safety concern for everyone inside the embassy.

She and her team had been in Nouakchott for almost two weeks. It was hard to believe she had only known Ellie for that long. Even with their disagreements, she felt closer to her than anyone she had ever met. Ellie was stubborn and opinionated, exactly the kind of woman she would normally avoid. And she had tried. Though maybe not as hard as she should have.

For so many reasons, Ellie was irresistible, but she was going to have to do everything in her power to admire her from a distance. It would be hard after the heart-stopping kiss they had shared. Especially since Ellie had made it clear she wanted more. It would take mental and physical ability to be the strong one from now on. More than her integrity was on the line. Ellie's life and those of many others were in her hands.

She dumped the remainder of her burger into the trash and made her way to Ellie's office. Stressful assignments were normal for her, but fighting a desire that threatened to consume her was uncharted territory. She didn't allow herself to have feelings for women and certainly not women involved in an assignment. She mentally strengthened her resolve as she walked, ticking through the possibilities of what could happen if she wasn't at the top of her game.

She groaned internally as she stepped to the open doorway of Ellie's office. The overhead lights were off and the lamp behind the couch barely lit the seating area. She paused for a second as her eyes adjusted to the dim lighting.

"Join me?" Ellie's voice was soft, slicing through Angel's barely formed willpower.

Ellie reclined against the back of the couch with both legs curled under her, her shoes discarded on the floor in front of her. Angel could feel Ellie's eyes on her as she crossed the room and took a seat opposite her. One glance told her all she needed to know. The green eyes were still filled with desire. Keeping physical distance was the only chance she had to resist the unspoken invitation.

She quickly filled Ellie in on the American who had joined the men outside. She stood when she finished, simultaneously relieved and disappointed that Ellie had remained in her seat, not even asking her to stay. The tea tray on the coffee table was untouched and she wondered if she was misreading the signs. Maybe Ellie was expecting someone else. Giving herself no time to waver, she turned and left. She preferred to think that Ellie was making an effort to honor her earlier request.

As she made her final rounds for the night, she glanced up at Ellie's window. Was Ellie watching? She couldn't tell. There didn't appear to be any light inside, but according to her tablet Ellie was still in her office. She made her way to the communications room and pulled up the live feed that focused on the street. Shepherd still sat on the wall. His head occasionally dipped in a random pattern as he dozed. It was almost midnight and he had now pulled the longest shift of any of the supervisors.

Although her bed was calling, she knew sleep wouldn't come. Between haunting thoughts of her lips on Ellie's and the change of events outside, there was no need to even try. Telling herself it was only for security purposes, she opened the embassy map on the next monitor. Ellie was safe in her office. She watched the blinking light pace the length of the office and then back again. In her mind, she could see the determined look on Ellie's face.

Knowing she should be focusing on Shepherd, she let visions of Ellie take over her subconscious. She ran scenarios in her head on what it would take to clear Ellie from her mind. The option she liked the best was to give in to the desire and let it fill her. Then she could move past it. She allowed herself to explore that idea for a few minutes and the thrill of it made her pulse race. She could feel Ellie's body beneath her fingertips and the weight of her breasts in her cupped palms.

Even as she envisioned the fantasy of pleasing Ellie, she was surprised to realize she longed for more than a sexual romp.

She wanted it all. Waking up with her, holding her at night, and sharing conversation. She had never considered sharing her life with anyone. Moving on to the next mission was the only thing she had really cared about.

She stood. If she continued allowing these thoughts, she would find herself at Ellie's door. *Focus.*

"Can I get a printed copy of this photo?" she asked the marine on duty, pointing to the feed of Shepherd on the monitor.

With a few keystrokes the whir of the printer across the room sounded. She grabbed the photo, thanked the marine, and left the room. She was happy to allow something else to occupy her thoughts, but it required a conscious effort to keep visions of Ellie away.

At the guardhouse, she gave the picture to the marines on duty with Eric and asked that they notify her immediately if Shepherd should approach the gate. She filled Eric in on the orders she had issued to Sarah earlier. Thankfully, Sarah had been focused on the mission at hand and not delved into her relationship with the ambassador. Being pressured to put her feelings into words wouldn't help right now.

She didn't normally discuss stuff like that with her team anyway. Sure, she talked with them about emotions they might have related to missions, but never about feelings unrelated to their work. She processed such things internally and that was how she would process her interest in Ellie. She would keep pretending Ellie had no effect on her and concentrate on her job.

As she returned to the building, she couldn't stop herself from glancing at Ellie's window again. The dark glass pane still protected whatever it held behind it, but she could feel Ellie's eyes on her. She wondered what Ellie would say if she showed up on her doorstep at midnight. She stepped into the shadow of the building and pulled out her tablet. Ellie's light continued to make the trek back and forth across her office. Would Ellie believe she was only coming to find out what was making her pace?

* * *

Ellie stopped at the window after she walked the length of her office one more time. She had seen Angel's GPS light in the communications room earlier and knew she wasn't sleeping either. The change in behavior of the men outside had her worried. It worried Ellie too. Unfortunately, that wasn't the only thing on her mind.

In two days, she would travel to the solar panel farm. That would be interesting, but what she was looking forward to the most was the drive there. Angel would be confined in the vehicle with her. She wouldn't be able to leave whenever the conversation wasn't one she wanted to have. Ellie couldn't wait for the opportunity to be alone with her. Well, except they would have a driver, of course.

She wasn't surprised to see Angel step out of the gatehouse and walk toward the embassy. As she had every day she had been in Nouakchott, she wore dark blue pants and a black Flagler shirt. Her hair blew across her face in the slight breeze, and she tucked it behind her ear. She knew she couldn't see her, but when Angel looked up at the window she felt like she was staring directly at her.

When Angel disappeared from her view, she sat down in her chair and tried to focus on the paperwork in front of her. After a few minutes of reading the same line over and over, she knew it was useless. She secured the papers back in the file folders and placed them in her desk. She pulled her office door closed and headed for her suite. She could pace anywhere, but maybe the walk to her suite would settle her mind and she might be able to sleep.

* * *

It was barely an hour into Saturday morning when Angel pushed open the door to the rooftop and settled on her stomach beside Arden.

"Morning, Tag," Arden said, gruffly.

She pulled her binoculars from her pocket and studied Shepherd. She was pretty sure the motion she had mistaken for sleeping was actually praying. The bowing of his head was too frequent to be random.

She sat up. She needed to talk with Ellie. This man had been on the wall for over fifteen hours and as far as she could tell he had not moved. No food breaks and no bathroom breaks. Something was definitely going down. She patted Arden on the leg to let him know she was leaving and hurried down the stairs. With the decision to go to Ellie made, she felt like a weight had been lifted off her shoulders.

She was met with a closed door when she arrived at Ellie's office. She pulled her tablet from her cargo pocket again. Ellie's light blinked inside her personal suite. She sighed and leaned against Chloe's desk. Going to Ellie's suite wasn't a good idea. She located Miller on the GPS tracking and was disappointed to see that he was in his room as well. She could talk with Eric or call Sarah, but they knew her too well. They wouldn't question her concerns, but they would see through her using work as a distraction from something else.

She returned to the Communications Center and compiled all the data on the men outside, looking for something to connect the supervisors to the dockworkers. When she couldn't stare at the words any longer, she gave in and sent a short text to Sarah. She wasn't worried about waking her. Sarah was a heavy sleeper. If she was asleep, Angel wouldn't hear back from her. Only a few seconds passed until Sarah responded, and Angel quickly dialed her number. She was inside her room by the time Sarah answered.

"What's up, boss?"

"Just wanted to see how the packing's going."

"It's fine. What are you doing awake?"

She weighed her options on how to answer. Sarah wouldn't judge her feelings for Ellie, but it wouldn't be fair to Ellie to share with anyone what had transpired between them.

"Shepherd still on duty?" Sarah asked.

She took the out, keeping silent about her other struggle. "He is."

"Makes you nervous?"

"It does." She smiled.

"I'm sure you have some scenarios playing in your mind. Do you want to share?"

"Feels like they're prepping for an offensive move."

"Or they ran out of staffing," Sarah offered.

"Or they simply ran out of staffing," she agreed, rubbing her face.

"You sound tired," Sarah said softly. "When's the last time you slept?"

"It's been pretty good until tonight."

"Things will play out however they will. You being awake won't make a difference to what they do. Besides I've seen you wake from a dead sleep and still hit your target at twelve hundred meters."

She laughed. That story would never be forgotten as long as Sarah was around. Angel had barely returned from an exhausting mission when Vince informed her that she was now a team leader. Her team was out on a training mission and she raced to join them. Her only thought was to show camaraderie as their new leader. While waiting for the rest of the team to move into position, she had fallen asleep. Sarah had been the only team member with her when the fire command came through. Quickly moving into action, she had forgotten she was there to supervise and had taken the shot. Over the head—and at a far greater distance than—the sniper on her team.

"So, go get some sleep." Sarah laughed with her. "Someone will wake you if you're needed. Oh, and Eric said there's an excursion planned for Monday?"

"Yes, but we'll see how the next forty-eight hours play out."

"Okay. Keep me posted. We've pulled in all nonessential equipment, so we can be ready to relocate with just a few hours' notice. Just say the word."

Angel slid her phone into her pocket and lay down on the bed. She had about two hours until she planned to be back on the roof. She closed her eyes and drifted into sleep with a sea-green haze the color of Ellie's eyes surrounding her.

CHAPTER EIGHTEEN

Ellie rubbed her tired eyes and took a gulp of coffee. The caffeine wasn't stimulating her like it normally did each morning. Angel's nervous tension was putting her on edge. When she had located Angel's GPS tracker this morning she had found her on the rooftop. The same place she had been when she had gone to sleep last night.

She sat her cup on the desk and walked to the window. She was supposed to check in with Micalah this morning, but telling her Angel had approved the outing wouldn't go well. If Micalah had her way, Ellie would have been ordered back to the States at the first sign of trouble. She knew Micalah hadn't forgotten the years they had worked together and that she could take care of herself. But she also knew if things didn't improve soon it would only be a matter of time before Micalah was on her doorstep.

Angel tapped lightly on the doorframe, and she turned, watching her walk in. The lines on Angel's face matched those she had seen in her own mirror earlier. Stopping in front of her desk, Angel made no sign that she intended to sit. She wanted to ask her how much sleep she had gotten last night, but instead she nodded for her to begin her briefing.

"He's still out there, but the men in the crowd have continued to rotate on a regular basis."

She didn't have to ask who Angel was talking about. She could hear the strain in Angel's voice. She resisted the urge to comfort her, fearing it would be rejected or, worse yet, accepted due to fatigue.

Turning her back to Angel, she stared out at the city surrounding her. Ignoring the crowd below, she concentrated on finding strands of color in the beige landscape that stretched in front of her. She could see the sun-faded blue entrance of the Olympic Stadium several blocks away and the green and yellow bleachers surrounding the red track. On all sides of the stadium were one- and two-story houses and businesses. Some were protected from the busy streets by walls in varying heights. Most structures were concrete and probably had been built by hand without the help of modern equipment. Despite the occasional crumbling wall, they radiated strength and durability, withstanding what nature and man could throw at them.

She felt the heat from Angel's body as she joined her at the window. It was like there was a magnet pulling them together. Angel held her tablet up showing a picture of a man's face.

"Do you recognize him?" Angel asked.

She studied his face and then shook her head. "This is the man outside? The American?"

"It is. His name is Craig Shepherd. He's from New York."

She only partially listened as Angel relayed his background before and after he had arrived in Mauritania. For the first time since Angel had mentioned the American on the wall, she remembered the conversation she had witnessed in the garage. She knew she should tell Angel, but she hadn't heard anything back from Shane. Maybe she had misread the situation and Farook had been telling her the truth. The guy in the picture wasn't the one she had seen with Farook.

"This is the first American that's been involved, right?" she asked, pushing aside any lingering doubts.

Angel nodded.

"Can we bring him inside the embassy for questioning?"

"I'd thought about that. We could claim it was for his own safety and maybe disrupt whatever they're planning."

"You think they're planning something?" she asked, repeating Angel's words in her question. Angel's nod reinforced her own growing fears. "I think you should bring your other team to the embassy before we leave on Monday."

"Yes."

She met Angel's eyes as they searched her face. She wasn't announcing defeat, but as ambassador it was her job to make sure everyone in the embassy remained safe. And she knew she couldn't do it alone. In the months that she had been in Nouakchott, she had learned to depend on others for so many basic daily needs. Being provided with informational briefings was fine, but now her food was prepared, her clothes laundered, and her suite cleaned by staff members. And the worst of it was that she no longer protected herself. Inside the embassy or out, she had become dependent on Shane and his marines.

Goose bumps erupted down her arms as Angel's fingertips reached out and slowly stroked her face. She rested her cheek against Angel's palm, welcoming the heat from her body. Angel's earlier inability to remain still no longer seemed to be a problem. She leaned into her touch, absorbing the strength and stability that flowed from her.

"I'll keep you safe," Angel said softly.

She nodded, taking a step back. She wanted nothing more than to fall into Angel's embrace and let her fulfill that promise, but she had a job to do. She was the ambassador.

"Thank you." She was surprised at the hoarseness in her own voice. "Do you need me to talk with Vince so you can bring your team in?"

"No."

"Okay, then let me know if they need anything." She knew Angel would shrug off her next words, but she said them anyway. "Please try to get some sleep today?"

"I will."

She glanced at her laptop and then back at Angel. "I'll be watching."

The smile on Angel's face warmed her again.

* * *

Angel was still smiling when she phoned Vince. She knew Ellie was watching her GPS light, and she hated to admit that she liked it. Ellie had touched a part of her that had been dormant for a very long time. She grimaced, knowing that telling her that would only make their struggle harder. Assuming she could even find the words to do so.

"Angel? What's happening?" Vince said, picking up on the first ring.

"The ambassador has agreed to move Sarah's team to the embassy."

"Then do it. Now."

"Done," she said, disconnecting the call.

She wasn't surprised that Vince wanted her to move quickly. His previous restraint was out of respect for Ellie. She knew he had been close to overriding Ellie's wishes each time they had spoken. She also knew if Vince had his way he would have been there with her. Entrusting the safety of someone you cared about to someone else was hard. She wished she could admit how much she cared about Ellie, but she wasn't sure if that would make Vince feel better or worse. She wouldn't do anything to risk being pulled from this mission.

She dialed Sarah. "You're coming in."

"All of us? When?"

She played the different possibilities in her mind. She could use her team as security escort for her and Ellie, but she felt like they would be better at the embassy. Taking marines familiar with the country made the most sense, but there wasn't any reason not to bring Sarah's entire team to the embassy. The safety of the embassy once she left would be their first concern.

"Bring everyone and get here as quick as possible."

"Okay. I'll let you know when we're on the road."

She disconnected the call and sent a quick text to Miller. He responded immediately, and they scheduled to meet in the break room outside the troop barracks. She texted Eric to join them when he could.

The break room was empty when she arrived, and she filled one of the glass mugs on the counter with coffee before taking a seat.

"How's things going?" Miller asked, walking in behind her and filling a cup before joining her at the table.

"Good, but I'm afraid we might have an issue in the future."

"Still no shift change for the man on the wall, right?"

She nodded. "It's weird. They've followed a consistent schedule for the last two weeks and now they're deviating. Add in the fact that the guy is an American."

Miller sat back in his chair. "Look, I don't want to add to your worries but I need to tell you about something. Apparently the other day when the ambassador made the little detour through the motor pool, she overheard something that bothered her."

She raised her eyebrows but forced herself to remain silent. With the off-and-on tension between her and Ellie, it wasn't surprising that Ellie had gone to Miller instead of her. She was disappointed, though. It was a harsh reminder that she needed to keep the air clear between them.

"Farook was talking with another man, possibly an American. They were both angry, but the other man was demanding Farook provide something he had promised. Something to do with a Conex to be shipped. She asked me to see what I could find out. When I asked my contact at the docks about an American who had a friend working at the embassy, he knew who I was talking about. He called me today to say that there has been a Conex departing every month under a diplomatic pouch stamp from our embassy."

"What?"

"Yeah, that's what I said. I was going to speak with the ambassador when you texted me."

"Thanks for letting me know." She stared at the dark television screen across from her. "Can you hold off on telling her what you found out?"

"Sure, but we should make sure the embassy really doesn't have something going out."

"I'll check with Chloe. I showed Shepherd's picture to the ambassador and she didn't recognize him."

"Well, that's good then. Now we know there's more than one American living in Nouakchott," Miller said, making her chuckle.

A surge of adrenaline flushed out the heavy fog of anxiety that had been weighing Angel down. She laughed a little harder. It wasn't so much what Miller had said, but more that he had even said it. His face still showed no emotion. His lips were pressed tight together and his jawline rigid.

"Good morning, all," Eric said as he took a seat beside her. His standard dark blue tactical pants and blouse were wrinkle-free and his face was shiny. A few blotchy spots on his neck showed that he may have rushed through shaving in a hurry to meet them. "What did I miss?"

She shook her head, bringing her laughter under control. She glanced at Miller and saw the edges of his mouth starting to curl. "Thank you. I needed that." She turned to Eric. "You missed Miller displaying his sarcastic wit."

Eric didn't look convinced and she didn't blame him. Miller's face was a mask again and had she not been there she wouldn't have believed it either. Turning her attention to the reason for their meeting, she told them about the pending arrival of Sarah's team and then laid out her plan for the additional team members.

"Adding a body to each of your current agents on duty will work well," Miller agreed. "What about for your trip?"

"I'd like to use my agents, but yours are more familiar with the terrain."

"No problem. My guys can cover for each other. Do you think four is enough?"

"I was thinking five, but I don't want to pull too many from here with what we're seeing outside. I'd put two in the lead and rear cars and one as my driver."

Miller frowned. "You might want to use local embassy employees for your drivers. They're familiar with the way people drive here. Plus you'll have several checkpoints to get through."

"That's what the ambassador said as well. Two to one wins. I guess four will do it then."

"I'd put two in the front and two in the rear, assuming you'll be armed."

She nodded.

"I'll send all four of them to you after the next shift change."

"I won't keep them long. It'd be good if you could sit in as well. I'd like to talk about the roads and what we might experience out there."

"Sure. See you back here in four hours." Miller gave them a departing wave after he refilled his coffee cup.

She tapped the email application open on her tablet. "I'm emailing you and Sarah the duty roster. I expect they'll be on their way to us within the next few hours."

"Let me know and I'll meet you at the gate," he said, standing. "Miller really cracked a joke?"

She chuckled. "It was more sarcasm than humor."

"I'm sorry I missed it, even though Sarah gives me more sarcasm than I ever need."

Although she often pretended to be irritated by Sarah and Eric's constant communication, it actually gave her comfort. They were almost like siblings when they bickered and traded jabs with each other. Then when she least expected it, she would find them huddled together under a poncho, blocking out the weather or keeping their light from giving away their position, as they worked through whatever was facing their team in the moment.

"I'd repeat what he said, but his stoic face is what sold it."

"I understand."

"I'm going to try to get an hour or two of sleep before I meet with Miller's team," she advised him. "But wake me if you need to."

"Okay. I'll walk that way with you. I want to do a little people watching from the roof."

She dumped her remaining coffee and cleaned her cup before heading back to the main building. She decided to stop on the second floor, and Eric continued on up to the roof. She wasn't sure she could sneak in and out without Ellie seeing her, but she was going to give it a try. Sam would probably be the best person to ask about embassy shipments. Well, aside from Ellie, of course, but she wasn't going to open the topic with either of them yet. They would ask too many questions. She was comfortable with Chloe and felt like she could get information from her without giving any. If Chloe didn't have the answers, then she would have to go to Sam.

Chloe's head was bent as she typed on her computer and Ellie's door stood wide open. She had checked the GPS application on her tablet on the way down the hall and she knew Ellie was inside her office. She approached Chloe's desk and waited for her to look up.

"How's it going?" she asked softly.

Chloe seemed surprised to find Angel's attention focused on her and she gave a shy giggle.

"Good. Can I help you with something?"

"Actually, you can. I need some information, and I thought you would be the person to ask."

Chloe giggled again.

She didn't like using her position to take advantage of people, but she wasn't going to make Chloe do or say anything that would get her in trouble. "I was wondering if the embassy sends any diplomatic pouches from the dock. Maybe on a regular monthly basis."

Chloe's face wrinkled in thought. "Not that I'm aware of. Do you need to ship something back to the US? We have an arrangement with the mail service."

"No. It'd be something large that needed to move in a Conex."

"A Conex?"

"You know, a large metal shipping container."

"I know what you mean, but we don't do anything like that. There's a book of diplomatic pouch approvals in the Defense Attaché's office that we're allowed to use, but it's certainly not on a regular basis. Sometimes when an employee transfers out, they'll use them for furniture and household stuff to avoid having to deal with customs." She grimaced. "I'm not really sure if that's allowed or not, but it makes their move go smoother."

She smiled. "It's okay. I'm not here to judge. I only needed to know if there was a regular shipment that was approved by the embassy."

"Any requests for diplomatic pouch approvals would come across my desk for the ambassador's approval, so I think I can safely say no."

"Thanks, Chloe. You've been very helpful."

She left quickly, relieved that Ellie had not interrupted their conversation. She didn't ask Chloe to keep their conversation a secret because she planned to tell Ellie about all of it. Exactly when, though, she wasn't sure.

She stopped in the communications room and pulled the exterior cameras up on what had become her computer. She dialed Eric, knowing he had already had time to survey the crowd. After confirming there was no change with the situation, she quickly scanned all the other cameras.

Returning to her room, she dropped on top of the bed. No need to remove any clothing or get under the covers. Sarah would be texting soon and she now had less than three hours before her meeting with Miller's team. She set her watch alarm in case she did fall asleep and stretched her arms behind her head. The last thing she remembered thinking was sleep wasn't going to come easy.

* * *

Ellie stepped out of her office and crossed to the coffeemaker. She poured hot water into her cup and dropped in a tea bag. She was hoping Chloe would volunteer information from her conversation with Angel, but it appeared that she wasn't going to. When she had heard Angel's voice outside her office, she had waited thinking she was coming in to see her. When she didn't, she had approached the door but only caught Angel thanking Chloe for her information. She couldn't imagine what information Angel would need from Chloe or why she wouldn't come directly to her.

"Did I hear Agent McTaggart's voice out here earlier?" she asked, hoping she sounded casual but knowing she didn't.

"Yes, she wants to ship something back to the States."

"What does she want to ship?"

"I don't know. Something large, I think."

She walked back into her office. Why would Angel need to ship something back to the States by embassy methods? Surely Vince would have a better plan in place.

She dialed the number she had been avoiding all day. Micalah would not be happy to hear she was leaving the safety of the embassy but not calling her would make Micalah even more worried.

"How are things?" Micalah answered, skipping a greeting.

"I'm fine and you?"

"I'm glad you're fine, but you know that's not what I'm asking."

"It's looking better." Her first lie. "So, we're moving forward with my planned visit to the solar panel farm."

"What?"

"Agent McTaggart approved it and we'll be returning before dark. The crowd outside the embassy isn't really a problem." Lie number two. She paused, knowing that she was talking fast and Micalah would know she wasn't telling the truth. "We sent someone out yesterday to meet with the fisherman and she didn't have a problem getting out or in."

"Have you thought that maybe they're waiting for you?"

"I think their problem is what I represent, as in the US, and not me directly."

"I hope you're right. What security is she taking?"

"Micalah, I don't know all the details yet. I'll make sure everything is properly planned. Now, what are you working on? Not something dangerous, I hope?"

Micalah groaned. "Point taken. I'm still going to worry, though."

"I wouldn't expect anything less."

She looked up as Chloe appeared in her doorway. "Mr. Flagler is on line two."

She nodded. "I have to run, Micalah. I'll call when we return."

"Okay. Be safe."

She disconnected the line and punched line two. "Vince?"

"How's my girl?"

She liked Vince's smooth, soothing voice. She took a deep breath, letting out the stress from her conversation with Micalah. "Your girl?" she teased.

"While you're under my protection, I'm allowed to call you that."

She laughed. "*Your girl* is feeling a little stifled."

"I thought you might be. With the change in scenery or lack thereof, I should say, I'm hoping this might mean more than the weather is changing. And for the better, I hope, but if not Angel will handle it. Just do what she tells you."

"Oh, you know me so well."

Vince chuckled. "Following orders was never your best skill, but trust Angel. She knows what she's doing and she'll keep you safe."

She thought about how wonderful it had felt to be wrapped in Angel's arms. She was pretty sure that was not what Vince meant. "I'll listen to her while we're out on Monday. I know the risks."

"I know you do. I'll talk to you both when you return."

She hung up the phone and studied the paperwork in front of her. She had barely accomplished anything in the two weeks that Angel had been around. Her mind wouldn't focus on anything for a solid length of time without thoughts of Angel drifting in or her attention being pulled away by the moving GPS lights.

And if that wasn't bad enough, now she had felt the thrill of her kiss. She wasn't sure she would ever be able to focus on anything again. There was no doubt in her mind that she wanted more than one kiss and there was no doubt that it was not an option. Her body surged with anticipation each time Angel walked into the room, and lately she had only to think of her to lose track of any clear thought.

After reading through a few pages, she finally closed the folder and tucked it back into a drawer. She was finished working at least for the moment. She checked Angel's GPS light and found her on the rooftop again.

"Call it a day," she said to Chloe as she passed. "In fact, I'm headed to the café. Why don't you join me?"

She had never invited Chloe to join her for dinner, but normally Chloe was headed across town to her own apartment. Living inside the embassy reduced her options. She hadn't heard any complaints from Chloe or anyone else for that matter. She was hoping that through Chloe she could get a feel for how everyone else was doing.

"I want to finish this and then file this stack before I go today, but thank you for the offer."

"Come on. You shouldn't even be here on a Saturday. Monday you'll have a complete day without me bothering you. You can catch up then."

Chloe stood. "Okay."

They took the elevator to the first floor and walked to the café. She stepped back and allowed Chloe to pick a tray and move through the line first. She liked Chloe's outfit today—dark pants with a purple and black striped shirt. The pants hugged her slim hips and she had tucked them into low-heeled black boots with a silver buckle on the outside. She couldn't help but notice that Chloe's fingernails were painted purple to match her shirt. She appreciated the amount of work it took for her aide to color coordinate her nails every day. It was something she had never desired to do. If she painted her fingernails, it was only with a clear polish.

She chose a piece of grilled chicken with a few pineapple slices on top and a side salad. She was really hungry, but tonight was movie night in the embassy and popcorn was in her future. She followed Chloe to a small table by the window. A quick glance at the darkening sky outside told her it was after five. She still had over two hours to kill before Angel's briefing.

Most days she didn't know where the hours went. Before Angel came into her life, she spent all of her time working. An occasional walk outside was something she had taken for granted. Maybe a leisure walk on the treadmill would do her some good.

"It looks like a nice night," Chloe said, interrupting Ellie's distracted gaze out the window.

"Breezy. I can see the flag blowing," she said as she cut into the chicken on her plate. "How are you adapting to being confined here?"

"It hasn't been too bad. Most of the people I hang out with after work are all here. I miss the food, though."

She chuckled. The café did tend to serve the same selections served in any US diner. "I think our cooks are so focused on making us feel at home that we never get a taste of Mauritanian cooking. Maybe I'll mention that to them. It would be fun to mix it up a couple days a week. I wonder what our local employees are eating."

"Probably a lot of rice and vegetables."

"Right." Ellie paused, taking another bite before continuing. "Chloe, I want you to know I appreciate the time you put into your appearance every day."

Chloe's brow wrinkled.

"I'm being serious." She reached across the table and touched her arm. "I've noticed that your outfits are always perfectly coordinated with your nails. I know how time consuming that can be every day."

Chloe blushed. "I actually enjoy it. It relieves my stress and it makes me happy. As a teenager, I used bright colors to piss off my mom. As I got older, I took more care to make sure I was color coordinated."

She followed Chloe's gaze as she looked at the other diners around them. She could tell Chloe was working up the courage to say something more.

"I did wonder if you thought it was too much for the embassy," she said shyly. "I'd never want to look unprofessional."

She smiled. "Everyone expresses themselves differently, and I look forward to seeing what color you'll have on each day." She ate another bite, giving Chloe time to relax into their conversation again. "The real question is how many bottles of nail polish do you have?"

"My spinning racks hold about fifty." Chloe grinned. "I have two of them now, but I just ordered a third. I blame my mom 'cause she sent me that coral-colored shirt for my birthday. She'd be horrified to know I bought polish to match."

"I won't tell her," she said, laughing.

CHAPTER NINETEEN

The front pocket of Angel's pants vibrated with an incoming call, and she rolled over to retrieve her phone. Above her, the blue sky had given way to purple and the horizon was a reddish orange. In another situation, she might have taken a moment to enjoy the view, but instead she pressed the phone to her ear and grunted a greeting.

"The embassy is in sight," Sarah said.

"I'll meet you at the gate."

She patted Rodriquez's leg as she rolled to her feet. She was anxious to have Sarah's team safely inside the embassy gates. She quickly sent Eric a text to let him know she was headed down; he met her as she reached the first floor. Together they exited the building and crossed the lawn.

"The crowd's moving. I think it's them." Eric said as they neared the gate.

She watched the crowd part to reveal a black SUV. Three more followed so closely that it looked like they were attached. One of the marines opened the gate and the vehicles drove through. Sarah rolled down her window, and Angel pointed them toward the motor pool. She and Eric waited until all vehicles were inside the gate and then joined them in the garage. Eric closed the roll-up door, blocking those outside the gates from seeing who or how many had arrived.

Sarah climbed out of the vehicle and grasped Eric's hand, pulling him close in a quick half hug. After greeting Angel the same way, she began giving directions to her team as they all gathered around.

Angel hadn't noticed Farook when they entered the garage but saw now that he was standing in the doorway of his office. His brow furrowed as he watched Sarah's team unload their gear. She was still forming an opinion of him. Neither his power play in Ellie's office nor his reaction when she had followed Ellie into the garage two days ago were normal or even friendly. It was possible, though, that the look of anger or disgust he displayed was only his normal expression.

His eyes locked on her as she approached him.

"Farook, these are members of my team. Can you take care of their vehicles?"

"Yes, yes." He nodded his head several times, but his brow remained creased.

"Great. I'll gather the keys for you."

It was good to have her team in one spot again. She turned the keys over to Farook with a smile that wasn't returned, and then she and Eric led the team to the barracks. She took a seat at the long table and waited while Eric helped them get settled. Sarah was the first to return.

"It's good to be here," Sarah said as she sank into the chair across from Angel.

"I'm relieved too. Although that safe house looked pretty nice."

"Oh, it was, but we also had neighbors on all sides. I made everyone wear a scarf when they went out so no one could tell the difference between any of us."

"Not a bad idea," she said taking Sarah's tablet and loading the GPS tracker page. She pulled ten bracelets from her cargo pocket and passed them to Sarah as she showed her the different lights. She pointed out critical locations within the embassy and Ellie's blinking light in the café.

When Eric joined them, she briefly ran through the distribution of team members and her plans for Monday. She sent them off to share information with each other as Miller and his team arrived. She shook hands with each marine, memorizing a face with a name. She took a seat as Private First Class Montgomery began to explain each phase of their trip. He had been a part of the team that had taken Sam on the two previous trips and his details were specific. He described their departure, checkpoint protocols, and the route they would travel.

"The solar farm is located on this side of Atar before the cut to Terjit Oasis. The only town of any size we'll pass through is Akjoujt. The road is paved all the way, but honestly you won't be able to tell most of the time because it'll be covered with blowing sand. You'll be able to see the Adrar plateau in the distance, but mostly you'll be surrounded by a flat desert with an occasional sand dune that relocates every time the wind blows."

He glanced at Miller and then back at Angel. "If I understand correctly, this'll be a fast trip. The ambassador will be on the ground for less than an hour?" He waited for nods and then continued. "That's good. We'll be able to clear the checkpoints going and coming during daylight hours. Baker and I will be in the lead car and Humphries and Ketterman will bring up the rear. For safest traveling, it'd be best to depart the farm by thirteen hundred hours."

He slid onto an empty chair. "Any questions?"

"Are there any formalities that we'll have to observe at the site?" she asked.

"The ambassador will have tea when she arrives, but it's understood that we're on duty and cannot join them. It wasn't a problem last time," PFC Montgomery answered.

"Good. Two of you should accompany us inside and the other two can wait with the cars."

Montgomery nodded. "Baker and Ketterman will go with you. Baker was also there before and is familiar with the facility."

She glanced at Miller. "I'll let you decide on the firepower we need. I'll only be taking my pistol."

"I'd like to mount a machine gun on each vehicle, but unfortunately local law enforcement frowns on that," Miller joked, and his marines laughed.

"Wouldn't that be nice?" She smiled. It seemed that his earlier sarcasm had breached a barrier between them. She liked this more jovial side of him. She had already seen he could be professional and diligent in his work, and his sarcasm wasn't bitter or mocking. She could see he brought a small amount of humor to what could otherwise be a dull and fatiguing assignment. "What are our other options?"

"We'll each have our standard pistol in plain view since we'll be in uniform, Agent McTaggart," Montgomery answered. "And a rifle hidden underneath the seat in both cars. Yours too, if you want."

She shook her head. "That's not necessary. We'll be traveling in diplomatic vehicles and I'm sure the distance between each vehicle won't be more than an inch."

"Standard quarter-inch gap," Miller teased.

"Sounds like we're good then." She stood. "Let's meet at zero six thirty on Monday morning. Everyone should bring an overnight bag in case we get delayed. I'm headed to fill the ambassador in now, but let me know if anything changes tonight or tomorrow."

She left the marines discussing the attractions they would be traveling near. Terjit Oasis seemed to be the one that had been visited and enjoyed the most. As hot as the summers were in Mauritania it wasn't surprising that a lush, hidden body of water would draw tourists and locals alike. She heard some regret that their current situation didn't allow for outside excursions.

What if she and Ellie were going sightseeing instead of working? Would they visit the oasis? She imagined Ellie in a bathing suit. It wasn't hard after seeing her in her workout clothes. Remembering the curve of Ellie's breasts and her muscular thighs had led to many hours of torture for her. She squeezed her eyes shut and quickly opened them to clear the vision as she pushed through the stairway door.

* * *

Ellie glanced at the clock for what felt like the hundredth time in the last ten minutes. Chloe had hurried off to meet friends after dinner, but she had returned to her office. With a lot of diligence, she had managed to make a small dent in her stack of work. The time had passed fairly quickly up until about ten minutes ago.

Finally it was time for Angel to appear. She put a pot of water on the heater for tea and paced behind her desk. She knew she could look at the GPS locator and see exactly where Angel was, but she also knew Angel was never late for a briefing. She glanced up as the sound of footsteps carried into her quiet office.

Angel stepped into the room and Ellie caught her breath. She still wasn't used to the way Angel's presence dwarfed everything around her. She turned away and took a calming breath. When she turned back, Angel stood at attention in front of her desk.

Angel's stance showed she was in professional mode tonight, and that was fine with her. She had started the teapot, but honestly she wasn't sure how much more push and pull her fragile libido could take.

"Good evening," Angel said softly, her voice conforming to the quiet room.

"Good evening. Anything new?"

"My second team has arrived and are beginning to double staff shifts immediately. No change outside the building, though."

She nodded. She hadn't realized she was moving closer to Angel while she talked.

"Are we ready for Monday's trip?" she asked as she slid between her desk and Angel. She could feel the heat from Angel's body, and it seemed to draw her closer.

"We are. I just met with our escorts and I'm happy to go over the details of the plan with you." Angel's voice was growing deeper with each syllable.

She placed a hand on Angel's chest, feeling her rapid heartbeat. She closed her eyes, expecting Angel to pull away. When she didn't, she forced her eyes open.

Angel was studying her face. She knew she shouldn't, but she slid her hand behind Angel's neck and gently pulled her forward. She felt the warning sparks and ignored them. As if no time had passed since the last time they kissed, their bodies instantly merged. She felt Angel's hands slide across her hips and knew they were probably gripping the desk behind her. Angel was fighting to resist. She could see it in her eyes.

She guided Angel's face closer until she could feel her breath on her lips. It was hot and fast and she breathed it in. When she thought she would explode from the anticipation, she finally pressed her lips to Angel's. The immediate response steadied her. She could feel everything Angel was too afraid to say. Caressing Angel's lips with her own, she deepened the kiss. Sliding her tongue into Angel's mouth, she moaned as Angel's tongue met hers.

Her body was on fire, and Angel was a wisp of oxygen stoking it hotter. The ridge of the desk cut into the back of her thighs as Angel's body pressed into her. Finally Angel's hands were on her, pulling her even closer. When Angel's fingers slid under her shirt and across her back, she felt her legs grow weak. She hated the clothes that stood between them. She wanted Angel's hands to be able to touch everywhere on her body.

With a groan, Angel broke the kiss, dropping her hands back to the desk. Her head hung limp over Ellie's shoulder. Her words were strained and barely audible. "I can't."

The anguish in Angel's voice dampened her desire. She wanted her so badly she had forgotten to respect what Angel had asked. She knew from Angel's response that their desire was the same. They both struggled with the boundary of professionalism, but Angel's was also one of integrity and honor.

She slid her hands down Angel's shoulders and gripped the muscles in her biceps. She could feel Angel's body trembling, and she wrapped her arms around her, squeezing her tight.

Angel responded, wrapping her in an embrace that left no room between them. The desire she had felt moments ago still poured through her, but she relaxed into Angel's arms. The strength of their connection was mind-numbing; she wanted to remain there forever.

All too soon Angel relaxed her grip and stood straighter, putting a small amount of space between them. She took Angel's hand and led her to the couch. When Angel sat, she took a seat across from her. Immediately she missed the heat from Angel's body, but she knew she needed to respect Angel's dedication to her job. Especially since her own life depended on it.

She poured them each a cup of tea and waited while Angel took a sip. Then she sat back with her own cup and watched her. Space she could give her, but she couldn't pull her eyes away. Angel's hair fell across her face as she stared into the cup of tea.

"There are no answers there," she teased.

Angel lifted her eyes and smiled. "If only there were."

They stared silently at each other until she finally forced her eyes away. She knew she was a complication Angel didn't need. She slipped off her shoes and pulled her feet under her.

Angel looked at the heels laying on the floor. "I still don't know how you walk in those things."

"With dignity and grace."

Angel laughed.

She watched the strain in Angel's face flow away as a genuine smile grew. She cherished her ability to cause Angel to lose control. From the breath-stopping passion moments ago to the easy laugh she had just heard. She was growing to like every part of her. She met Angel's eyes and watched as they went from caramelized brown to dark chocolate.

Angel's words were soft and filled with desire. "You rock my world."

"You really can't talk like that if you want me to remain at a distance. I'm at the edge of my restraint."

Angel gave her head a shake. "When I'm away from you, it's easy to convince myself I can be close, do my job, and resist my desire for you." A few seconds passed before she continued. "But it seems I can't. Nor do I want to."

Ellie watched the struggle play out across Angel's face.

"Stopping that kiss was the last thing I wanted to do," Angel continued. "But then I remembered that you could be in danger, especially when we leave the embassy. I need my head to be clear and I'm not sure I can do it." Angel rubbed a hand across her face. "I'm going to send Eric with you instead."

She had met Eric and she had no doubt he was good at his job, but there was no way she was leaving this building without Angel beside her. She would say it, but she knew she needed to convince her too. "I need you beside me."

"My head is not where it needs to be."

"I have no doubt by Monday morning you'll feel differently. There isn't anyone in the world I would trust with my safety over you." She wasn't surprised by the words or the fact that she meant them with all her heart.

"Vince," Angel said softly.

"Not even Vince. Your desire to keep me safe transcends all normal responsibility. I couldn't feel safer with anyone else."

Angel nodded. "Thank you." A slow smile returned to her face. "About those shoes, do you think you could find something more appropriate for Monday?"

"It depends on my outfit."

The office door burst open and a small girl ran in, jumping into Ellie's lap. "It's movie night," she squealed excitedly.

She glanced at Angel and almost laughed at the panic on her face. She wasn't sure if it was the child or the thought of what she might have interrupted a moment ago if they hadn't stopped.

"This is Sam's daughter, Brittany." She laughed at Angel's raised eyebrows. "Her entrance is always a surprise. Just ask her father." She squeezed the little girl. "She's in charge of picking the movie tonight. What will we be watching?"

"*Finding Dory!*" Brittany exclaimed.

"Oh, yes, lots of talking sea creatures." Ellie winked at Angel. "It's a good movie. Maybe Agent McTaggart would like to join us."

Brittany bounced excitedly on Ellie's lap. "Would you? We could make space for you on the couch."

Ellie raised her eyebrows in mock surprise. "Oh, I don't know, Brittany. Do you think there's room?"

Brittany nodded eagerly.

"That's a big honor, Agent McTaggart. She doesn't let just anyone sit on the couch with her."

Angel grimaced. "I think I have work to do."

Ellie laughed as she slid the little girl from her lap. "Go save me a seat."

Brittany sprinted from the room.

"You could join us if you want," Ellie coaxed.

Angel's eyes narrowed. "A dark room with you?" She shook her head. "I don't think so. Not even with a pack of children." She set her empty cup on the table and stood. "I should get back to work."

CHAPTER TWENTY

Angel stepped around the corner from Ellie's office and leaned against the wall. She had lost control, and this wasn't a feeling she was accustomed to. Ellie did more than rock her world. She took away all thoughts and cares. She heard Ellie's office door close, and she hurried to the stairs. Right now, her plan was to keep a solid distance between them.

As she walked she pulled out her phone to text Sarah and Eric. She was surprised to see that almost an hour had passed while she was with Ellie and she hadn't even briefed her on the plans for Monday. She had missed the vibration of a text from Eric. Both he and Sarah were waiting for her on the roof. She sprinted up the stairs.

She pushed through the fire door and took in the scene. Sarah, Eric, and Miller were prone beside Rodriquez and Arden. She joined them, taking a position beside Miller as she pulled out her binoculars.

"What's going on?"

"Another man has joined Shepherd. He arrived about thirty minutes ago," Miller explained.

"Do we know anything about him yet?" she asked.

"No. Sarah was getting ready to head down and dig into it. I'll take her to the communications room," Miller said.

Angel pulled back from the edge and stood. "Let's go. I want to know who he is."

An hour later, she motioned to the other three to follow her out of the Communications Center. They had identified the man as Randy Barnes, another US citizen, and she was ready to get her team moving.

"Sarah, keep an agent with each of Eric's but add a roving patrol through the night."

"I think it's time to pull Agent Connor in," Miller added.

"See if she can meet us."

Miller dialed and they waited while he spoke to her. Pocketing his phone, he informed them, "Agent Connor will meet us now outside the barracks."

"I'll go set up the roving patrol and check on my guys." Sarah stopped at the foot of the stairs, turning toward the gatehouse. "I'll catch up with you when I finish."

Angel nodded. "Eric, go with her. From now until I return I want you guys to stay together."

In the last couple of weeks, Angel had come to respect Miller and his competence. She made a quick decision as she watched Sarah and Eric walk away. "They'll report to you while I'm gone."

"I'll keep everyone in the loop."

They walked in silence through the double doors into the break room. Angel made a fresh pot of coffee and poured them both a cup. "I have to say that I'm at a loss with what they might be planning. They have to know we're watching them and that making changes like that would definitely put us on guard. It's like they want us to know they're planning something."

Before Miller could respond Agent Connor arrived. Angel quickly filled her in and asked for her assistance in increasing security.

"You can have both of my agents. Just tell us where you need us to be."

She nodded. "We appreciate that." Her phone buzzed with a text message and she glanced at it.

"What is it?" Miller asked.

"Sarah has additional information. Randy Barnes is married to Ronald Pigott's sister."

"Wait." Connor held up a hand. "His company is installing the solar panel farm."

"You're correct," Angel said with concern. "I think it's time to brief the ambassador. Maybe she can be convinced to at least postpone her trip."

Miller and Connor nodded, but neither one looked optimistic.

* * *

Angel pulled the copy of Randy Barnes's picture off the printer and located Ellie's GPS light on her tablet. She was in the conference room down the hall from her office that was converted once a week to the movie room. It had been over an hour since they had parted earlier, so Angel was hopeful that the movie would be ending soon. She absolutely was not going to pull Ellie from a group of children unless the building was on fire. Angel opened the door quietly, slipping inside.

She leaned against a rear wall until her vision began to identify shapes inside the room. Ellie was seated in the middle of the couch with children on both sides of her. Several more children sat on chairs around them and a few lay on the floor. As her eyes adjusted to the lack of light, she was surprised to see Ellie turned in her direction instead of watching the movie. When Ellie started to stand, she quickly motioned her back down.

Ellie leaned down and whispered something to the child beside her. The child scurried toward Angel. She recognized Brittany and bent down to hear the message she was coming to give. Instead, Brittany took her hand and led her back to the couch. The spot Brittany had vacated was too small for her so she dropped to the floor in front of the couch.

Her stomach gave a flutter as her back came in contact with Ellie's legs. Warmth quickly spread through her body. She pulled her legs up in front of her and casually rested her arms across her knees, forcing herself to focus on the swimming characters on the screen in front of her. The pressure of Ellie's hand on her shoulder was gentle and for a moment it settled her. Then she felt the slightest of touches as Ellie's fingertips reached the skin beneath her hair.

Goose bumps erupted down her legs, making her toes curl inside her boots. She stared stoically but unseeingly at the movie screen, the photograph of Randy Barnes folded and forgotten in her pocket. The stroking fingertips pleaded with her to give in to the ecstasy they promised. She closed her eyes, allowing herself a moment to forget what they were facing outside the embassy.

All too soon, she felt the children around her begin to move, and she opened her eyes to the glare of the overhead lights. The movie was over. She quickly stood, hoping she didn't look as guilty as she felt.

The mischievous smile on Ellie's face told her she knew exactly what she had done. She wanted to be annoyed with her, but it took all of her strength to stop her stomach from spinning cartwheels. Taking a deep breath, she pushed aside her physical turmoil.

"Can we talk in private?" she whispered.

Ellie nodded, walking toward the door. She followed at a distance, giving Ellie time to say good night to each child. In the hallway, Ellie took her arm, leading her through the crowd of parents. The sound of the office door closing behind her reverberated in her head. They were alone again.

Focus.

She stopped in front of Ellie's desk as Ellie continued to the other side.

"What's going on?" Ellie asked.

"There's been another change outside." She pulled the photo from her pocket. "Randy Barnes has joined the first man on the wall. Another US citizen."

"Randy Barnes? That name doesn't sound familiar." Ellie stepped around her desk and took the photo from her.

A flash of recognition crossed Ellie's face, and she held back her response, giving Ellie time to explain.

"I want to see him," Ellie demanded.

"No."

"From the roof."

"No."

"I want to see his face in real time. Not a printout."

"How do you know him?" she pushed.

"Let me see him, and then I'll tell you."

She forced out a breath of air. Against her better judgment, she gave in to Ellie again. "Fine, but you have to do exactly as I say while we're on the roof."

The flash of satisfaction that crossed Ellie's face was a brief irritation. The truth was she needed to know exactly what Ellie knew. She had already learned the hard way that Ellie would be more forthcoming if she yielded first. She wasn't sure she had ever met anyone as hardheaded as Elizabeth Turner.

She pulled open the door to find Sam sitting in Chloe's chair. He stood when they stepped out.

"I saw you at the movie," he said looking at her and then at Ellie. "So I assumed something was going on."

"You...you should have knocked," Ellie blurted.

Angel held back a chuckle at the slight blush spreading up Ellie's face. Of all the times, they had been behind closed doors this was an innocent one.

"I didn't mind waiting." Sam held out a folder to each of them. "I put together some notes from my last visit. A little insight for your trip on Monday."

Angel nodded. "Thank you. Every tip helps. Especially when you aren't sure what you're facing. I'll catch up with you tomorrow if I have questions."

"Sure, anytime. Is everything okay?"

Angel pulled the photo from her pocket. "Do you know this man?"

"He looks familiar. Should I?"

"His brother-in-law owns the company installing the solar panel farm."

She heard Ellie's gasp but didn't look at her. Instead, she watched Sam study the picture.

"I need to think on it," he said, glancing up.

"We'll be right back." She led the way to the elevator.

As the doors slid closed, she squeezed Ellie's arm gently. She wasn't upset and she wanted her to know it.

"Why is it that you always take the stairs unless you're with me and then it's the elevator?" Ellie asked teasingly.

She glanced down at Ellie's shoes.

"Really?" Ellie raised her eyebrows. "You think I can't take the stairs in these shoes?"

The elevator doors opened and Ellie stepped out.

Through the rush of wind, she faintly heard Ellie's words.

"You're wrong, very wrong."

She quickly stepped in front of Ellie, bringing them both to a stop. There was only one nearby building that was as tall as the one they stood on now. She pulled her binoculars from her pocket and quickly scanned the other rooftop. Seeing no one, she motioned for her agent on that side of the roof to keep an eye on the building. She quickly glanced around to see if there were other risks to the ambassador that she needed to evaluate. Seeing none, she moved forward until she was prone at the edge of the roof.

Following her, Ellie showed no concern for her blue dress pants or her cream-colored shirt. They lay on their stomachs, taking turns looking through her binoculars. She looked around at the other agents and the marine. Each was focused on their own position and showed no surprise at having the ambassador on the roof with them.

After a few minutes, Ellie handed the binoculars back to her and crawled back into a standing position. Angel patted Arden's leg as she moved to join Ellie. The wind whipped Ellie's hair across her face, masking whatever expression she was wearing. Ellie opened the fire door, and she followed her into the stairwell. It was hard not to notice that Ellie had chosen the stairs over the elevator.

Sam was waiting on the couch in Ellie's office and she took a seat across from him. This was going to be a long conversation and probably not one she was going to enjoy. Ellie paced behind her desk, finally coming to rest on the edge of her desk. Angel wasn't surprised that Ellie chose to remain standing.

* * *

Ellie wasn't afraid to tell Angel that she had gone behind her back to ask Shane for help. She was, however, not sure how to prepare for Angel's definite disappointment.

Sam looked back and forth between them. "I've seen this guy."

"Where?" Angel asked.

"He was on the docks the day I met Inspector Asker about maintaining their customs requirements."

"Did you talk with him?" Angel asked.

"No. He was with a group of guys. I assumed they were dockworkers. They seemed interested in knowing if Asker would agree with us or not."

Angel's intense gaze zeroed in on her. She felt her palms begin to sweat.

"Let's hear it," Angel demanded.

Ellie took a deep breath and explained exactly what she had overheard in the garage. She glanced at Angel a few times, but her face was unreadable so she focused on Sam.

"I knew Shane had contacts at the docks so I asked him to look into it," she finished.

Angel rubbed a hand across her face.

Sam spoke first. "Ellie, why didn't you come to me? You know the dockworkers are the ones outside. Maybe this is all connected."

She grimaced. Sam was right. She should have brought everyone in on what she heard. She was so upset with Angel that day for following her that she had forgotten to put everyone's safety first.

"Have there been any problems with the solar panel farm?" Angel asked. "Any regulations you've pushed to enforce or anything that would make them unhappy?"

Ellie searched her memory. She would love to be able to make the connections and put all of this behind her. "I can't think of anything."

"Me either," Sam agreed. "It's actually been surprisingly smooth. The same company installed a smaller version of this field at the edge of Nouakchott about two years ago so they already knew all the ins and outs."

"Okay. Then why is this site visit so important?" Angel asked.

"The last two progress reports they submitted to the Mauritania government not only failed to include a completion date but also lacked important details," Sam explained. "The main item missing was documentation showing what items have been imported. The Mauritanians aren't pushing back since it's a US-based company and they don't want to upset us or the company doing the construction. The plan was for Ellie to casually ask them to fill in the missing details. Just a friendly chat, no arm twisting."

Sam paused and Ellie jumped in. "My predecessor pushed hard for the small solar farm here in Nouakchott. Blackouts were a common occurrence because the city planners didn't account for how fast the city would grow. Severe droughts over the last ten years have also forced people into the city. Even the nomadic Arab-Berbers. Because of its location outside of Akjoujt this solar farm will allow farmers to cultivate crops and raise animals again."

"Okay. I understand, but why can't we postpone your visit?" Angel suggested.

"No," Ellie insisted. "It's taken hours of coordination to schedule this visit. Their supply trucks are moving back and forth to the docks every day, and our visit disrupts their work as well as that of the men on site. The management gives most of the workers the day off when we visit and that has to be worked into the flow of supplies arriving. I will not cause them to lose more than one day of work by rescheduling."

"I have to agree with Ellie," Sam added. "The efforts made to allow us to visit are extensive. It would hurt our relationship with them if we didn't show up when we said we would."

"It doesn't bother either of you that the man outside is connected to the company building the facility? This man or whoever he's working for is unhappy with something you guys are doing."

"Maybe he's one of the paid dockworkers being used for hire. Maybe he doesn't have anything to do with the bigger reason," she argued, watching Angel rub her face again. The few hours of sleep that she might have gotten earlier in the day had done nothing to ease the fatigue from her eyes.

"Fine. We're done here then." Angel stood. "Ambassador, I'll see you Monday morning. Sam, stay in close contact with Sergeant Miller while we're gone."

Sam nodded.

She watched Angel disappear from the room, wishing she would stay. Even though Angel was upset with her, having her nearby was comforting. She wished they could spend time together without the pressure of their jobs. She had almost forgotten Sam was still in the room when he spoke.

"You guys need to clear the air between you before your trip."

"What?"

Sam stood and walked toward her. "I like to think we've become friends during your time here, so please don't be upset that I'm sticking my nose where it might not belong. I've seen plenty of nice men pass through here, and no one even turned your head. And although I haven't seen anything unprofessional from you or Agent McTaggart, it's clear that there's something between you."

She shook her head. "There's nothing between us. How could there be? She's here to do a job. I can't get in her way."

Sam took her hand and led her to the couch, his fatherly concern melting her resolve. "Let's have some tea and talk about all the reasons you should get in her way. After this mess is cleared up, of course."

* * *

Angel descended the stairs slowly. She wasn't even sure Farook would be available at this hour, but according to his GPS light he was still in the motor pool. This was not a visit she was looking forward to. What she really wanted to do was tie him up and interrogate him, but she was fairly sure Ellie wouldn't like that. So she would play the diplomat.

She pushed open the heavy fire door into the motor pool and looked around. Three black Toyota SUVs sat in a single line directly in front of the closed roll-up door, apparently waiting for their trip on Monday. There was another SUV and two sedans along the far wall, but all the other vehicles were gone. She didn't see Farook so she crossed the room to his office. The door was open and she stuck her head inside as she knocked on the frame of the door.

Farook's head flew up at her knock and he quickly stuffed the papers in front of him into his desk. He stood, blocking her from coming into his office.

"Why are you here?" His frown faded into an eerie smile as he adjusted his question. "How can I help you?"

He slid around her and out the door, leading her away from his office. Whatever he had been doing at his desk was not something he wanted anyone to see. And she wanted to see.

"I wanted to check with you about the ambassador's trip on Monday. Are the vehicles ready?"

"Yes, yes. I have them all lined up."

"We'll be down about six thirty Monday morning to load up. Please let me know if there are any problems."

"Yes, yes. Everything will be ready."

She debated her next move. Showing Farook the picture of Barnes could show their hand and make things worse, but she really wanted to hear what he would say about their connection. She pulled the picture from her cargo pocket.

"Do you recognize this man?"

"No. No."

"You've never seen or spoken to him before?"

"No. I don't know him."

She stared at him for a few seconds before folding the picture and placing it back in her pocket. "I'll see you Monday morning."

She walked across the concrete floor to the stairway door. She wasn't sure about her course of action now that he had flat-out lied to her. She didn't know him very well, but she did know body language. His actions when she arrived and the sheen of sweat now covering his forehead made her believe he was up to something. However, that something might have nothing to do with the ambassador or their trip.

She texted Miller and Eric the details of her conversation with Farook. She had no doubt that Farook wouldn't make it two steps without one of them following him. It was the best she could do for now. She would tell Ellie about his denial tomorrow, and they could decide together how to have him removed. For now, she felt more comfortable keeping an eye on him.

She made one more swing around the embassy, checking in with all of her agents. Eric and Sarah had fully briefed everyone, but she needed to keep moving a little bit longer. When she finally returned to her room, she kicked off her boots and stripped quickly. She took a hot shower and dressed in her standard uniform. Stretching out on her bed, she checked on Ellie's GPS light. She had noticed earlier that Ellie had returned to her suite, but she needed to see that again before she could relax. The importance of Ellie in her life was not something she wanted to think about. She had never needed anyone, except maybe Vince. Though they had a professional relationship, he was still very much like a father to her.

Thoughts of Ellie's gentle touch during the movie made her stomach flutter, sending chills throughout her body. No woman she had ever met before could compare with Ellie. Not that she would ever compare Ellie to anyone. It wouldn't be fair. Ellie was strong and determined. She had accomplished things in her life that few women had dared to attempt. Ellie had been in this country as a teenager. She knew the challenges she would face, and she had volunteered to come back here anyway even though it meant fighting for respect from men who considered her from a lower class. And it was all to make changes for their good, not for herself.

Ellie was certainly a better person than she was. She was quick to write people out of her life if they didn't agree with her. Ellie rose above that to prove that the people she worked with could be better people too.

She tried to block the personal thoughts of Ellie from her mind and play the scenario for their trip. She mentally traced their course to the solar farm and their safe return, trying to anticipate possible security and natural hazards.

Those were not the only things she had to worry about, of course. Ever since Ellie had mentioned this trip, she had been fighting to avoid thinking about being trapped in a car with her for ten hours. It horrified and thrilled her at the same time. There would be no walking away from any conversation, and she couldn't even think about how close they would be to one another in the backseat.

CHAPTER TWENTY-ONE

Angel's eyes flew open, shocked to see she had slept through the night. She couldn't remember the last time she had slept as late as seven. Jumping out of bed, she grabbed her phone and checked for messages. There were none. Apparently Miller had everything under control. She quickly showered and made her rounds, checking in with Eric and Sarah before appearing promptly at eight in front of Ellie.

The same as it had been the previous Sunday, the embassy was surprisingly quiet considering the number of people living inside it. As if it were any other day, Ellie was dressed in a perfectly tailored suit with her jacket hanging over the back of her chair. She closed the folder in front of her and stood when Angel arrived.

"You look refreshed." Ellie smiled.

She returned her smile. Whatever had Ellie in this jovial mood seemed to have reset their relationship once again. "I got a few hours of sleep. How about you?"

"I slept. I assume everything is quiet outside."

"It is. Shepherd and Barnes are still out there together." When she had left Sarah moments ago, she was wiring an amplifier to see if she could pick up any conversation between them. She would provide Ellie with details if it yielded any information.

"Did you meet with our marine escorts?"

She removed her tablet from her cargo pocket and pulled up the meeting notes from the previous night. Ellie walked around her desk and motioned her to take seat. Angel took her usual seat at the end of the couch and was surprised when Ellie sat beside her. She was hit by a subtle yet intoxicating smell of coconut and something else. Maybe lavender.

"Are you okay?" Ellie asked, the hint of a grin playing on the corners of her mouth.

"What? Yes."

She placed the tablet on her knees so Ellie could see as well and quickly covered each point, the warmth from Ellie's body slowly seeping into her. She pushed against it. Today was her day to focus on their trip, not to lose herself in the feel of Ellie's body. The pressure of Ellie's thigh against her own sent her into overdrive, pushing her closer to the edge. The smell of coconut reminded her of the beach, which reawakened lingering thoughts of Ellie in a bathing suit. She fought the images flashing through her mind and stood. Her mind was at war with her body and she needed to be alone.

"I'll have more information this evening," she choked out, moving toward the door.

"I'll be here."

She hurried from the room. She had forgotten to mention Farook's denial, but she definitely was not returning now.

* * *

Ellie couldn't remember ever seeing Angel move so fast. She hadn't thought of what sitting beside Angel might do, only that she wanted to be close to her. The last two weeks had been an emotional roller coaster. Keeping secrets and holding back feelings was starting to take its toll on her. She wanted to feel their connection again. To relax in the safe and comfortable net Angel cast around them. To shed her ambassador skin if only for a moment and be herself.

She poured a cup of tea from the pot in front of her and leaned back into the couch. Angel was such a mystery. The dossier that she had shredded one night after Chloe had left might have offered some clues, but nothing came close to providing the kind of information she was after than firsthand observation could.

She wondered if she would be so intrigued if she wasn't so desirable. Sam was convinced they would be perfect together, and she thought about how her life would change if she was dating someone. It wasn't something she had ever considered before and it made her a bit nervous. She certainly wouldn't be able to move a partner or spouse into the embassy, but Angel would never be that person anyway.

Tying Angel to one spot wasn't going to happen anytime in the near future. Even though her body reacted to Angel each time she was near, it didn't mean they could have a future. Their bodies were in sync, not their lives. Every inch of her craved to give into the temptation. Could she convince Angel to spend the day in bed instead of preparing for tomorrow? She gave a rueful laugh. The way Angel had bolted from the room moments ago, she wasn't sure she could convince her the sky was blue much less to give in to her desires.

She sat her teacup on the coffee table and stretched out on the couch. She had tossed and turned most of the previous night, and this was supposed to be her lazy day. In a few minutes, she would return to her suite and change into something more comfortable. She had a book she had been wanting to read. Something about women and romance, of course, and the life of an LA movie star, but for a moment she allowed herself to think about Angel. How their bodies had fit together when they kissed. How she had wanted to wipe her desk clear and let Angel take her right there. She closed her eyes and let her imagination run wild.

* * *

Angel followed the sidewalk around the four-story embassy building. Stepping close to the building, she ran her fingers over the jagged stone of the exterior wall. It was rugged and unaffected. The opposite of her reactions to Ellie's touch. She shook her head. She needed to block all distractions from her mind while she prepared for tomorrow's trip. She took a deep breath. The fresh air and sunshine coursed through her body, giving her strength.

She tracked the roving patrol on her tablet and intercepted them behind the barracks. A quick discussion with them told her everything was going smoothly. She circled the maintenance building, taking the long way back to the gatehouse. A check of all posts hadn't revealed anything amiss, so she made her way to the break room outside the barracks. She filled her coffee cup before sitting at the table to work on tomorrow's plan. She was thankful for a quiet day in which to review everything on her tablet and get familiar with the course. After an hour, she was starting to feel comfortable with her plan. She stood and stretched, relieved for the break when Miller walked in.

He tossed a folded square of paper on the table before filling his cup. "I brought you a topographical map to take tomorrow. For some crazy reason, we've had a hard time getting these so we only have a few."

"Thanks. I'll get it back to you as soon as we return tomorrow." She rubbed her face. She had been fully rested, but the potential scenarios playing in her mind were wearing on her.

Miller sat down across from her. "What's got you worried? Here or the trip?"

She grinned. "Both."

"Right."

"I've been thinking about Barnes and what his involvement could be. We know he's talking to Farook, so we should assume he knows the ambassador will be leaving the embassy tomorrow. If their goal is to reduce the number of security agents with the ambassador, then I look for them to move on us as soon as we exit the embassy. But if we make it past the crowd without incident, then you guys should prepare for an assault."

Miller nodded. "It's hard to believe they could be ramping up for an assault when the random gunfire stopped after your arrival. I thought things were growing calmer, not escalating."

"I don't think anyone could argue with the fact that the crowd is definitely not angry and is completely unmotivated for an assault. It's the motives of the men behind the crowd that could force the issue."

Miller shook his head. "I'm having trouble seeing the men outside climbing the fence or throwing grenades. Even if someone orders them to."

"I agree, but if it's not one of those options, then what's their angle?"

Angel sat silently and Miller seemed lost in his own thoughts too. When her cup was empty, she stood.

"I'm going to the gym," she said. "Maybe I'll figure something out there."

"Concentrate on your trip. We've got the embassy covered."

She made a quick check of Ellie's location and was relieved to see her back inside her suite. She quickly changed into workout clothes and climbed the stairs to the gym. She paused outside the entrance to Ellie's suite and imagined herself knocking on the door.

* * *

Ellie held her breath as Angel's GPS light moved in her direction and then stopped outside her door. Angel hadn't been inside her personal living space since the first day she'd arrived. Her heart raced with the possibility of a social call, knowing that Angel wouldn't hesitate to knock if it wasn't personal.

When the light moved, Ellie released her breath. The gym, of course. She was going to the gym. It was stupid for her to think Angel would stop by for a social visit in her suite.

She tried to return to her book, but disappointment kept interfering with her ability to follow the story. She wanted to be close to Angel. She changed into workout clothes and quickly headed for the gym. She had to move fast. Angel would probably leave if she noticed her moving in that direction.

She opened the door to the gym and gave Angel a smile. Sweat glistened on Angel's face as her long legs stretched the length of the treadmill. She began walking on the treadmill beside Angel's, trying hard not to watch her in the mirror that covered the wall in front of them. Angel was dressed the same as she had been the previous time Ellie had passed her leaving the gym. The baggy gym shorts slid up and down her thighs in a seductive rhythm.

When Angel reduced her speed, she pleaded, "Please don't leave."

Angel gave her a quick glance and then stared straight ahead, her attention focused on something Ellie couldn't see. The treadmill motor roared as Angel increased her speed again.

She let a small smile of satisfaction spread across her face. Putting in her earbuds, she started a recorded sitcom episode on her treadmill screen and settled into a relaxing pace. When it ended, she let the tape continue and watched a second episode. The steady movement from Angel's body beside her brought a sense of comfort and excitement at the same time.

When they each reached to reduce their speed at the same time, she met Angel's eyes and they laughed. Removing her earbuds, she glanced at Angel.

"Nice run?"

"Not as mind-clearing as I'd hoped, but I can't complain. The company was good."

She smiled. "I was thinking the same thing. Are you almost finished?"

"As soon as my cooldown ends."

"I'm starving. Would you join me for a late lunch?"

Angel hesitated so she pushed a little harder. "Early dinner?"

"Okay," Angel said, giving in. "Shower first?"

She felt her face blush as she imagined Angel's question as an invitation. Oh, yes, she would love to shower with her. Instead she glanced at her watch. "The café's going to close in less than an hour. We better skip the shower for now."

* * *

Angel couldn't remember much about their lunch conversation. Ellie had pulled on a zippered sweatshirt that was barely zipped halfway, displaying a large portion of her chest and tank top. Though she tried not stare, she had a hard time keeping her mind on the topics they were discussing. She was so disoriented that by the end of the meal she even agreed to meet Ellie in her suite for their evening briefing.

She showered and had a final meeting with her team and Miller. After discussing with them the potential for what might occur, she felt as comfortable as she could with leaving them the next day. Shepherd and Barnes had each disappeared for a short break after the midday prayers, but the monitors in the Communications Center showed that both were back again and in the same spots. She paced inside the small room and watched the seconds move closer to the time to meet Ellie. Noticing on the second-floor camera that several kids were running down the hallway, she moved closer to the marine in front of the terminal.

"What's wrong?" she asked.

"Just a Sunday evening scavenger hunt," the corporal answered.

"Scavenger hunt?"

"There are always activities for the kids on the weekends and especially now that we're all confined."

"Is the ambassador there?" she asked as she watched the monitors switch from camera to camera, catching more running children.

"Probably, but Deputy Patone is overseeing it."

She remembered Sam's daughter, Brittany. He probably needed a lot of activities to keep her entertained.

"I'm going to check it out."

She heard the marine laugh as the door closed, but she didn't care. She desperately needed a distraction for the next thirty minutes. She found Sam outside the ambassador's office with Chloe. They were checking items off a list as a boy about ten years old danced in front of them.

"Okay, Jeremy. You still need the last two items on the list." Chloe leaned close to him. "Try Conference Room Two."

After the boy took off at a sprint, Chloe held up his paper. "Wonder how long it will be before he realizes that he forgot this." They all laughed when Jeremy ran back into the room, grabbed the paper from Chloe, and ran out again.

"I think he needs my help," Chloe said, following him.

"Did you come to join the fun, Agent McTaggart?" Sam asked.

She smiled. "I was in the communications room and saw the kids running around on the monitor. It looked like I should check it out."

"Just having a little fun."

"I can see that."

Sam sat down on the couch across from Chloe's desk. Resting his arm along its back, he turned toward her.

"Are you ready for tomorrow?" he asked.

"As ready as I can be. Thanks for the background information, by the way." She leaned against Chloe's desk and tried to rein in her nervous energy. "The entire trip seems like an unnecessary risk."

"You security-minded people would never let us do anything if we didn't push. You need us to balance you out."

She chuckled. "I can see how you might think that."

"Ellie's a good woman. She's already accomplished more in six months than her predecessor did during his entire term, but she has more to do. Bring her back safely."

She liked it when those close to Ellie spoke up for her. It eased her mind when she thought about leaving.

"I will."

Sam studied her. "She's not as difficult as she seems."

"Nope, you can't convince me of that. She's the most hardheaded woman I've ever worked with."

Sam laughed. "You only think that because she wins you over to her side without you even knowing it."

"You're right on that. Sometimes I can't even believe what I agree to." She smiled at him. "And on that note, I'm off to give my nightly briefing. Have a good night."

"You too, Agent."

As she walked away, she heard Sam's parting words. "She trusts you, and when it counts she'll do exactly what you tell her."

His words slowed her pace, but she didn't turn around. She wanted to believe him. He knew Ellie better than anyone in the building. If she didn't believe what he said at least a little then she shouldn't take her through the gate. She had to believe that Ellie wouldn't question her authority. But if a battle of wills did occur, she had to be the only winner.

As she climbed the stairs, she contemplated Ellie's reasons for briefing in her suite instead of in her office. Surely she must have resisted, but honestly, she couldn't remember disagreeing. Being alone with Ellie without fear of interruption was exactly what she wanted. In another time or place, maybe. Tonight, though, she needed to avoid all physical contact. She swiped her badge on the outer security access door and entered Ellie's private hallway.

Ellie opened the door before she knocked, making it clear she had been watching the GPS app on her tablet.

"I hope you didn't cheat for any of the kids," Ellie teased.

"Chloe's taking care of that."

"I'm not surprised." Ellie motioned to the small seating area that was her living room. "Can I talk you into joining me?"

Without a thought, Angel took a seat on the small loveseat facing a thick cushioned green chair. A book lay open on the cushion, and Ellie moved it to the coffee table between them. She tried not to think about the fact that the room behind Ellie held a queen-sized bed with a thick white comforter. This would be a true test of her resolve. She wasn't sure she could spend time inside Ellie's domain without losing her head.

Ellie was dressed in light blue sweatpants with a white drawstring at the waist. The baggy bottoms swallowed her feet as she pulled them up on the chair beneath her. Her white tank top was covered by a long sweater-style jacket that she wrapped around her chest. Her hair hung loose, making the shadows from the lamp dance across her face.

"Are you ready to see some of the countryside tomorrow?" Ellie asked.

"Will there be something more than sand?"

Ellie smiled. "There'll be plenty of desert but a few mountains and probably a camel or two as well. I wish we could detour to see more than Highway N1, but I'll take the time to show you around when all of this is over."

"I look forward to it."

If Ellie was surprised by her willingness, she didn't show it. The conversation quickly progressed to the beauty of the country with Ellie eagerly sharing her personal stories about places she had visited as well as about the everyday activities that took place at the Port de Peche in Nouakchott. Forgetting about the briefing she was supposed to be giving, Angel let Ellie's excitement draw her in.

"Oh and you missed the Tabaski last month. It's an Islamic festival known as the Sacrifice Feast. We closed the embassy for three days and on the final day we had a huge party downstairs. For the Muslims it's about prayer, but for us it's mainly about eating and giving gifts to the children."

"It's a celebration of something?"

"It is. It commemorates the willingness of Abraham to follow God's command and sacrifice his son. The dates change each year because it depends on the sighting of the moon, but I believe it's always in September."

Without thinking, Angel spoke the first thought that crossed her mind. "That story has always bothered me. How could anyone kill their own child?"

"He didn't do it. God stopped him."

"Yes, but he asked him to do it and Abraham didn't know he was going to stop him."

Ellie shifted on the cushion, pulling her knees up to her chest. "Are we into the black and white viewpoint again? It's about belief and trust. You have to believe that Abraham did know God wouldn't let him sacrifice the son he had waited so long for."

She shook her head. "I guess next you're going to tell me that the twenty percent of Mauritanians still in slavery believe they're doing God's will?"

"I believe they're doing what they've been raised to do."

"Slavery was abolished here in 1981 but it took over twenty-five years for it to become illegal to own slaves." She knew she was pushing Ellie again, but she couldn't stop. These were the hard questions she wanted answers to. She knew Ellie was a good person and she wanted to understand.

"Ending slavery is not about enforcing the laws. This country is a vast desert and that would be impossible. It's about changing the belief that slavery is a part of the natural order and providing the ability for freed slaves to support themselves."

"So you think it's irrelevant that only one in four thousand cases are reported. The only government agency allowed to submit legal complaints on behalf of the slaves doesn't submit any. And the nongovernmental anti-slavery activists are arrested, prosecuted, and convicted."

Ellie took a deep breath. "You've been doing your homework, Agent McTaggart. I never said things were perfect here. There will always be room for change. I have the ability to raise public awareness. And to provide funding and protection for those nongovernmental agencies."

What had she done? Ellie was sharing the positive, beautiful side of this country, and she had dragged them both into the darkness. She stood. "I'm sorry, Ambassador. I didn't come here to beat you down about this country or your beliefs. I'm impressed with your desire to make changes. We need more people with your passion in the world."

Ellie stood, too, bringing their bodies closer together. Only inches apart.

She looked down into turquoise eyes filled with compassion. Ellie could have been angry with her. She wouldn't have blamed her. But that wasn't what she saw. She saw a strong woman who wanted to make a difference and was willing to do the work. She could understand how Ellie was so successful in swaying others to see her side of things.

"I've enjoyed talking with you tonight," Ellie said, touching her hand. "Maybe when we come back from this trip we can spend more time getting to know each other."

"Let's get through tomorrow. Then we can try to find a common ground we can agree on."

"Conversations aren't always about agreeing, you know?"

"I'll keep that in mind."

CHAPTER TWENTY-TWO

Angel showered and dressed in her usual cargo pants and Flagler shirt. Strapping on her pistol, she threw an extra clip and a change of clothing into an overnight bag. She pulled on her matching dark blue blouse to conceal her weapon. Sometimes displaying her weapon would show strength, and other times it would only instigate tension. She would adjust as the day progressed, based on what she encountered.

She had not received any calls during the night, but she had allowed enough time to check in with every post before she met the marine detail in the motor pool. She had no doubts about leaving them, only a desire to keep them safe. Miller's ability to act in a high-stress situation was an unknown, but her time with him the last few weeks had given her confidence that he would respond appropriately.

After checking in with her agents, she swung by the café. Her stomach wasn't keen on food yet, so she added a loaf of bread and some crackers to her bag. Her decision to make Chloe her last stop was rewarded when she passed Ellie entering the café as she was leaving. She forced a relaxed smile on her face as she entered the office.

After exchanging a cheerful greeting, she leaned close to Chloe, whispering. "I need you to do me a favor."

"Of course," Chloe said enthusiastically.

"You have access to the ambassador's suite, right?"

"I do." Chloe's smile began to fade.

"The ambassador's in the café and I need you to pack an overnight bag for her. No dress shoes. Hiking boots would be best, but running shoes will do. And a comfortable change of clothes." She paused and then quickly continued as Chloe's face arched into a frown. "It's only a precaution. I'm not expecting anything to happen, but I want to be prepared. If we can do this without causing any stress to the ambassador, then that's good for both of us, right?"

Chloe stood. "I'll do it."

"Great."

* * *

Ellie was surprised to find Chloe's desk empty when she stopped by her office after asking the cooks in the café to pack a snack bag and sandwiches for each car. She left Chloe a quick note and almost had stepped into the elevator when she remembered Angel's criticism of her shoes. She looked down. She had chosen a pair of black loafers with a sculpted two-inch heel to wear today. They were stylish with a strap across the top of the foot and comfortable. To make her point that they were also practical, she took the stairs instead.

When she stepped through the fire door into the garage, the acrid smell made her nose wrinkle. The underground garage had an excellent ventilation system but still always smelled of motor oil and gasoline. The smell of exhaust from the running vehicles was worse than the lingering old scents.

Angel was giving instructions to the marines standing with her. She was an imposing figure psychologically as well as physically. As the roll-up door in front of the first car was opened, a gust of fresh air swept inside, pushing Angel's dark hair across her face. She flicked it out of her eyes without a pause in what she was saying. When she finished, she turned toward where Ellie was standing, meeting her gaze. Patting the nearest marine on the back, she crossed to meet her.

Ellie liked observing Angel in action as much as she liked staring at her across the desk. The way her body moved as she walked toward her took her breath away. She was smooth and elegant, holding Ellie's attention captive with each purposeful step. She wanted nothing more than to pull her in for a kiss. One that they wouldn't have to stop.

Angel came to a halt directly in front of her, stopping Ellie's mind from continuing to strip her of all clothing. Angel's eyes searched her face for a second before turning to survey the scene around them.

Ellie had a feeling that Angel had a good idea about what she was thinking, but she said it anyway. "You're beautiful, you know?"

"No."

"No, you're not beautiful, or no, you don't know."

"Yes."

Ellie laughed. "This conversation is going nowhere. Are we ready to go?"

"Yes."

"I assume we're in the middle car."

Then it hit her—maybe Angel wouldn't have them in the same vehicle. Maybe Angel would think she would have a better view from the lead vehicle or the rear vehicle rather than riding in the middle with her.

With a little more panic in her voice than she expected, she asked, "You're riding with me, right?"

"Yes, and yes."

She shook her head. If this was going to be the extent of their conversation, it was going to be a long ten hours. She dropped one bag from the café in each of the cars and then took a seat in the rear of the middle vehicle. Her driver slid into the front seat and greeted her.

"Good morning. How are you?" he asked in English.

"Good morning, Nasri," she replied. "Did you volunteer for this outing?"

"I did. Yes."

Nasri Haik was one of four embassy drivers, but he also worked as translator when needed. He spoke several dialects of Arabic as well as English.

"Thank you. How are you doing being away from your wife and children?"

"I am fine. They are safe with my family outside the city so I do not worry."

"I'm very glad to hear that. We appreciate you being here."

Their conversation stopped as Angel joined them, and their caravan began to move.

"Both men are still outside on the wall?" she asked Angel.

"They are."

"How much range does your cell phone get?"

"We'll see."

"Enough that they can let us know if things change when we leave?"

"Yes."

Ellie pulled her tablet from her bag and put her headphones on. Watching a movie seemed to be her best choice. She had thought—hoped, anyway—that there would be some conversation, but clearly Angel wasn't in agreement. She wasn't going to sit here and beg her to talk. Maybe if she gave her some time, she would be more engaging on the return trip.

Beside her, she felt Angel slide her pistol from its holster. She didn't ask if everything was okay. She had learned during her time as a senator to ignore all potential risks around her and let her security do their job. Angel, she was certain, would do everything necessary to keep her safe. Angel held the pistol in her lap as their vehicle passed through the men outside the embassy. Ellie kept her gaze on the small screen in front of her.

* * *

Angel's eyes flew open as Ellie sighed, pulling her headphones from her ears.

"Are you okay?" she asked. Her voice gravelly from the hours of silence.

"I'm fine. I can't believe I fell asleep so quickly."

"Neither of us have been getting much sleep lately."

"Were you sleeping?" Ellie asked.

"No, just resting my eyes." She glanced out the window. "Not like there's anything but sand to look at out there."

She had secured her pistol in its holster once they left the city behind and desert was stretching in all directions around them. The large plateaus she could see in the distance stood high above the flat plains, but she was pretty sure most of them were farther than they were traveling today. Here there was nothing more than some tufts of grass, a few trees, and an occasional small sand dune to break the monotony. Safety wasn't an issue when she could see someone approach from miles away.

"There'll be more to see soon." Ellie leaned toward her to peer out the front windshield. "That's Akjoujt in the distance."

"Yep."

"Was there any change outside the embassy after we left?"

"Nothing."

The silence stretched heavily in the car between them. The usual tension was back. She wanted to blame it on the stress of the day, but she knew it was her fault. She had constructed a large mental wall between them to avoid the risk of a disagreement. Now she knew that was the wrong approach. Ellie needed communication to know everything was okay.

She studied Ellie's hand as it lay on the seat between them. Her fingers were long and delicate with short, perfectly cut nails. The blue veins on the back of her hand stood out against her pale skin. She found Ellie's hands alluring and could easily imagine what it would feel like to have them touching her.

To keep her mind from wandering down paths it shouldn't she turned her gaze on their surroundings. On the edge of the town they were approaching, strips of connected buildings alternated with an occasional stand-alone shack made of stone and wood. Splashes of color danced throughout as children ran and played in the distance. If the streets were paved, she couldn't tell, due to the amount of sand that had been blown around. The streets were crooked, winding around houses and other structures. Electric poles leaned on street corners, connecting a maze of wires raised barely high enough for vehicles to pass underneath.

She placed her hand on top of Ellie's. She wanted to ease the tension between them, but instead she felt a charge of electricity. When Ellie didn't respond, she glanced at her, squeezing her hand. "Are we okay?"

Ellie met her eyes. "We're fine. I'm just trying to understand you. Maybe if you weren't always so stubborn."

"Me!"

"Yes, it's—"

Ellie's response was cut off by a thundering explosion in front of them. A ball of fire roared where the engine had been in the lead embassy car. Angel bounced in her seat, looking in all directions. It felt like an ambush, but she couldn't see anyone closing in on them. She turned back to the front car as the marines climbed out and surveyed the damage to their vehicle and the road. Once they had checked the area around them, they motioned Angel's driver to pull forward. Protocol dictated they would leave the car where it sat, and each marine would join the other two cars.

She saw the young men's bodies convulse as gunfire erupted.

She reached for the door handle. She had to get out there and pull them to cover. Ellie grasped her arm, stopping her. She looked into her panicked face.

"You can't go out there," Ellie cried.

Angel shook her head, clearing it of the yearning to take care of the men. Her responsibility was Ellie and keeping her safe. Inside the embassy car they would be protected. "Get moving!" she yelled, slapping the seat beside their driver. When the car didn't move, Angel hit his arm. "Move!" she demanded.

His body pitched forward against the steering wheel. It only took a second for her to realize a bullet had pierced the supposedly bulletproof car, and she shoved Ellie onto the floorboard.

"What the hell!" Ellie yelled as Angel pinned her to the floor with her body.

"Get ready to move. We have to get out of the car!"

Ellie squirmed below her. "What? No! We're protected here and we need the car to get back to the embassy."

"I'd rather have you alive." She popped the door open and slid to the ground, pulling Ellie with her.

"I don't understand. We're safer in the car. It's armored."

"Not this one. We have to move."

"Nasri—" Ellie cried.

"We can't help him. He's dead. Now move."

With cover from the marines behind them, she pulled Ellie to her feet and held tight to her hand as they ran toward the closest building. She pushed Ellie deep into an alley and collapsed against the wall as the third car in their convoy exploded. She could still hear gunfire, though. She fought the urge to join them in the battle. For now, she had to keep Ellie safe and that meant not drawing attention to their location.

Ellie tried to walk toward the opening of the alley, and Angel grabbed her arm.

"I only see two gunmen. Why aren't you firing back?" Ellie exclaimed.

She pulled her back against the wall beside her so they could both see the edge of the alley. She pointed to the rooftop across from them.

"There are at least three men on that rooftop and who knows how many more I can't see. If I fire, it will draw attention to us. For now, I'm hoping we managed to get away without them seeing the direction we went."

"Oh." Ellie was silent for a few seconds, and when she spoke her voice was calmer. "Who do you think they are? Do you think they know who I am?"

Angel turned to face her. "I'm not sure, but right now I'm not willing to risk your life to find out."

"But if they realize who I am, they might stop firing."

Ellie stepped forward again, but Angel quickly pulled her into her chest, covering Ellie's mouth with her hand as she pulled them back into the shadows. She strained to hear the conversation of two men as they passed the opening of the alley.

"She's not in the car. Did you see which direction she went?" the first man asked.

"No, but we'll find her."

"Damn right, we will. Lars was clear that we wouldn't be paid until she's eliminated."

Ellie kicked against Angel's body, but she held her tight, pulling both of them further down the alley and behind one of the buildings. When they were safely out of range of the men, she released Ellie and quickly stepped away from her, letting Ellie vent her rage.

"That son of a bitch." Ellie stomped back and forth. "I can't freakin' believe it. That was Farook."

Angel let her pace for a minute and then reached out a hand to stop her. "I know you're angry, but we have to get our heads together if we want to survive. They're going to search this town and we can't be here."

* * *

Angel knew she was taking a risk, but she didn't have a choice. She hoped Ellie was smart enough to stay inside the empty storage building they had found. This was a task she had to complete alone. The gunfire had stopped and the streets of Akjoujt remained empty, but she knew that wouldn't last long. She maneuvered the several blocks back to where they had left the embassy vehicles. All three still sat blocking the roadway. Quickly crossing the open street to reach them, she pulled the dead marines from the lead car and Nasri into the shelter of a shack behind the street.

An eerie silence pervaded the area. There was no sign of the town's residents. They'd been smart enough to clear the scene as soon as the first explosion hit, no doubt. She removed the dog tags from around the marines' necks, squeezed the cool pieces of metal in her fist, and closed her eyes for a few seconds. There was nothing more she could do for them at this moment.

There were no other bodies, she was glad to see. Wondering briefly which direction the other two marines had fled and wishing the best for them, she ran to the vehicle they had been traveling in and popped the trunk. After pulling their overnight bags from it, she spotted a light blue shopping bag through the open back door. She reached in, grabbed it, and stuffed it inside one of the other bags. Glancing around she saw three men in the distance talking heatedly with a Mauritanian national guardsman and pointing up and down the street. He was nodding. Angel wondered if he was part of their group or if they had told him a lie to get him to work with them. At the moment it didn't matter. She couldn't count on anyone to assist them.

CHAPTER TWENTY-THREE

Ellie's heart thudded in her chest. She was scared, but more than that she was angry. Farook's voice at the end of the alley talking about putting an end to her had sent her over the edge. Apparently the deaths of the two marines and Nasri hadn't knocked him to his senses and she would make him pay for his betrayal when she returned to the embassy. For now, she needed to help Angel get them out of this town.

She crept around the stone shack, listening intently for any voices or sounds. She was several blocks from where they had been hit and hopeful that any occupants had been smart enough to flee the area.

She pulled two lengths of fabric from the clothesline and stuffed a handful of money into the remaining pants pocket still on the line. She didn't like to steal, but they needed to cover themselves if they wanted to get out of this town unnoticed. She was sure Angel would have a plan, but for her own sense of self-respect she needed to contribute.

She quickly returned to the spot Angel had left her. Angel came around the corner at the same time. She ignored the annoyed look Angel gave her and reached out to help her carry the bags in her hands. She was relieved they were back together.

Angel led her silently to the rear of a store. A small overhang there blocked out the sun and offered a sliver of shade.

She glanced inside the bag she held and then looked at Angel. "These are my clothes. Did you pack this?"

Angel shrugged.

She could feel rage and fear bubbling back to the surface. She knew she wasn't angry at Angel, but she lashed out anyway.

"Did you go through my personal belongings?"

Angel, peering intently into the window of the store, made no move to answer.

"Look at me," she demanded. "Were you in my room without permission?"

Angel turned from the window as Ellie's words registered. "What? No! I asked Chloe to pack you an overnight bag in case we needed it."

She wanted to be mad. She wanted the heat coursing through her veins. It kept her moving and she needed to keep going right now. She searched Angel's face and saw only compassion. She knew her angry words weren't covering her fear. She leaned against the side of the store and took a deep breath. "I'm sorry."

Angel reached out tentatively, pulling her into a hug.

She wanted to cry. She wanted to pretend they weren't stuck in the desert, hours from the safety of the embassy, and that three or more men hadn't died on her watch. She relaxed into the strong arms, letting Angel's confidence strengthen her.

Angel's voice was soft when she finally spoke. "I know you're scared, but I *will* get you out of here. Together we'll come up with a solution."

She nodded. Though she wanted to stay in Angel's arms, she stepped back and picked up her bag again. She began inventorying the items inside. Tossing a pair of jeans and a T-shirt beside her on the ground, she pulled out her hiking boots. They made her smile.

"I could have worn my heels," she muttered under her breath as she began removing her suit. She heard Angel chuckle, but she didn't look up. Beside her Angel was stripping as well, and despite the direness of their situation the last thing she needed at this moment was to see Angel partially dressed.

* * *

Angel knew fear when she saw it. Even with Ellie's CIA background, it was clear she wasn't accustomed to feeling afraid. And the anger she was feeling would only carry her so far. They both needed a plan to feel in control. One that gave them confidence in their survival.

Angel peered into the window again, seeing through the store to a front window where she could see national guardsmen scanning the street. There was no sign of their pursuers, though. Her eyes brushed over the man and woman huddled behind their sales counter. She nodded at them. Her original intent had been to enter the store so they could change clothes and regroup, but when she saw them, she hadn't wanted to frighten or endanger them further.

She concentrated on figuring out what their next steps should be. One of their challenges would be communicating with people who might be able to offer assistance. Luckily, Ellie would be able to help with that. Which meant that she'd need to be more forthcoming with her than in the past.

"Farook and his friends have already talked with the Mauritanian national guardsmen and I'm afraid we might not be able to get through any checkpoints."

Ellie sighed. "That explains why there wasn't a gendarmerie checkpoint before Akjoujt. They must have been paid off."

"I saw their tent before the explosion, but there wasn't anyone in it."

Ellie picked up the lengths of fabric she had taken and handed a blue one to Angel, keeping a red and orange one for herself. "These might help."

"Thanks for staying put like I asked," she said sarcastically.

Ellie gave her a small smile. "I needed to do something to help and I saw the clothesline. Wearing mulafas can help disguise our appearance."

Arguing would have only been time wasted. She followed Ellie's instructions and wrapped the mulafa around her body and over her head.

"There's an old truck behind that house." Ellie pointed to a small block building without a door.

"I could hotwire it, but the noise might draw attention."

They glanced at each other as a vehicle started in the distance. Angel grabbed their bags. "Let's give it a go."

She let Ellie lead the way to the little sun-faded blue truck. It was an early 70s model with rust spots along the bottom of the doors. There was barely enough room for the two of them and their bags in the front seat. She lay across the floorboard and traced the wires leading to the ignition switch.

"It's eerie how empty this town is," Ellie stated, nervously making conversation.

"Yeah, explosions and gunfire tend to scare people away."

The old truck made a grumbling sound as the engine fired. She slid behind the wheel. She hated stealing someone's vehicle, but she would make it up to them when this was over. Right now, she had to get Ellie out of this town.

She glanced at the dashboard gauges and saw there was barely a quarter of a tank of gas—assuming the gauge worked. It wasn't enough to take them back to Nouakchott. But it was enough to get them to Atar. Plan B it was. She would share the first phase with Ellie.

"I don't know what we'll face in Atar, but if we can get ahead of Farook and his friends I'm hoping we'll be able to clear the checkpoints. What sort of communication do you think they have between checkpoints?"

"I'm not sure. There's no cell service, so a GPS phone would be the only thing that might work out here."

Ellie grew silent and Angel knew what was coming. The one thing that might prove to be her biggest mistake in the end. She maneuvered the truck onto the sandy road.

"Did you bring a GPS phone?" Ellie asked softly.

Communications should have been the first thing on her mind when the first shot went off, but Ellie's safety had blurred all logical thought.

"Montgomery had one, but it wasn't on him when I went back to the car." Neither was his rifle, but she skipped mentioning that.

Ellie nodded.

"I'm hoping the marines from the rear car picked it up and have already called in the situation. For now, though, I'm afraid we're on our own."

"So…they weren't killed too?" Ellie asked hesitantly.

"No. Only the two marines in front of us and Nasri." She gave her thigh a quick squeeze. "Let's concentrate on one task at a time. Miller gave me a map. It should be in my bag. Can you get it out?"

She turned down a side road running parallel to the main street.

"N1 is the main road and that runs directly in to Atar. If there are any side roads they don't show on the map." Ellie's voice was muffled as she fought with the paper map.

They hadn't passed or seen any vehicles on the road before the explosion, and it didn't appear that anything was moving in Akjoujt either. She pulled the truck slowly to a stop on the eastern edge of town where their path connected with N1.

"I see four men standing in the street," Ellie said, looking into Akjoujt.

"All clear my way." She pulled onto the sand-packed road heading east.

"Maybe they'll keep looking for us in Akjoujt," Ellie said as she unwrapped the fabric from around her face. "Are you hungry?"

She wasn't, but she let Ellie take back some control, even if it was small.

"Yes, and water, too, please."

Ellie handed her half of a sandwich and an open bottle of water. She ate the sandwich in three bites, barely chewing. It was like sandpaper going down, and she quickly downed half of the bottle of water before handing it back to Ellie.

"I only brought six bottles of water so we should try to pick up more in Atar if we can."

"There are two in the café bag as well," Ellie added.

"That was good thinking. And on the food, too."

Ellie smiled apologetically. "Thanks for the change of clothes."

She stretched her hand across the seat and took Ellie's. "One step at a time."

"Okay, then what's our next one?"

"We should have enough gas to get us to Atar. If we can refill the truck, we'll keep moving."

Ellie squeezed her hand. She took that to mean the plan had met her approval. The road in front of and behind them remained empty. She held her breath and let it out slowly. She had been in worse positions before. She couldn't let herself dwell on the bodies she had left behind. Her responsibility was to keep Ellie safe.

She glanced at Ellie. Her jaw was tight as she studied the map folded in her hands. The panic they had both felt earlier had been replaced with a resigned acceptance of the position they were in. She drew strength from Ellie's calmness. Together they would do whatever it took to survive.

The desert view was changing fast as they traveled farther into the Adrar Region. Two brown and pink mountain ranges stretched north to south, standing tall above the vast desert. The huge rocks gave way to occasional glimpses of thicker vegetation to the south.

"What are you doing?" she asked when Ellie began placing the items from their bag on the seat between them.

"I'm moving all the necessities to one bag in case we have to leave the truck. We might be able to use some of the food to barter for safety or travel."

"You speak the language here, right?"

"I speak French and Hassaniya Arabic, which is mostly spoken in Nouakchott. There are many dialects of Arabic as well as three other national languages. I think we can get by with what I know, though."

"I hope so because I see a gendarmerie checkpoint coming up fast."

"I was afraid of that," Ellie said, glancing up.

"We're still a good distance from Atar, so sort the food and see what we have to offer them."

"I have some money, too. That'll probably work best with the gendarmerie."

"We'll try both."

Angel's mind raced with scenarios about what they were going to face. She shifted slightly and felt the cold steel of her weapon through her shirt. She didn't want to have to use it especially on the gendarmerie or national guardsmen who were only doing their job. It had taken all of her willpower not to pull it when they were attacked, but if she had they probably wouldn't have gotten out of Akjoujt.

"Okay, here we go," she said as she began to slow for the checkpoint, a small green shelter at the side of the road that was barely large enough for two men to sit inside. Only one man appeared as they approached.

She put her hand to her forehead as if to block the sun and tilted her head away from the man. She stared straight ahead and let Ellie lean across the seat in front of her.

"*Ish haal li-mgiil.*" Good afternoon, Ellie said.

The guard nodded and reached out his hand.

Ellie responded with a stack of bills rather than their papers. He frowned but stepped back inside the small shelter.

"He's checking with his supervisor," Ellie said softly.

She watched Ellie's face as they waited for the guard to return. Her ambassador persona was in place. Regal and stoic. It was a side of her Angel had grown to love. And hate. It was the ability to care about people and still hold them at a distance. To argue for a cause that might not be your own. She was a part of Ellie's embassy family now. She was on the inside looking out. She had seen both sides of Ellie and she felt nothing but admiration for her.

She heard the tent panel flap beside her and was careful not to look in his direction. With any luck, he would assume she was a male companion since women wouldn't normally travel alone.

"Go," Ellie said urgently. "Slowly but go."

Angel dropped the truck into gear and began to pull forward.

"He gave us a wave so I'm going to assume the money was acceptable."

She was glad she hadn't pulled her weapon or even rested it on her lap. The checkpoint had been easy. If the gendarmerie had been advised to watch for two women, they had either fooled them or the men didn't care. Ellie stared out the side window. She reached over and grasped her hand again. It was the only comfort she could offer.

Ellie pulled the map from her bag and spread it across her lap. Never releasing Angel's hand, she studied it like it held all the answers. A few low, sand-colored buildings and lots of shiny objects began to grow out of the desert in front of them.

"That's not Atar, is it?" Angel asked.

"No, that's the solar panel farm."

She watched for any movement inside the chain-link fence. There was nothing and the stillness felt sinister. A ghost town of flat panels where buildings should be. She could feel Ellie's body stiffen beside her.

"Looks like no one is there."

Ellie sighed. "They give everyone the day off when outsiders visit. I wish we could use their phones."

"Not a chance."

Ellie didn't question her decision. The surprise of seeing Farook and the words they had overheard had quashed any thoughts of this attack not involving the ambassador directly. Angel wished she had taken the opportunity to be harder on Farook back at the embassy. There would be plenty of time to beat herself up over her actions later. She caressed Ellie's hand with her thumb, a simple reminder that they were in this together. Ellie took a deep breath and settled back into staring at the map.

The comfortable silence returned between them as they left the solar panel farm behind. Before long the land around them began to rise, giving way to flat-topped mountains with layers of serrated rock. The heat was stifling under the intense sunshine and it created a misty blue effect on the horizon. She watched the landscape change and couldn't help appreciating its beauty. It wasn't the first thing Ellie was right about, and she was pretty sure it wouldn't be the last.

The truck began to stutter as they reached the first buildings on the streets of Atar. She quickly swung the wheel to the right and pulled them to a stop at the side of a small block building. It appeared to be a store, but the lot was empty. A few vehicles moved on the road farther into the city, and she could see the ripple of people walking in the distance. Nearby, a small group of people in robes stood with a national guardsman.

"They may not be letting anyone pass."

"They're nomads," Ellie explained. "The guardsmen shouldn't have a problem with them. Probably just chatting."

"Yeah, maybe. Let's see if we can find another vehicle," she said as she pulled Ellie away from the main street.

Atar was a city of about twenty-five thousand people, and she had expected more activity. She wondered if the quietness they were encountering off the main street was normal. They kept walking until the larger block buildings gave way to a scattering of small wooden huts. Behind one, they found a sand-dusted truck. It was even older than the previous one they had borrowed. She pulled open the door and lay across the floorboard. There wasn't even a grind when she tapped the wires together. She tried it a few more times with no success. As she climbed out of the truck, she saw an old man standing at the window of a nearby hut. He slowly shook his head. She gave him a smile and a shrug.

"This isn't going to work. Let's start walking."

She straightened the fabric around Ellie's head and then took one of the bags she carried. The door on the small hut screeched open, and she quickly stepped in front of Ellie. The old man from the window shuffled out and held up a robe. Angel stepped forward and took it from him. Ellie reached around Angel's body and handed him a few bills. He took the money and shuffled back into his house.

Wrapped inside the robe was a bright blue skirt, which Ellie immediately pulled on over her jeans. Angel slid into the robe and then Ellie wrapped the mulafa around her upper body like a scarf, covering Angel's face.

"Do I look okay?"

Ellie took a few steps back and then walked around her. "A little more like a man. That might be good."

Though Ellie's mulafa looked okay, Angel couldn't resist the chance to touch her. She straightened the cloth around her head, covering her blond hair, and then slid her hand inside, stroking Ellie's cheek. Time seemed to stop as she stared into her eyes.

"You have a new plan?" Ellie asked softly.

"Of course."

She touched Ellie's lips with her fingertips and then adjusted the fabric across her face, masking her lighter skin as much as possible. Pulling a blanket from her bag, she wrapped both of their bags inside it. In hobo style, she swung it over her shoulder and took Ellie's hand.

"Let's blend in with the nomads."

Ellie nodded. "Maybe we'll be able to walk right out of town."

* * *

Ellie's breath caught as Angel pushed her against the building, covering her with her own body. They were on a side street waiting for the opportunity to slide into the group of nomads. Her pulse quickened at the sudden movement and pressure of Angel's body. Knowing her actions were not meant to affect her libido, she tried to push the reaction of her body to the recesses of her mind for later analysis.

"Was that Farook?" she asked softly, holding in the panic.

"Him or his men." Angel relaxed her hold on Ellie and took her hand. "Let's move farther down before we try to merge with the group."

Angel led them quickly down the alley and onto the back street that ran parallel to the main road. Peering around Angel, Ellie could see two people in the distance, both dressed in traditional robes. She was pretty sure neither of them was Farook. Following the sandy path behind the stores, she waited as Angel carefully checked each opening before they crossed.

Movement caught her eye as they passed between buildings. There wasn't anywhere for them to hide. She felt protected with Angel in front of her, but she hated that Angel was left exposed.

She watched the man walking toward them. He wore pants and a T-shirt covered by a traditional boubou. The boubou was a bright green and looked like a large sheet wrapped around his body. His dark hair and the stubble on his face made him appear more menacing than Ellie wanted to believe he was. Even after everything she still wanted to believe that these men weren't willing to harm her.

Taking a deep breath, she stepped around Angel and went face-to-face with the man. "Why is Farook doing this?"

The man chuckled. "Farook is not giving any orders."

His English was broken, and she could hear an Arabic accent. Angel's arm stopped her from walking any closer to him and she grasped it for support. Her pulse quickened as he pulled a knife from his belt.

"Thanks for making my job easier," he sneered.

"Why are you doing this?" she demanded. "I'm an ambassador. I'm here to help make things better. What can I do for you?"

"Do for me? You can keep your nose out of our business. Killing you will make things better." He waved the knife in the air as he moved toward them.

A cry escaped from Ellie's throat as Angel pushed her against the building. The scene unfolded faster than anything she had ever watched and yet time seemed to slow. Angel was behind him, grabbing his hand and sliding his knife across his throat. Before she could utter another sound, Angel dropped his bleeding body to the ground.

She had seen death before and even been the one responsible for it, but as a CIA analyst she had never been on the scene as it transpired. Thankful that the man's face was planted in the sand, she watched him, waiting to see if he would stand and come at her again. Angel stepped between them and turned Ellie's body away, giving her a nudge to begin walking.

"We need to get out of here before his friends find him," Angel said firmly.

"Is he dead?" she asked softly, turning back into Angel.

Angel pulled her into her arms, holding her tight.

"He was going to kill me," she mumbled into Angel's neck. The truth of her statement hit her as she said the words and her body shook.

"I won't let that happen."

She squeezed her eyes shut, sucking in a breath. That man, a man that didn't even know her, had wanted her dead. And without Angel, she would probably be. Sinking into Angel's arms, she counted to ten and then took a step away. She said the only thing she could at that moment. "We need to move."

CHAPTER TWENTY-FOUR

Angel's head ached. Her body was tight with tension and adrenaline was the only thing keeping her moving. She remembered every detail from the one other time she had been forced to kill with her hands. Fight or flight. Kill or be killed. Faced with a deadly situation, protecting herself had been the only option. This time was different, though. There was no doubt in her mind that he would have killed Ellie. Even incapacitating him and letting him live would have meant risking Ellie's life.

To ease the pain in her head, she focused on getting as far away from the deadly scene as possible. She took Ellie's hand without looking at her. She couldn't stand to see the disgust she knew would be displayed in Ellie's face. Ellie might never be able to forgive her. Her heart was crushed even though she knew she had done what had to be done. She focused on that, allowing only the thought of protecting Ellie into her mind.

She led Ellie in a circle as they watched the nomads from a distance. The small group they had seen earlier had grown significantly. Animals and people moved together at a meandering pace. The national guardsmen were walking toward the southeastern edge of town away from the group of travelers. She tightened her grip on Ellie's hand and pulled her forward. For the moment, she was thankful for the silence between them. She needed time to work things out in her head.

She had heard her team talking about the ore train that ran along the northern border of Mauritania from the mining city of Zouerat, which was mostly unreachable by car, to Nouadhibou on the west coast. One passenger car was available, but purchasing tickets would draw attention. The locals rode on top of the iron ore, which wasn't ideal, but the ride was free. It would be the safest way for them to travel back to Nouakchott. It would avoid all checkpoints and in Nouadhibou she would have cell service again. She wasn't sure Ellie would agree to her plan, but she felt good about it.

Now, she just had to figure out how to get them sixty miles over harsh terrain to the city of Choum, where they could catch the train. She adjusted her scarf and noticed Ellie doing the same thing. They quickly emerged from the alley and slid into the middle of the group. Receiving a few nods from the other travelers, she studied their faces for someone that might refuse their presence. No one seemed concerned and she relaxed her grip on Ellie's hand. An elderly woman patted Ellie's shoulder consolingly and gave her a soothing grunt. Keeping her face hidden under the scarf, Angel was relieved to see others in the group protecting themselves from the blowing sand as well.

She calculated their trip in her head. Choum would probably be at least three or four hours by vehicle. Walking sixty miles would take almost a week, but the Mauritania desert would be unforgiving and not an option. This group was moving west now and that was the opposite direction of Choum. She kept her eyes alert for another vehicle they might be able to borrow. The men at the front of the group took a path to the left. She tried to access the map in her mind and remember where this road might go.

She leaned into Ellie and spoke softly, "Can you ask where they're headed?"

Ellie turned to the elderly woman beside her.

Angel studied the group, watching it stretch into an almost parade-like travel procession while she listened to Ellie's conversation. She guessed there were about fifty or so adults and a handful of children. Most of the men had moved into the lead. The women were walking slower, giving the children space in the middle to play. A few young men followed at the rear with several goats and a camel. She knew she was probably making it obvious she wasn't a man, but she wasn't willing to separate from Ellie.

"They're headed to Terjit Oasis for the night," Ellie whispered.

"That's what I was afraid of. We need to go the other direction."

"Toward Choum?" Ellie asked.

She nodded as she started to move them to the left of the group. The elderly woman reached out and grabbed Ellie's other hand. She grunted something and Angel looked to Ellie to translate.

"She wants us to have dinner with them," Ellie explained.

Angel considered this offer. Terjit Oasis was in the opposite direction of where she wanted to be, but it wasn't too far out of their way if she remembered correctly. Maybe this wasn't a bad idea. Getting off the road might take them out of sight of the men chasing them as well. She waited for a break in Ellie's conversation with the woman and then she touched her arm to get her attention.

"Let's go with them for the night."

Ellie nodded. "We might find someone there to catch a ride to Choum with."

She had a feeling that Ellie knew her plan, but she was glad that there wasn't any hint of disagreement from her yet. She studied Ellie's face as she turned to speak with the woman again. She wondered what Ellie was thinking. Was she upset that she had killed the man? She desperately wanted a moment alone with her so they could talk, but staying with this group was the best idea.

The thought had barely crossed her mind when she noticed the gendarmerie checkpoint ahead. She gripped Ellie's hand tightly.

"Checkpoint," she said softly.

"What do you want to do?"

"Let's move to the rear of the group and see what happens when the lead men approach."

"There's nothing but sand around us. It's not like we can separate from them now."

"I know," Angel said between gritted teeth. She was angry at herself. They had left the town on foot and now had nowhere to go.

Together they started to move toward the back of the procession. She stopped when Ellie pulled away from her.

"What?" she whispered. She looked from Ellie to the elderly woman beside them.

The woman shook her head and maintained her tight grip on Ellie's arm.

"She doesn't want us to move."

They moved back to their original positions, and the woman patted Ellie's arm as she released her grip.

She held her breath while the lead men cleared the checkpoint and began to move forward. The group had tightened their ranks as they waited, and now she was jostled from all sides with each step. She held tight to Ellie's hand and noticed the woman had grasped Ellie's arm again too.

Angel took a quick glance as they passed the two soldiers at the checkpoint. They were dressed in green woodland fatigues and black boots, the same as all the others they had seen. They each carried a rifle slung across their back and a pistol strapped to their waist. Once they had passed them with no trouble, she realized she was still holding her breath. The woman smiled broadly at them and released Ellie's arm again.

"Wow," Ellie breathed.

"Yeah, that was too close for comfort."

The women spread out from the men, and the children began to play again. Older kids swinging sword sticks battled back and forth across the road amidst games of tag and chase. Occasionally Ellie contributed a few words to the jovial conversations around them. Mostly they walked in silence, appreciating the small feeling of safety they felt in this group of strangers.

The scenery around them began to come alive as they entered the little village of Terjit. Nestled between two tabular mountains, it was the gateway to luscious date trees, palm trees, and other vegetation. The village was only a few small shacks that seemed totally abandoned. The road was easy enough to walk on and clearly marked between the tall rock walls. Against the base of the mountains, wind-blown sand reflected the evening sun, creating a spectacular display of raging fire—and offering a welcome contrast to their perilous situation.

At the edge of the village, the group stopped to drink at a shallow stream. It wasn't much more than a trickle that came down out of the mountain. Angel pulled a bottle of water from her pack and passed it to Ellie. She drained the remaining liquid when Ellie took a long drink and handed it back. When it was their turn at the stream, she refilled all their empty bottles and dropped in water purification tablets. The locals might be okay drinking mountain water, but she wasn't going to take the risk.

The woman beside Ellie hadn't said more than a few words since they left the checkpoint, but she kept them close by her side, steering them forward into the shadows of the many date and palm trees. The air around them became cool and damp. Water dripped from the cliffs above in a soothing rhythmic pattern. The sound of children playing echoed off the rock walls and as quickly as she heard it, it stopped. On all sides of them, everyone began dropping to their knees facing the last rays of the setting sun. Ellie pulled Angel to the ground beside her.

"Pretend to pray," Ellie commanded harshly.

She suppressed a sarcastic chuckle. *Why pretend?* They were stuck in the desert with men who wanted to kill them. If there was ever a time in her life that she wanted assistance from a higher being, this was it. She closed her eyes and bent her head to her knees. Instantly her thoughts returned to the dead marines she had left behind. Her eyes burned with the memory. Vince had drilled into her head that you never leave a man or his body behind except to protect the living. She prayed that they would be able to retrieve their bodies and Nasri's as well, when this was all over. *When it is over? When will it be over?* She knew the decisions she would make in the coming days would be critical to their survival. She inhaled deeply and slowed her breathing. She could do this. A plan began to form in her mind, and she saw them safely at the embassy again.

She felt Ellie stand beside her and she quickly jumped to her feet. She didn't know how long they had been praying, but she was surprised at the peaceful feeling that had come over her. Her mind was focused, and her body was no longer tense. Small groups of people were beginning to separate from the mass. Little fires began popping up all over and the smell of cooking food drifted around her. Ellie pulled their loaf of bread from her pack, offering it to the woman they had been traveling with. It was met with exuberance and disappeared into the food preparation.

The woman placed a small rug on the sandy ground and motioned for Ellie and Angel to sit. Very little time passed before a man and two boys took up seats around the rug with them. She hadn't heard or seen any type of signal to call the family to dinner, but clearly they knew when to arrive. Ellie spoke with them in soft tones and Angel tried to pick out words she understood.

"In the next couple of days, they'll head back west to be closer to Nouakchott for the winter. There'll be more food there," Ellie relayed. "They were going to stay in Atar for the night, but the rumblings of trouble changed their minds."

She appreciated Ellie's ability to appear comfortable in this diverse setting. Sitting with her legs crossed in front of a campfire, making conversation with people from another country. She had pulled her mulafa down to her shoulders and her blond hair fell around her face when she leaned forward. Angel thought she looked more beautiful in this desert surrounding than in her expensive suit inside the embassy. The two boys seemed fascinated with her and tried to cut into the conversation at every chance.

The area around them was dark now except for the little fires placed here and there between palm trees. There was a dense area of vegetation a little farther away from the base of the cliff where they had stopped. She could imagine the cool water of the oasis and she longed to strip down and plunge into it.

Before the meal was served, a bowl of water and soap were passed to each person. Angel followed Ellie's lead and washed her hands and face. The woman preparing the meal produced several little metal plates and scooped some of the mixture from the pot over the fire onto each. A piece of bread from Ellie's loaf was placed on each plate before passing it along. When everyone had a plate, the man recited what she assumed was a prayer and they began to eat. She watched them use pieces of the bread to scoop up the mixture and she carefully did the same. She was thankful for the whispered reminder from Ellie to only use her right hand to eat.

The first bite was surprisingly tangy. The flame from the fire didn't provide enough light for Angel to analyze what was in the stew. She had seen the woman picking dates from the trees surrounding the oasis and they certainly provided the sweetness. The other flavor was something like soy sauce. The rice was nothing like store-bought. It was filled with taste that exploded in her mouth. She could identify carrots, potatoes, and maybe okra, but she was most pleased that there was no unidentifiable meat.

When the meal was almost finished, the man stirred the coals in the sand and placed a teapot over them.

"Mauritanian sweet tea is served after meals. Typically, Chinese green tea is used. Three glasses are served to each person. Mint and sugar are mixed into the tea after each glass," Ellie whispered softly.

Finally, the man sat up on his knees, raising his arm with the pot about two feet high as he poured the tea into another pot and then back into the original pot. He repeated the same process with each glass.

"That's called tea pulling. It aerates the tea and creates a thick frothy foam on top. It's a true art and takes quite a bit of practice to get it perfect." Ellie picked up her first cup. "The saying is that the first glass is bitter like life."

Angel took a sip of the strong tea. She agreed with the saying. It was very bitter, and she set the cup back down.

Ellie slurped her tea loudly and nudged Angel. "You have to drink it all and let them know you're enjoying it."

Angel picked up her glass and attempted to imitate Ellie. By the time she finished the glass, she was laughing so hard she could barely drink without choking.

The family seemed to understand she was new to this ritual and joined in with the laughter. Ellie picked up her second glass. "It'll get better with each glass. This one is said to be strong like love or some say sweet like love."

Angel sniffed and then took a sip. She couldn't even look at Ellie and think about love at the same time. She glanced at the family watching her and wondered if they understood anything Ellie was saying. They seemed to be enjoying their tea and the show. At least, Ellie was right. This glass was a little better. The mint and sugar made it easier to drink.

"Since Muslims don't drink alcohol and it is not allowed in Mauritania, some people believe the copious amount of sugar can create a high and the tea is sometimes called desert whiskey."

"I can definitely feel a sugar high coming on," Angel mumbled.

Ellie slurped beside her, sending Angel and the two boys into fits of laughter again. Although everyone else had leisurely sipped their glasses, she hurried to catch up when she was able to get her laughter under control.

Ellie held up her third glass. "The third glass is gentle like death or the end of all things, to which we all will come."

"Okay, now that's depressing. I can't drink to death, but I can drink to the end of this trip."

Ellie nodded. "I can drink to that too."

Angel actually enjoyed the final glass. She was getting used to the sweetness and she enjoyed Ellie's production of sharing the tea ritual with her. Much too soon the woman began gathering their dishes and Angel downed the last of her tea, surrendering her glass. With all the dishes bundled into a blanket, the woman shuffled off toward the sound of the stream. Ellie followed to help her wash them. The man had wandered into the darkness; Angel assumed he was going to visit with others. She stood to follow Ellie. She wasn't concerned for her safety among this group; she only wanted to stay close to her in case they needed to leave quickly.

The two boys moved to each side of her and tugged her back into a sitting position. The taller of the boys, probably about twelve or thirteen years old, produced a bag of multicolored beads and split them evenly between the three of them. She ran her fingers through her stack of beads. Some were shiny and smooth, and others were filled with ridges and bumps. They were all brightly colored and the firelight made them sparkle. She was surprised when the younger boy, she guessed his age to be about ten, pulled a deck of cards from his pocket and began to shuffle.

Though they couldn't communicate by words, the boys demonstrated the game and she nodded her understanding. She quickly lost the first two hands and her bead pile was depleting quickly. She had never played poker, but she imagined that what they were playing was some form of that. The third hand she won a few beads back, but the fourth took all of them away. She threw up her hands and started to stand. She really should find Ellie. She looked around but could see nothing but darkness outside their fire.

The boys shook their heads and divided the beads evenly among everyone again. She laughed. This game could go on all night. A few minutes later, she felt Ellie sit down close behind her. A clean fresh smell wafted from her and Angel turned to look at her. Ellie's hair was wet, and her face looked relaxed.

"Taslima showed me the oasis." Ellie smiled. "When you finish here, I'll take you."

She turned to face the boys again. "It won't take me long to lose. I'm very good at it."

Ellie leaned around her and stopped her from playing the card she had selected. She pulled her glasses from her pocket and studied Angel's cards. "Play that one." She pointed at the five of hearts.

She shrugged. "If you say so."

She won the hand and Ellie nudged her with her shoulder. "See what happens when you listen to me?"

With Ellie's help, she won the next couple rounds. She hated to leave the game when the boys were losing, but they seemed to be enjoying the game either way. She held up her finger to tell them one more game. She shrugged off Ellie's recommendations and let one of the boys win the next game. Then she divided her beads between them and stuck out her fist. The boys giggled and bumped it with their own.

* * *

On Ellie's instruction, Angel stripped down to her sports bra and boxer briefs. Thankful she wasn't wearing some skimpy underwear, she couldn't help but wonder what Ellie had worn. She tucked her pistol between the layers of folded clothing and glanced up as Ellie lay her mulafa on the ground.

"Are you coming in?" she asked, her pulse quickening.

"No." Ellie sat on the mulafa at the edge of the water. "Probably not a good idea."

She couldn't see her face in the darkness, but she could hear the smile in her voice.

"Take as long as you want. I'll be right here."

She waded into the cool water. In the heat of the day it probably felt wonderfully refreshing, but the temperature had dropped after the sun set. She shivered as she submerged beneath the water. When she surfaced, Ellie tossed her a bar of soap. It had a refreshing citrus-like smell that Ellie had returned with earlier.

Covered in goose bumps, she quickly washed around and beneath her underwear. Ellie offered her mulafa as she walked out of the water and Angel wrapped it around her shivering body.

"Chilly?" Ellie asked with a laugh.

"A bit, but still refreshing." She dried enough to pull on her clothes, and they returned to the warmth of the fire.

The fire appeared to have been recently stoked though there wasn't anyone around. The belongings of the family they had dined with were still laying nearby so Angel knew they would return at some point. She sat down as close to the fire as she dared and absorbed the warmth. Ellie sat beside her, their legs touching.

She waited to see if Ellie would talk first. She knew the events of the day were weighing heavy on her and she wanted to give them both a chance to share their thoughts. Even if the consequences of that conversation would be learning that Ellie felt disdain for her now. After several minutes, she gave up and broke the silence. "Are you upset with me about what happened earlier?"

"Upset, yes, but not with you."

"Because he's dead or because I killed him?"

Ellie remained silent.

Angel took a deep breath. "I did what I had to do. Talking wasn't going to work and using my pistol would have revealed our location." She paused, not sure how much to say but wanting to make things better between them. She needed Ellie to understand that killing someone wasn't easy for her. "Taking someone's life is not something I take lightly...but I'd do it again to protect you."

"Thank you." Ellie's voice was deep and filled with sorrow. "I'm sorry you had to do that on my behalf."

She put her arm around Ellie and pulled her close. "It's my job, but you have to know I'd do anything to keep you safe."

The question she wanted to ask wouldn't come out of her mouth. She feared the answer. Did Ellie feel differently toward her now? Without the answer, she could still dream about their future.

* * *

Ellie shifted the makeshift clothing pillow under her head, looking for a softer spot. She could feel the occasional deep breaths from Angel and knew she was still awake too. Aside from the perilousness of their situation, she had really enjoyed their evening together. She was glad they had started talking about what happened in the alley, though. She still had so much emotion churning inside her and the man's death played like a video each time she closed her eyes. The way Angel had taken him without hesitation had surprised her. She would be forever grateful, though, because she knew she would not be alive right now otherwise.

From the moment she had met Angel, she had felt protected in her presence, but now she felt truly safe. There had been no discussion about their sleeping arrangements, but she had been relieved when Angel lay down close beside her. Most of the small fires scattered around them had disappeared hours ago, but she could still hear the occasional murmur of conversation. The ledge that they lay under protected them from the desert winds, but she still felt a chill. She pushed her back against Angel's body, searching for warmth.

"You need to sleep," Angel whispered, rolling toward Ellie and pulling Ellie's back against her.

"I'm trying."

"Think about happier things and your mind will push away the bad images."

The silence lingered between them as she thought about Angel's words.

"How did you know that's what I was thinking about?" she asked.

"We'll both be haunted for a while."

"But I'm glad he's dead."

"Me too."

Angel squeezed Ellie's body tighter against her own.

She held back a moan of contentment. She couldn't help wishing they were back in the embassy. If they were, she wouldn't hesitate to take advantage of Angel's closeness. But they weren't.

They were stranded in the desert, and the level of excitement she was feeling wrapped in Angel's arms was inappropriate.

Angel had killed a man today. Killed a man to protect her. She squeezed her eyes shut, reliving the moment again and again. She knew what Angel did for a living, but seeing her act so quickly made it all so much more real. She wanted to ask Angel how many people she had killed, but the question seemed so heartless. The depth of sadness displayed in Angel's eyes throughout the day told her more than words could anyway. Angel didn't enjoy what she had done even though her words were devoid of any regret.

"Do you see a lot of death working for Vince?" she asked softly.

She felt Angel's intake of breath.

"You don't have to answer that if you don't want to," she quickly added.

"I've had a lot of people in the crosshairs of my rifle, but thankfully I didn't always have to pull the trigger." Angel took another deep breath. "Do you feel differently about me now?"

"Feel differently? Because you sacrificed yourself to save my life? Of course I do. But not the way you're asking. I'm so thankful to have you with me. I wouldn't be here right now if you weren't the person that you are." She pushed up on her elbows and turned toward Angel. The darkness surrounded them like a blanket of protection, and she could barely see the pale outline of her face. "How are you handling all of this?"

"Mostly I'm sad that you saw me take someone's life." Angel's voice was barely audible.

"I'd never judge you."

"No matter what I feel, I'll always follow through with what I've been trained to do. Every time I'm sent on a mission, I know the risks."

"But how do you deal with the outcome?"

"Right now, I'm just concentrating on getting us out of this mess. I'll resolve any additional baggage when it's all over," Angel said with conviction.

She knew that was the Flagler agent talking and not really Angel, but she would respect the suppression of her feelings for now. Angel knew what she needed to do to move forward; now wasn't the time to make her process her emotions. She rolled onto her side, snuggling back into Angel's arms.

"During my time as an analyst, I gathered intelligence for others to use in the fight against terrorism. I saw the aftereffects of war mostly in pictures. On a few occasions, I came face-to-face with the enemy, but it was always after they were in our custody. I took moderate risks, but I never really felt fear until today. I've been trained on what to do if I ever found myself in a life-threatening situation, and I have to trust that I would have done it today. If you wouldn't have been there."

"I'm sure you would have."

"I've always been better at the fight end of things than the flight part."

Angel's body shook with a chuckle, and Ellie could feel her own tension start to dissipate. Their time together had been fraught with disagreements and clashes about their beliefs. Now their future was uncertain, and it felt good to be on the same side.

"We're going to be okay," Angel said softly, her lips close to Ellie's ear.

"Because you have a plan?"

"Of course."

"I'd follow you anywhere."

She waited for Angel to explain her plan, but instead she felt her steady breathing of either relaxation or sleep. She wasn't sure why Angel was being evasive about her plan. She knew this country better than Angel did. She knew they were headed for the ore train in Choum. It made the most sense. Even if they could find a reliable vehicle to make the return drive, they would be vulnerable on the road alone. Clearly Angel believed she wouldn't be cooperative about what she had planned, so why should she make it easy on her? *Oh yeah, because it felt good to be on the same side.*

"Are there snakes out here?" Angel asked.

She was surprised at Angel's voice and the question but held back a chuckle. "Of course, there are, but I'd be more concerned with the scorpions. They like dark, enclosed spaces like sleeping bags or shoes."

"What?" Angel tried to get up, but Ellie pulled her back down, openly laughing now.

"Don't worry, the deathstalker scorpion only gets up to four inches in length and they prefer drier areas so we're probably safe around the Oasis. It's hyenas and jackals that I'd worry about. They get really hungry in the desert and all animals come to water."

"You aren't making me feel better."

"Is that what I was supposed to be doing? Telling you a bedtime story?"

Angel was silent for a few moments. "Yes, after the day we've had I'd like to hear something good."

"Okay. Here you go, my little angel," she said softly. "Are you familiar with the scimitar or Sahara oryx?"

"That's a deer-like animal?"

She chortled. "Yes, kind of. It's a spiral-horned antelope that stands barely three feet tall. Their coats are white with a reddish-brown chest and they have black markings on their forehead and nose."

"Sounds pretty."

"Be quiet and try to go to sleep." She felt Angel's chuckle but continued her story. "Years ago, they inhabited all of North Africa because they had a built-in cooling mechanism and needed very small amounts of water. With the changes in climate and hunters wanting their horns, they were declared extinct in two thousand."

"That's sad."

"The local folklore has many tales of unicorns being sighted, and I'd tell you one but apparently you can't remain silent long enough."

"I'll try."

Ellie laughed again. "Truth is the unicorn myth probably originated from sightings of an oryx with a broken horn."

"Way to ruin the story."

"Hush."

CHAPTER TWENTY-FIVE

After morning prayers and breakfast, Angel began to gather their belongings while Ellie assisted in the cleanup from the meal. She planned to have Ellie talk with their hosts and see when they would be headed back into Atar. It was important to conceal their return as much as possible.

"I found us a ride to Choum!" Ellie exclaimed as she slid to a stop beside Angel.

"How?" The excitement in Ellie's voice made her grin. "That's great news."

"We have to meet Nafisa now, though. She came to Atar to shop yesterday and is headed back to Choum in a few minutes."

"She doesn't mind giving us a ride?"

Ellie chuckled. "She doesn't mind sharing the cost of her taxi."

"Oh. A four-hour drive in a taxi sounds lovely. Let's go check out this vehicle."

There were only three vehicles in the area outside the dense vegetation of the oasis, two large Toyota Land Cruisers and a small red sedan. Of course, Ellie crossed to the sedan and gave a customary hug to a woman clad in a flowing multicolored mulafa. Ellie was dwarfed by the large dark-skinned woman as they stood side by side talking animatedly.

She was pretty sure traveling to Choum by car instead of SUV wasn't a good idea, but it seemed Ellie had already made the decision. The only other option was attempting to hotwire another vehicle when they returned to Atar. No matter the condition of the taxi, it would at least have the gas and an experienced driver to get them through the desert.

"Nafisa. Angel," Ellie said, introducing the two women as they climbed into the backseat. "Tariq is our driver."

Angel nodded her greetings and slid in beside the driver. He was small in stature with a trace of brown hair above his lip that was barely discernable against his skin. His hands gripped the steering wheel tightly as the car started off, bobbing and weaving across the road. He wasn't talkative, but he had a broad grin, the kind that showed all of his teeth. She liked him immediately.

When they reached the edge of Terjit, the cab slowed to approach the checkpoint. Angel didn't want to produce their paperwork, but she wasn't sure money would work this time. She pulled out the stack of papers Chloe had prepared for them to travel with.

She wasn't sure what paperwork Nafisa or Tariq would have. She held her fiche out to Tariq, but he waved it away. Pulling to a stop, he began chatting with the soldiers as if they were old friends. After a few minutes, he pulled through the checkpoint.

She glanced at Ellie and shrugged. They had received another gift from a Mauritanian. Not having to show their paperwork on the trip to Choum would be a huge win for them.

To say thank you, she attempted a bit of social conversation. Her small amount of French allowed them to talk about the view around them. In the morning light, the sun shone down on the table-shaped mountains, reflecting the golden light across the desert rock and sand dunes at their base.

"Five hundred meters," Tariq said.

Angel nodded. Five hundred meters was over fifteen hundred feet, which was more than four times the size of Britton Hill, the highest point in Florida. The varying geography was one of the reasons she liked the Florida panhandle, where flat land was fronted by barrier islands and sandy beaches as well as low rolling hills.

Out of things to talk about with him, she listened to Ellie and Nafisa chat in the backseat, straining to catch a word she understood. After a few minutes, she gave up. Glancing over the seat, she caught Ellie's eye. Her smile was contagious, and Angel returned it. If only for a short time, Ellie could forget about their situation and the threat to her life.

Angel wasn't surprised that Ellie was enjoying her conversation. She already knew that the ambassador was able to handle many situations, but she was the most comfortable communicating on a personal level. Content that Ellie was safe and secure in the backseat, she returned to her own thoughts. The next phase of her plan required perfect timing. The train came through Choum every day, but it would only be stopped for a short time, possibly only minutes. They would stand out and be easy to locate if they had to wait for tomorrow's train. Catching today's train would be the safest option as would hanging back until the last minute to board. They would be able to lay low there until they reached Nouadhibou.

She wasn't completely sure what to expect with riding the train which delivered iron ore to the cargo ships on the coast. Ellie could probably fill in some of the blanks, but she hadn't shared her plan with her yet. Since she was determined not to purchase passenger tickets, they would have to sit on top of the ore with the local travelers. Conditions there would be extremely chilly and windy through the night and sweltering hot under the sun the next morning. They would need additional clothing or blankets for protection.

Her thoughts moved on to what would happen once they arrived in Nouadhibou. She had to assume the men chasing them would be watching the train station there, but she was counting on the two-mile length of the train to help cover their escape. She also hoped that they wouldn't be expecting them to arrive so soon. If they could get safely off the train without being seen, her top priority would be to find somewhere to charge her cell phone. It seemed doubtful that it would have any power left by the time they arrived tomorrow.

Once her phone had a charge, they could contact the embassy and someone could be dispatched to pick them up. It would take time for her team to reach them so they would need a place to hide out for a few hours. According to the map she had studied earlier the Banc d'Arguin National Park was located along the coast. It might provide some shelter away from the regular travel paths. It was closed to motor vehicles, so anyone attempting to follow them would have to do so on foot.

Ellie's laughter drifted into the front seat and Angel's thoughts turned back to her. Ellie had become more than someone she was here to protect. Though she had vowed not to allow herself to get close to her, she had to admit that she had been unable to accomplish that. She liked the way Ellie's touch made her feel and the way her body reacted to her. Her life wasn't conducive to having a relationship and certainly not one that would likely have to be maintained with a stretch of thousands of miles between them. Why she was even thinking about this was a mystery to her. She should be focusing on getting them back to the embassy safely.

Ellie touched her shoulder. "Nafisa would like to stop for lunch in Atar. There won't be anywhere to eat along the road to Choum."

She shrugged. Stopping in Atar after what had happened yesterday made her uneasy, but if Nafisa was correct they would need food before the trip.

"I think traveling with them will cover us enough to be okay," she said, hoping she sounded more positive that she felt.

The streets of Atar were crowded with donkeys pulling carts and flocks of goats as well as people. There were more people than vehicles and the streets were narrow. There were no sidewalks and the vendors were set up directly on the street. Tariq drove slowly and carefully, avoiding running children and animals. When they reached the northeastern edge of town, he stopped in front of a white stone building with a handwritten sign that read OPEN in multiple languages. This end of town was quieter, and the four of them quickly decided to select a table in the outside courtyard.

"It's a hotel too," Ellie whispered. "It's owned by a Dutch man and his German wife. They're very welcoming to Westerners. I've always wanted to come here. I've heard they are both amazing chefs."

Angel nodded, taking in their surroundings. The garden terrace's six wood and stone tables currently were all empty. The wooden base of the tables and chairs were painted with leaves in a brilliant green. An occasional red berry dotted the fake vegetation.

"I've heard this place has great food," Ellie said to Nafisa and Tariq in what sounded like Arabic, translating for Angel when she raised an eyebrow.

They both eagerly responded, and Ellie smiled. "They've both been here before and thought it was very good," she relayed to Angel.

When the woman arrived to take their orders, Ellie ordered for Angel. While they waited for their food, Ellie carried the conversation, translating between everyone. Angel tried to participate as she watched the road for anyone passing that could cause them problems.

Angel glanced at the square plate that was set in front of her. It had a piece of meat that looked like flank steak but was probably goat in a gravy or sauce with a yellow ball of rice or grain of some kind. She cut a piece of the meat and was surprised at the tenderness and the taste.

Ellie bumped her shoulder. "It's okay?"

She nodded. "You can tell me later what I'm eating. I'm hungry and it tastes good, so don't ruin it."

Ellie shook her head. "I'm happy to broaden your horizons."

She smiled, focusing on her plate. Everything about Ellie had broadened her horizons, and it was getting harder not to show it each time she looked at her.

* * *

The drive to Choum passed quicker than Angel had anticipated, even though the tarred road had ended soon after they left Atar. The sandy path was hard to follow and at times she wasn't even sure they were still on it. Tariq was experienced and drove fast, swerving back and forth across the road to avoid rocks and boulders. When the sand got too deep, he stopped and let some air out of the tires to keep them from getting stuck.

As they approached Choum the last rays of sunlight hung on the horizon, illuminating houses and shops made from mudbricks and the train which stretched into the distance like an ancient metal dinosaur, carriage after carriage heaped with black iron ore. As it slowed to a stop, the lines of people waiting began climbing aboard quickly.

Angel jumped from the sedan before it came to a complete stop. Grabbing their bags from the trunk, she slung them across her back. She turned so Ellie could tuck the blankets Nafisa handed them into their packs. Waving goodbye to Nafisa and Tariq, she pulled Ellie toward the already moving train.

"Hurry."

"You can't be serious." Ellie yelled over the rattle of the railcars as they began to move again.

"It'll take us back to the coast and within cell range of help."

Ellie pulled her to a stop. Her jaw clenched as she watched the railcars inch past them. "I knew this was your plan, but I certainly didn't expect the train to be moving when we boarded."

"We really don't have time to debate this."

"This was your plan all along?"

She sighed. Given a choice, this wasn't what she would have chosen. She couldn't defend this plan, but she could give Ellie a few seconds to work through her fears. "We have a narrow window. Once the train gains speed, we won't be able to get on."

"Then we'll catch it tomorrow?"

"We would draw even more attention, and I'd rather not spend another night in the desert."

The wind from the train whipped their hair and the rattle of the cars grew louder as it began to pick up speed. She leaned close to Ellie. "You go first. Grab one of the ladder rungs and keep climbing. I'll be right behind you. Trust me, okay?"

Taking a deep breath, Ellie nodded. "Let's do this."

She stayed on Ellie's heels as they started to jog. When Ellie reached up and grabbed the rusty orange ladder, she followed, grabbing the rung above her. She pulled her legs up onto the lowest bar and put an arm around Ellie's waist. Holding on tight, she turned their bodies so they could grab the rungs with both hands.

"Climb," she yelled into Ellie's ear.

Ellie tentatively began to move up the railcar. She stayed tight against her, keeping Ellie's body between her and the car. She hadn't come this far to let Ellie fall to her death. When they reached the top, she did her best to block the wind while Ellie swung her leg over and into the car.

The ore was piled high, but it sloped down to the sides of the car, leaving barely a foot of metal to block the wind, which was brutal. The ore wasn't rocky as she had expected, but more like a very bumpy sand. They needed to create more shelter for themselves or they wouldn't survive the night here.

She grasped Ellie's arm and pointed to the corner, motioning for her to go first. They crawled slowly, keeping their bodies close to the ore. Angel pulled her scarf up around her face and saw that Ellie had done the same. The ore dust was already coating their bodies and seeping through her clothes. When they reached the corner, she began digging into the ore to make a pocket big enough to hold both of them. Ellie watched long enough to figure out what she was doing and then began helping.

Angel finally had a space large enough to stretch out her legs. Exhausted from digging, she lay on her back with their bags stacked on her stomach, staring up at the beautiful sky as her eyes traced the stars of the Milky Way. Darkness had come up on them fast as the lights from Choum faded behind.

She was surprisingly comfortable tucked into their shallow pit. She pulled two blankets from their bags, handing one to Ellie. Her eyes were starting to adjust to the lack of light, but she could see little more than the outline of Ellie's face before the blanket covered her. She unfolded her own blanket and burrowed beneath it. Reaching out her hand, she found Ellie's. She closed her eyes and let the gentle sway of the carriage car rock her to sleep.

* * *

A few hours later, Ellie awoke with a chill deep in her bones. The wind was now an artic breeze and had penetrated her blanket with ease. A shiver rippled through her body and she shifted closer to Angel.

Angel stirred and Ellie rolled over to face her. She pulled the scarf from over her eyes so she could see Angel. In the darkness, Angel's brown eyes were a deep midnight black. She found herself quickly lost in them. Their faces were inches apart. She wondered what Angel would do if she removed their scarves and kissed her.

"This isn't the way I imagined getting close to you," Angel's voice was soft, almost getting lost in the roar of the wind and the train.

"You imagined getting close to me, huh?" she teased.

"Maybe once or twice."

Her body shivered again, though more from the closeness of Angel now than the chilling wind.

Angel lifted her blanket to cover both of them, rolling partially on top of Ellie. With Angel's body blocking the wind, she removed their scarves and snuggled her face into Angel's neck. Even with the smell of sweat and iron ore, Angel's scent lingered. It flooded Ellie's senses. The weight of Angel's body pressed hard against her like the safety of a cocoon. Beneath their blankets, she wrapped her arms tight around Angel.

Arousal burned through her and her hips, acting on their own, pushed into Angel's thigh. She felt Angel's shoulders tense as their eyes met. With only the moon and the stars for light, her night vision had kicked in, and she stared directly into the raging fire in Angel's eyes. This time was different. Angel wasn't going to put the brakes on this time, she knew, and her body pulsed in a rush of excitement. She wanted to feel their lips pressed together. She didn't wait for Angel to make the first move.

The metallic taste of iron ore lasted only a second and then the sweetness of Angel's mouth consumed her. Unlike their first kiss, this one was slow, traveling gently to a place of unrestrained desire. She wanted to rush it, to feel Angel's tongue in her mouth, but she fought her impatience and let Angel fan the flame. The agony was delicious, and she knew in a second what she had been waiting for her whole life.

This woman. With all her annoying rules. This woman. Willing to risk everything to protect her. This woman. With her softness buried deep beneath layers of strength.

When Angel's tongue finally traced the edge of her lips and then slipped inside, she couldn't hold back her moan. She felt like she had been waiting hours instead of seconds to feel Angel's gentle stroke. Her body was hypersensitive to every ounce of pressure Angel applied. She found enough space between them and slid her hands underneath Angel's robes. She could feel the pebbles of sand and ore from her dirty hands and she resisted the urge to slide her fingers beneath Angel's shirt. Slowly she brushed her thumbs across Angel's taut nipples, feeling them grow harder beneath the layers of clothing. She pressed harder with each stroke.

Angel's hips shifted, applying pressure to where their bodies connected, causing them both to gasp. She wrapped her arms around Angel, gripping her shoulders.

"Oh," she moaned, breaking their kiss. "Do that again."

Angel followed her command immediately with several rapid thrusts.

She couldn't believe how wonderful Angel made her feel. She felt almost giddy. Like a teenager in the backseat of her parents' car. The thought almost made her laugh until she looked into Angel's eyes again. Deep, dark, and devouring. This time she was unable to look away.

Angel rocked against her again, setting a slow, gentle pace, a rhythm that matched the movement of the train and pushed her closer to the impending explosion. Each stroke of Angel's thigh brought every nerve in her to the surface, even through their layers of clothing.

She embraced the fire coming from Angel's body. Her eyes locked with Angel's as their bodies crested together, exploding into oblivion. Angel continued their pace for a few more seconds before relaxing on top of Ellie.

"I want my mouth on every part of your body," she demanded.

Angel chuckled. Her voice was gravelly when she spoke. "Yeah, that's probably not the best idea at the moment."

She squeezed Angel hard, digging her fingers into Angel's back. She buried her face in Angel's neck again.

"I want you naked," she groaned.

"I promise when we get back, I'll make that wish come true."

* * *

Angel bent her head and kissed Ellie. Tasting the iron ore on her lips, she realized their blanket was no longer covering them. She pulled it up over their heads before settling beside Ellie.

Her heart was still running on overdrive. She couldn't believe what had happened between them. Something so different from anything she had ever experienced. She had known when Ellie kissed her neck that she wouldn't be able to hold back. Not this time.

"That was amazing, you know," Ellie's voice was muffled as she snuggled deeper into Angel's neck.

"You're amazing."

Ellie lifted her head and kissed her. It was deep and full of promises.

She answered Ellie's kiss with a vow of her own. Keeping Ellie safe was more than her job. It was her life. It was in her blood. With no Ellie, there would be no Angel.

CHAPTER TWENTY-SIX

Angel awoke with the blazing sun pounding down on her back. In their sleep, the blanket covering them had shifted, leaving them exposed. She turned away from Ellie to grab her sunglasses from her bag.

Ellie groaned, covering her eyes with her hands. "My eyes are being sliced with a paper knife."

"Are your sunglasses in your bag?" she asked.

"Yes, please. The front pouch, I think."

She passed Ellie her glasses and considered leaning in for a kiss. Before she could put her thoughts into action, Ellie leaned up on her elbows and kissed her.

"Good morning," she said, slowly drawing out the syllables and making Ellie laugh.

"Good morning back," Ellie said still laughing. "I'm going to visit the bathroom. Can you make the coffee?"

She was glad to see Ellie could find humor in their situation. "I would love to make the coffee, but would you settle for some date and hibiscus jam without bread and maybe a little unidentifiable meat jerky?"

"That sounds yummy, but what are you going to do about my need for a bathroom?"

She sighed. "That's a bit tougher. The train won't stop again until we reach Nouadhibou, but I've felt it slow occasionally. I'm not sure why, maybe a small town that's not on the map. If it happens again and we're ready, we'll have a few minutes on the ground. You'll have to be really quick."

"I can do it," Ellie said, sitting up.

She wrapped her scarf around her head as she raised up to check their surroundings. Several robed figures sat at the edge of the car, their attention focused on buildings in the distance.

"You might get your wish faster than I thought."

Ellie crawled to her side. "Finding a bush is going to be hard. I wish we could go off the other side. Do you think it's true that the ground north of the tracks is filled with mines?"

"I'm not sure, but we're not going to risk it."

Ellie laughed. "Somehow I knew you would say that. You'd rather these men be blinded by my moon."

She laughed too. "I will protect your moon as much as I can, but I'm afraid I have my own agenda on this mission." She grabbed her pack and handed Ellie hers. "Let's take these and we'll catch a car farther back."

She was already thinking ahead to their arrival in Nouadhibou. Two hundred cars would be a lot for Farook's men to watch, so the farther away they were from the station the better the chance they might have to avoid detection. She put her arm around Ellie as they crawled closer to the edge. One of the men looked at them and a flicker of surprise passed over the exposed portions of his face. He began quickly talking to the men around him.

"What's he saying?" she asked Ellie softly.

"He knows we're women."

She watched the man and his friends crawl away from the ladder, motioning for them to go first.

"*Shukran.*" Ellie said "thank you" in Arabic.

As the train started to slow, she swung a leg over the side and braced herself on the ladder. She opened her arms and Ellie slid between her and the side of the train. They slowly made their way down the car. When her feet were on the last rung, she noticed men from other carriage cars already jumping. She took a deep breath.

"Here we go," she called, giving Ellie one last squeeze.

She jumped, collapsing her knees as soon as her feet hit the ground. She rolled into a standing position ready to assist Ellie, but she didn't need it. Ellie executed a perfect PLF or parachute landing fall, something that was taught at all parachute jump schools to prevent broken legs or other injuries. She'd have to ask her about how she acquired that skill later.

She grabbed Ellie's hand and they ran toward the side of a mudbrick building. The few pieces of vegetation were low standing and provided no protection. She dropped her pack and quickly unwrapped her mulafa, holding it completely opened in front of her body. She positioned Ellie between her and the building.

"That's the best I can do, Madam Ambassador," she said.

"I'll take it."

She watched the train continue to crawl along. Hot chills ran across her bare arms as she thought about the movement of their bodies last night. The way they had fit together without any effort. The kisses that had left her breathless and a little lost.

Ellie grabbed the blanket from her as they traded places. She moved quickly and was grabbing the mulafa back from Ellie before the last cars were even in sight. She wrapped it around her body and grabbed her pack as Ellie did the same. They raced toward the slow-moving train.

Following the pattern they had used previously, she protected Ellie's body from the wind and a potential fall. When they swung their legs over the top, she stopped to look around. The car wasn't very crowded, but all the corners were already filled with other travelers. She began digging beside the ladder. It wasn't ideal, but it would give them a faster departure when the train reached Nouadhibou.

Ellie helped her move the iron ore until they had a little depression to drop into. Laying down was the only way to block the wind so she lay on her side, leaving a space for Ellie beneath her. Ellie held up her toothbrush.

Great idea, but she knew it wasn't going to be an easy task. The air around them was filled with floating ore and sand. She pulled her brush and a small tube of toothpaste from an outer pouch in her pack. Sharing her paste, she watched as Ellie slid the toothbrush under her mulafa. She did the same and began scrubbing her teeth.

When Ellie leaned near the edge, she quickly stopped her. Demonstrating, she dropped her head beneath the rim of the car and spit where the ore met the wall of the train car. Ellie did the same.

She packed everything away and then lay back down. Ellie slid into the spot beside her. She leaned close and whispered into Ellie's ear. "Spitting into the wind would have brought it back on us or someone else."

Ellie laughed. "Guess that's why everyone gets off the train to use the bathroom."

"Right."

She took a drink and then passed the bottle of water to Ellie. They shared a protein bar dipped in homemade jam and a piece of unidentifiable meat jerky. Food wouldn't be an issue when they reached Nouadhibou, but she saved her last protein bar anyway. Ellie still had two bottles of water left and she had one. They would drink most of it during the remaining ride. The raging sun would dehydrate them quickly.

She pulled off her sunglasses and tucked them into the pack she was lying against. She studied Ellie's face. The small amount of exposed skin around her eyes was black with iron ore; she looked like a raccoon. She had to imagine she looked the same. She pulled her mulafa down and removed Ellie's, kissing her gently. In a few hours, she would be the security agent again and be forced to block out the way Ellie made her feel. She would take advantage of this private time with Ellie now while there was nothing else they could do to advance their escape.

Ellie's lips responded to her touch and the kiss deepened as their tongues touched. She rested her hand on Ellie's stomach. She could feel the warmth from her body even through her clothing or maybe it was only her imagination. Either way it set her mind at ease and she relaxed against Ellie. They kissed and joked, letting the time pass around them. Long before she was ready to break their contact, she felt the train begin to slow. She slid on her sunglasses and raised up to look ahead. The sandy desert stretched all around them, but in the distance, she could see a growing town.

"Time to go," she said with a final kiss.

She glanced at her watch. It was almost noon. She pulled her phone from her bag and turned it on. It still had a small amount of power and a single bar of reception. She quickly texted Eric.

Both okay. In Nouadhibou. Contact again in hour.

Hopefully by then she would have access to power and be able to talk instead of text. She waited for the text to send and then turned the phone off. She looked up to find Ellie watching her.

"I have a small amount of reception."

"How much power?"

"Some."

Ellie narrowed her eyes. "How much?"

She knew she had to be honest with her if she wanted them to work together.

"Just a little. I told him I would turn the phone on again in an hour. If we're lucky, we'll find somewhere to charge. If not, we have enough to send him one or two short texts."

Ellie nodded. "This close to the border there are a lot of people traveling back and forth. I think we'll be able to find somewhere."

Finding it was one thing. Staying out of sight would be their challenge. The train had slowed considerably, and she wanted to get off sooner rather than later.

"Let's go," she said as she swung her leg over the side of the train.

Ellie didn't argue.

* * *

Ellie followed Angel and hugged the metal ladder rung. The feel of Angel's body wrapped around hers was wonderful, and if they weren't being chased by men who wanted to kill them, she would be content to stay in this position. Much too soon Angel began her descent and she had no choice but to move with her. After so many hours with the movement of the train beneath her, she was a little relieved when her feet hit solid ground.

She knew Angel had a plan to get them back to the embassy and she trusted her to recognize when they needed a new plan. With their scarves completely wrapped around their faces, they followed the crowd toward the small whitewashed train depot in the distance. The sounds of traffic and people were surprisingly loud after the many hours with only the hum of the train and the wind in her ears.

She squared her shoulders and prepared to face the reality of people wanting to kill her. Anger boiled inside her again. It was hard not to take it personally, but she knew it wasn't her fault. They weren't actually fighting against her but against what she represented and what she could do. Maybe Farook's men wouldn't be here. Maybe they could catch a cab back to the embassy and everything would be over.

Angel pulled her away from the crowd moving toward the train depot. They followed others headed directly into the city.

"Did you see something?" she asked, matching Angel's increased pace.

"Possibly."

"Okay."

The walk to reach the first busy streets wasn't short, but she didn't mind. Her muscles were stiff from so little movement and the chance to move away from a potential threat was welcome. She had enjoyed the moments alone with Angel, but she couldn't forget what had brought Angel into her life and the danger that followed them.

"Can you ask him if he can take us to a cybercafé or whatever they call it here?" Angel pointed at a minibus taxi waiting in front of what appeared to be a hotel.

"I'll do my best."

She approached the open window of the taxi with Angel close behind her. The male driver turned the radio down and nodded eagerly to her request. They slid onto the bench directly behind his seat, keeping their scarves in place. The drive to the café was bumpy as they followed the road, dodging people and animals. Their driver turned right past a green building simply labeled BANK and then drove across what appeared to be an empty field. Back on a paved road, he made a left, swerving across traffic before pulling to a stop in front of a large building housing several businesses. Years of sun, sand, and salt had turned the vibrant red building to a pale pink.

She passed a few bills to the driver and they slid out of the bus. The door on the right advertised cell phones and accessories. They went inside and purchased a small device that would give them one hour of phone charge.

Next door was a small café. Two other patrons were sitting near the short counter where orders were placed. Angel led them to a table in the back corner. She plugged the charger into her phone and motioned for Ellie to stay with their stuff.

When Angel returned with two cups, Ellie asked, "What did you order?"

"I have no idea," Angel said distractedly as she searched through her pack, pulling out the map.

She chuckled, sniffing the steamy brew before taking a sip. She couldn't identify the spices inside, but it was definitely tea. Though the air inside the café was stuffy with the early afternoon heat, the tea warmed her on the inside.

She checked her watch as Angel dialed Eric. It hadn't been quite an hour, but she was glad Angel wasn't waiting.

"We're okay," Angel said into the phone. "Fill me in quickly."

She tried to read Angel's face while she listened to Eric. Whatever he was saying didn't require a response from Angel. She wanted her to ask if everyone at the embassy was safe, but she knew Angel would get as much information as she could in the short time they had. For the moment, it was enough to know that Angel's team was on the other end of the line.

"Okay. Pick us up at Banc d'Arguin National Park."

Banc d'Arguin National Park was one of the first excursions her father had taken her on when she arrived in Mauritania. She studied the map on the table. The park was over four thousand miles of protected area for migratory birds. It was filled with sand dunes, coastal swamps, small islands, and shallow coastal waters. Sitting along the western coast of Mauritania, it was separated from Nouadhibou by the Bay of d'Arguin.

Angel's voice drew her attention.

"As soon as you can...we'll be fine."

She took another sip of the tea, but it no longer offered any comfort. She could feel the tension growing in Angel's body even though her face held no signs to what she was hearing.

Angel powered the phone off and dropped it on the table. She watched her pick up her cup of tea, sniff it, and then set it down again.

"They're coming?" she asked.

"They're on the road already. They left as soon as we texted."

"How are things at the embassy?"

Angel frowned.

"What?" she asked with growing concern.

"Everyone is fine, but within several hours of our departure the crowd dispersed."

"What?"

"They just walked away." Angel rubbed her face. "My guess is they believed you were being...handled."

She fell against the back of her chair. "My death would have made everything better for them." She shook her head. "What were they up to?"

"I've been thinking about that. I think its smuggling. Something they were trying to get out of the country by way of the port."

"Smuggling what?"

"Food, drugs, people." Angel stood. "Let's grab something to eat while the phone charges."

She pulled Angel back down and motioned at the cups of tea. "I'll get the food."

She could see Angel wasn't happy with this arrangement, but she was. She was starving and needed something she could actually eat. She ordered two plates of *thieboudienne* and carried them back to the table.

"What is that?" Angel asked.

"It's the Mauritania national dish. Just eat it."

"I will, but what is it?"

"It's fish and sweet potatoes over rice. The sauce is made of pureed onions and tomatoes."

She watched Angel take a bite, chewing slowly. When Angel dug in for a second bite, she began eating too.

This close to the coast, the majority of meals contained some sort of fish. Apparently, Angel was okay with that. They ate quickly in silence and left the café as soon as they finished.

On the street, they flagged down another taxi. She wasn't surprised to see Angel being vigilant again. She didn't see anyone she recognized or anyone watching them, but she followed Angel's lead. If there was one thing she had learned on this harrowing adventure, it was that she could trust Angel with anything and everything.

Angel showed the map to their driver and pointed to the northern end of the national park. He nodded his agreement but quickly began negotiating for a higher fare. Their request wasn't unusual, but it did take the driver away from the city and other fares, so she nodded for Angel to agree to the price.

Their course took them north, off of the peninsula where Nouadhibou was located and then south toward Nouakchott. The taxi dropped them at the edge of the park before the first entrance where very little vegetation dotted the sandy landscape.

"We can't stay out in the open like this," Ellie stated after they had walked for a few minutes. "This is a mating area for migratory birds and there are regular police patrols. Tourists are never in this area."

"Let's move closer to the base of that cliff," Angel suggested, pointing away from the water to their left.

She could see the sandy cliff stretching up at least twenty or thirty feet into the skyline. Small low-growing vegetation in a rich emerald green color dotted the ridge along with a few small trees. As they got closer, she could see small red and white flowers growing close to the ground.

"How will your team find us?" she asked.

"In another hour, I'll turn my phone back on, and Eric will track our GPS signal."

"We need to find a paved road then, because they won't be able to drive on the beach."

They stayed close to the base of the cliff in case they needed to find cover, walking in silence as pelicans, flamingos, and many other types of birds that she couldn't identify fluttered around them.

She had wanted to visit the park since her return in Nouakchott, but this wasn't the way she had imagined. In the distance, she could see a wooden boat with a large sail and makeshift huts dotting the shoreline. When she had visited with her father, he had taken her to an Imraguen village. She remembered how antiquated their fishing boats had been. The no-motor rule along the park coastline encouraged more sustainable but less profitable traditional fishing methods.

"Is that a boat?" Angel asked.

"Yes, that's the Imraguen tribe. They are the only ones allowed to fish inside the park."

Angel smiled at her. "Tell me more."

She knew Angel was only distracting her, but she enjoyed sharing cool facts about the country.

"They move their entire village up and down the shoreline following the schools of mullet. The men stand in the water and surround the fish with their nets. In the past, the dolphins helped herd the schools of mullet toward their nets. I'm not sure if that's still true or not."

Angel bumped her arm. "I can see what you were talking about. The country is fascinating and beautiful."

She laughed. "You mean you liked the desert too."

"Yeah, I guess."

Despite their situation, she enjoyed the peacefulness that settled between them. At the base of a cliff, Angel guided her to a spot hidden by vegetation. They drank water and shared another protein bar. Angel leaned against the rock behind them and closed her eyes.

She leaned against Angel, settling into the crook of her arm. One thought had been weighing on her mind while they walked.

"What happens when we get back to the embassy?" she asked.

"We'll figure out what's going on at the dock and then we'll stop it."

She wasn't trying to put Angel on the spot, but she needed to know where they stood. "And what happens with us?"

She felt Angel take a deep breath. She couldn't go back to pretending that there was nothing between them. She wanted more and she needed to know if Angel did too.

"I'm looking for something more than a fling," Angel said softly.

She shifted away and turned so she could study Angel's face. There was a shyness there that she had never seen as Angel's eyes focused on a distant spot in front of them. This wasn't the reaction she had been bracing herself for. It was great to hear that they wanted the same thing. She moved until Angel's eyes were focused on her.

"Me too," she said.

She could barely keep the happiness from her voice. She watched the slow smile spread across Angel's face and then it was gone. She watched her unfold the map from her pocket and lay it in front of them. And just like that Angel was back on task.

"Any idea on how we can manage that?"

"We'll figure something out. Right now, we need to find an area accessible to vehicles."

She ran her finger along the coastline on the map. "Based on the cliffs behind us, I think we're about here. We need to go a little farther south and then cut east."

"That doesn't look too far," Angel said as she folded the map and stuffed it in her pocket.

"I can't wait to sleep in a bed with you."

"I won't object." Angel stood and pulled her to her feet. "Let's keep walking. They should be here soon."

CHAPTER TWENTY-SEVEN

Angel could have screamed in celebration when the black SUVs came into sight. She texted Eric and he confirmed that it was her team. She wanted to run toward them, but she managed to maintain a fast walk. Ellie didn't seem to mind the pace.

"It sure is great to see you," Eric said as he flung the door open, allowing them to climb in.

"We're happy to see you guys too," she said as she tossed their bags into the rear compartment and climbed in beside Ellie. She patted Pollock's and Toma's shoulders in the front seats as Eric settled in beside her. She took the opportunity to press a little closer to Ellie, resting her hand partially on Ellie's knee.

Eric handed her his phone. "You know who you need to call."

She dialed Vince and he picked up on the first ring.

"Angel."

"We're fine, Vince. Eric's here and we're safe."

"What the hell happened?" Vince demanded.

"After the ambush, we just kept moving. We caught the ore train back to Nouadhibou."

"That explains your appearance," Eric mumbled beside her. She elbowed him.

"Great job, Angel. Put Ellie on."

She passed the phone.

Ellie listened for a few seconds and then responded, "I'm fine...really...everything you said about her was true."

She watched Ellie's face, straining to hear Vince's words. Ellie's eyes connected with hers as they filled with tears.

"Thank you for sending her," Ellie continued, her voice hoarse with emotion. "I'll call you tomorrow."

Ellie disconnected the line and passed the phone back to Eric. "Thanks for reminding us that we need to shower."

Eric smiled. "Do you need to call anyone else, Madam Ambassador?"

"No, I assume my staff knows I'm okay."

"Deputy Patone and Ms. Allen have been kept informed. Everyone else thinks you spent the night in Atar."

"Thanks for picking us up," Ellie said, resting her head against the seat.

"Tell me exactly what happened while we were gone," Angel asked Eric. She returned her hand to Ellie's knee as she tried to get a handle on what had transpired while they were gone.

"About two hours after you left, a car picked up both men on the wall. Once they left, the men in the crowd began to wander off. It was weird, but we got it all on video. It was clear they didn't have a purpose anymore and no one was there to make them stay. Sam contacted Inspector Asker and he sent a team to talk with them. He stopped by himself a few hours later and said that the men were told their job was over that they should report back to the docks today. By that time Miller's marines had phoned in and we knew about the ambush."

"They made it back?" she asked with relief.

"The two who survived the attack. I'm sure you know about the two in the lead car, right, and the driver?"

She nodded and felt Ellie's body tighten beside her. So much had happened since that first moment of the attack that they hadn't talked about the men they lost. She was sure Ellie felt responsible since she had insisted on making the trip.

"So there has been nothing happening outside since everyone left yesterday?"

"Nope. The streets are quiet."

She rubbed her face and then looked at the black dust on her hand. She couldn't wait to wash the ore and the pain away.

"Farook Kassib was in Akjoujt. He was definitely involved," she said, forcing her mind to focus. She needed to fill in the gaps. Maybe then it would all make sense. "Have you seen him?"

"No. He snuck out of the embassy not long after you left. We had his access badge deactivated immediately."

As he continued to fill her in, she used the feel of Ellie's head on her shoulder to keep her grounded. Everything they had been through in the last two days as well as the last several weeks, and these men had walked away like it was over. Well, it wasn't over for her. Or Ellie. She would find Farook and everyone else involved.

She wanted to work out a plan, but she found herself drifting off to sleep instead. When she awoke, they were pulling to a stop at the embassy gates. The empty street around them seemed unnatural. The sun was setting behind the walls of the embassy, and it painted a golden shimmer across the lawn.

She climbed from the vehicle and offered a hand to Ellie. Chloe grabbed Ellie in a huge hug as soon as her feet hit the ground. Ellie gripped her back and then hugged Sam too. Her face was unreadable as Angel watched her greet each of them. Ellie had been through so much and Angel knew she wouldn't share the hard parts with either of them.

"Let's get you into a shower," Chloe said as she pulled Ellie toward the entrance.

She turned to meet Miller's eyes and again felt the immense pain at the loss of his marines. There weren't enough words to express her sadness. She shook his offered hand and pulled him into an embrace. "I'm so sorry, Shane."

"We're all glad to have you and the ambassador back safe."

She could feel the sincerity in his words, and she longed to offer him comfort. She slipped the two dog tags into his hand. He embraced her again before walking away.

She turned to Sarah, who had patiently waited her turn. Pulling her into a hug, Sarah squeezed her tightly.

"I never stopped believing you'd come back," Sarah whispered softly.

"We're fine now."

Sarah stepped back and looked at her curiously. Whatever Sarah had heard in her voice, she knew she wouldn't push her in front of everyone.

"We'll talk later?" Sarah asked.

She nodded. She would need to debrief at some point, and she knew Sarah would be there for her.

"Angel?" Ellie had stopped and was looking back at her.

She wanted nothing more than to go with Ellie, but she couldn't. She needed to talk with her team and figure out their next step. Now that she was back at the embassy she needed to focus on her mission. Once the men involved were caught, she would be able to enjoy Ellie's attention.

"Go with Chloe and I'll catch up with you later."

"I thought…" Ellie's voice dropped.

She took the few steps to Ellie's side and guided her away from everyone. Turning her back to the group behind her, she bent her head and spoke softly.

"Can I see you tonight?"

Ellie's face brightened. "Yes."

"It might be late. I need to get a handle on what's happening here." She hesitated. "Then I'll find you."

Ellie nodded.

She gently touched Ellie's face, wiping a black streak from her cheek. She longed to kiss her, and she hoped Ellie was reading everything she was trying to convey. With a last glance at Ellie, she quickly turned to face her team.

* * *

Angel rubbed her face for the hundredth time. The five hours they had been back had been devastating and frustrating. She was relieved to hear that the bodies of the deceased marines and the driver had already been retrieved. She would never forget them or their sacrifice.

She stepped from the stairwell and leaned against the wall. She had stopped by her room earlier to secure her pistol and change clothes. It had taken all of her strength to leave without a shower. The truth was she wanted Ellie more than she wanted a shower. She wanted to crawl into bed with Ellie and hold her tight.

She pushed off the wall and took the few steps to Ellie's door, knocking softly. The door opened immediately. Ellie stood in front of her. Her skin shone with a fresh clean scrub and her white long-sleeved T-shirt hung from her shoulders, barely reaching her thighs. She was captivated by her beauty and unable to move.

Ellie reached out and touched her arm, sliding her hand into Angel's. "Come inside."

She stepped into the dimly light room. "You're beautiful."

"You certainly know how to charm a woman."

Ellie slid her arms around Angel's neck, pulling her down into a kiss. Her lips were soft and demanding. She wanted to explore them further, but the sweet smell of Ellie reminded her that she hadn't had a shower yet.

"I came straight here. Can I use your shower?"

"Only if I can join you."

She smiled. "Sounds wonderful."

She followed Ellie into the bathroom and dropped her dirty clothes into a pile. The moment for shyness had passed the night before in the darkness on a moving train. Now, her only thought was having Ellie in all the ways she had dreamed about.

Ellie's touch was gentle as she washed the dirt and the pain away. She braced herself on the shower wall and easily surrendered to Ellie's touch until she could no longer stand.

Though her body and mind longed for sleep when she crawled between the sheets, everything was forgotten with the touch of Ellie's skin. As she moved on top of her and fit their bodies together, every part of her awoke. She took her time, enjoying the softness of Ellie's skin and the sound of her voice as they both rode the wave of desire over and over. Better than anything she had ever imagined; Ellie's healing touch was now forever imprinted on her body.

* * *

Ellie felt the bed shift as Angel quietly slid to her feet.

"Are you sneaking off?" she asked, jokingly.

Angel stepped into her pants and pulled on her boots. "As much as I'd love to lie in bed with you all day, I have to get back to work."

She sat up, pulling on her T-shirt. "I need to get back into the flow of things here too. Sam only checked in for a second last night, and I'm sure he was holding back."

Angel sat on the edge of the bed. When she cupped Ellie's face, running her thumb along her cheek, Ellie leaned into her touch and slowly ran her tongue along Angel's lips. When she finally slid it inside her mouth, the warmth of their kiss melted her.

"Do I have your attention now?" she asked.

"You've always had my attention."

Angel jumped to her feet as the door to Ellie's bedroom burst open and Micalah barged into the room.

"Micalah!" she exclaimed in surprise. "What are you doing here?"

"I got on a plane as soon as I heard you were missing." Micalah's eyes locked on Angel. "But I can see I'm too late."

Angel studied Micalah for a few seconds and then looked at Ellie. "Briefing at eight?"

She nodded. Closing the door behind Angel, Ellie turned to face Micalah.

"What are you doing here?" she demanded. "Better yet, how did you get into my room?"

"It came to my attention you were missing, and no one could tell me where you were. Including your beloved Vince. Oh, and I bribed the nice marine."

"Unfortunately, we weren't able to make contact until yesterday. Thankfully everything is fine now."

"It's not fine! Someone is trying to kill you," Micalah exclaimed.

"There is that." She took a deep breath and dropped to the chair. "I'm hoping there'll be some information on that at this morning's briefing."

"Okay, but what about *that* woman?"

"*That* woman saved my life."

Micalah gave her a suspicious glance. "Somehow I'm not buying that she just dropped in this morning."

She smiled. "I'm not going to discuss that with you."

"No need. You've answered my questions. I hope you're being careful."

"Careful? Seriously."

"You aren't exactly in gay-friendly territory."

"I'm being discreet, Micalah. Besides it's all new and no decisions or discussions have been made at this point. So, let's talk about something else." She walked into the bathroom and turned on the shower. "How long are you staying? Do you want to sit in on the briefing this morning?"

"I'm here until you're safe, and yes, I want to hear what *that* woman has to say."

She stuck her head out of the bathroom. "Play nice or I'll send you home."

"I only want to make sure she's doing her job and not just you."

"Not funny."

* * *

Angel slowed her pace as she approached Ellie's office. She could barely contain her anticipation of seeing Ellie again. All morning she'd struggled with her desire to run to her. The memory of last night played through her mind.

"Angel?"

She glanced up at Sam approaching from the other direction, his red tie standing out against his white shirt. The eagerness of his message portrayed on his face.

"You have news?" she asked.

"Maybe." He motioned toward the ambassador's office. "Shall we?"

She worked to hold her face still as she made eye contact with Ellie. Sure that no one could see her, she gave Ellie a wink, looking away quickly when Ellie's face flushed slightly.

Ellie cleared her throat and motioned for them to take a seat. "Sam, Angel, this is Micalah Cutter. She is a CIA analyst, but she's here as my friend."

She turned to see the woman who had barged into Ellie's room earlier sitting on the couch behind them, her arm resting along the back of the couch, giving a relaxed impression. She had read only concern in Micalah's face this morning, which was the only reason she had left them alone. The look on her face now showed more than concern. It was clear to Angel that Micalah wasn't going to remain silent during the discussion to come.

"Madam Ambassador," Sam began formally. "Minister Aboye finally allowed us to search the containers waiting to depart to the US. Inside one of them we found water, blankets, and food."

"Human smuggling?" Ellie asked.

"It looks that way. A container from the same company with our diplomatic pouch paperwork left port two weeks ago destined for the US."

Ellie turned away and then spun back again. "I'll assume this is Farook's work. How in the hell did he manage to gain access to diplomatic pouch paperwork? Do we know where this container is? Can we stop it?"

"A very pissed off Chloe is working on finding out how he accomplished this as well as getting your signature. I'm not sure what we can do about stopping the container, but we should be able to figure out which ship it's on." Sam stood. "I'll stay on it."

As Sam left, Angel stepped forward. "Sam and I are working with the police force to track down Farook and identify Lars. So far, unless Vince approves me to dispatch my agents to assist, I don't hold much hope of finding him. Randy Barnes and Craig Shepherd have left the country. We believe they might be headed to the US, but for the moment they're off the radar."

"I want Ronald Pigott in my office today. I want to know if he knows what his brother-in-law has been up to," Ellie demanded.

"I'll let Sam work the diplomatic route, but if he's unsuccessful I'll push Vince to allow me to send agents to bring him in."

Ellie nodded.

Sam rushed back into the room, holding up a piece of paper. "I've got it. It'll cross into US waters sometime next week."

Micalah stood, but Angel quickly pulled the paper from Sam's hand. "I'll handle that."

She leaned against the wall outside Ellie's office and pulled her phone from her pocket. From memory she dialed her friend Stacey's number. Stacey Blake was a Flagler security agent working undercover in a Manhattan dress shop. The shop specialized in imports from China, and Stacey was working a possible human trafficking angle. Stacey was also a bulldog. She wouldn't let any tip pass by without following it to the end.

"Angel?"

"Hey, I need a favor." She read the information from the piece of paper in her hand to the woman on the other end of the call.

"Okay. I'll check this out personally. If possible, we'll intercept the container now, but depending on how they are stacked on the ship we might have to let it get to port before we can reach it. You're sure they have supplies."

"From what we can see on this end, we believe they're given enough to keep them alive."

"Okay. I'll call you."

Angel listened to the silence on her end of the line for a few seconds before sliding the phone back into her pocket. She had complete confidence in Stacey. She returned to the ambassador's office. Micalah stood beside Ellie, and everyone looked up when she entered.

"I've contacted a fellow Flagler agent and the container will be located as soon as possible. Sam, let's get Pigott in front of the ambassador."

* * *

"Okay, she's more than arm candy. I'll give you that."

"Seriously. 'Arm candy.'" Ellie rolled her eyes. "She's efficient and competent."

"And beautiful."

"Isn't she?" Her face flushed again. She wanted to gush about how wonderful Angel was, but it would be inappropriate. And she wasn't the gushing type. Was she? Well, she had never been before. She pulled Micalah back to the couch and sat down across from her. "What am I going to do?"

Micalah laughed. "Now you want my opinion. You couldn't listen to me before you fell in love with her?"

"Fell in…no. I'm still getting to know her. I can't be in love with her."

"I just sat here and watched you both avoid looking at each other through a briefing. There's no need to deny it. You're in love with her and she feels the same."

She couldn't be in love. Not yet. They needed time to get to know each other. Didn't they? She stood. "I need to work."

She ushered Micalah out the door and took a seat at her desk. Who was she kidding? She wasn't going to be able to work. Her work life was in turmoil due to a few lying, cheating men, and her personal life was spiraling out of control too.

She took a deep breath. That wasn't true. Angel had a handle on the Conex and the threat to the embassy seemed to be gone. For the first time in her life, she had someone that made her insides flutter. Someone she respected and was as strong as she was. She thought about the way Angel had taken control of the situation. Today she was wearing the same color and style of uniform that she had since the day she arrived at the embassy, and yet, something was different. Closing her eyes, she called to mind the way Angel's face had looked as their eyes met earlier. The lines of stress that had been evident in the last couple of weeks were gone, and the hint of a smile played on her lips. She was seeing another side of the real Angel. One without the strain of performing a job and keeping everyone at a distance. Oh, how she liked this woman.

* * *

"Have you been avoiding my call?"

Vince didn't sound angry, but Angel could hear the distress in his voice.

"No."

"I've left several messages for you and spoken to Eric and Sarah."

She sighed. She couldn't lie to Vince, but telling him the truth about how she felt about Ellie was not something she was looking forward to. Her only reprieve was that at this moment she wouldn't be able to see the disappointment on his face. She'd hear it in his voice, though, and that thought had kept her from returning his call immediately.

"Things are going well. Pigott will arrive within the hour and Ellie's friend from the CIA will help me grill him. We'll get to the bottom of this before the day is over." She took a deep breath. "I called Stacey Blake and she's tracking down the shipment container. Hopefully she'll be able to rescue the occupants before it makes port. We—"

"Angel, stop. What's going on?"

She sighed. Vince had always encouraged her to speak her mind. To never hold things in. It was time to face the music. "I might be in love with her."

"Stacey? I didn't know you guys were close."

"Not Stacey. Ellie."

Vince was silent.

"Vince? Please don't be upset with me?"

"How could I be upset with you? You brought her back safely." He exhaled loudly. "I should have expected this. I threw the two of you together. I should have known you would find each other intriguing. That's a recipe for disaster."

"Disaster? Are you serious?"

"Well, maybe, disaster isn't the right word." Vince chuckled. "I'm not upset with you. I've never tried to tell you what to do and I certainly won't try now. I trust you to work things out professionally even if that means I'm going to have to give you more time off to work on your long-distance relationship."

* * *

"I want to question him too," Ellie demanded.

Angel's desire for the woman in front of her surged. Of course, her CIA side would want to question anyone involved in the plot on her life. Luckily, she didn't have to answer.

"Absolutely not," Micalah countered. "We expect you to sit there and be quiet."

She nodded her agreement, though it brought a frown to Ellie's face.

"Madam Ambassador," she said softly. "When all of this is over, you'll still have to work with this man and the people in this country. Let us handle this."

Ellie groaned. "Why do you always make sense?" She dropped into the chair behind her desk.

The door to Ellie's office opened and Sam walked in along with Ronald Pigott.

Tense introductions were exchanged and then Angel stepped in front of him. She refused to wait a second longer to force this man to cooperate.

"Do you know why we didn't make it for the visit?" she demanded.

"No, I don't. I was very disappointed. We stopped production for the day. We've made a lot of improvements since—"

"Your brother-in-law tried to kill the ambassador."

"What? No!"

"Randy Barnes hunted us from Akjoujt to Terjit. There is no mistake."

Micalah stepped forward. "Farook Kassib, an embassy employee, was assisting him and stealing from the ambassador."

"I don't know this man."

"Really?" Ellie stood, placing her hands on the desk in front of her. "Let's drop the façade."

"You can't stop us from completing this farm."

"No, we can't, but we can make sure this will be your last project inside the borders of Mauritania. You'll also need US support to win the bidding for new contracts in any country."

Pigott dropped his head in defeat. "My brother-in-law has ambitions that I don't share. He's hungry for money."

Ellie looked around the room. "We understand that you can't control his actions, but you can help us find him now."

"I'll help you. What do you want me to do?"

Ellie turned her desk phone around to face him. "Call him and find out where he is."

"I'll send him a text," he said, pulling a cell phone from his pocket. "I haven't spoken to him since—in about a week."

Angel waited while he sent the text and then she was on him again. She shoved him into a chair and stood over him, forcing him to look up at her. "Three good men were killed. Tell us everything you know about Barnes's operation."

"Three? No." He shook his head. "I told Randy I didn't want to know." He paused before leaning around her and addressing the ambassador. "I like working in this country. I feel like I'm really helping out."

He seemed to think any sympathy would come from Ellie, so Angel stepped to block his view. "I'm sure the ambassador appreciates your sincerity, but now she wants to hear something solid. Who is Lars?"

She saw recognition in his face at the name and she leaned closer. "Tell us who he is."

He shook his head. "I don't know him, but I've heard Randy and Craig talking about him. He's a horrible person. Not someone I would associate with," he said as he leaned to the side again, trying to bring Ellie back into the conversation.

Angel crossed her arms over her chest as Micalah joined her to block his view of Ellie.

"Did you sponsor Barnes's and Shepherd's work visas?" Micalah asked.

"Yes, but I didn't know they had ulterior motives for being here. As soon as I found out they were doing such horrible things, I fired them."

"What horrible things?" Micalah continued to press him.

"Shooting guns outside the embassy, of course," he said as if she should know.

Angel jumped back in. "Oh, so the smuggling of young girls was okay with you?"

His face paled.

She looked at Micalah. "Guess he didn't know we knew that."

He cleared his throat. "I didn't like it, but it didn't involve me."

"There's some logic for you," Micalah said, shaking her head.

"I mean, I wanted them to stop. Once they linked up with Lars, I blocked all their access to any means of transport through my company. I thought that would stop them."

"Well, it didn't," Ellie said, standing again. "But I think you knew that. Why did you think they were firing guns outside the embassy?"

"They told me they were only trying to distract you, but when I talked with Randy last, he mentioned he was having trouble keeping the crowd in place."

Ellie nodded as if everything made sense now. "I'm finished with this. Sam, please turn Mr. Pigott over to the DSS agents outside the door. They'll keep him company until Barnes returns his text. He can spend his time writing down every known location his brother-in-law might be at."

Angel sank into the chair in front of Ellie's desk and waited until the door closed behind Sam. "So, your pressure to stop the kickbacks on the docks must have been working."

"Yes, I guess so," Ellie answered with a sigh.

"And then Barnes and Shepherd decided to kill you when their distraction plan wasn't working."

"Right," Micalah said, jumping in. "So, a simple distraction plan gone bad?"

"Yes, but not so simple," Ellie answered.

* * *

Angel walked silently beside Micalah, wondering how long it would take her to put her concerns into words.

"I'm not going to lecture you," Micalah finally said, breaking the silence.

"Good. There isn't anything you could say that I haven't already said to myself."

Her phone rang and Stacey's name displayed on her screen. "I need to take this."

Micalah nodded and stepped away, walking to the end of the hallway.

"What did you find?" She listened while Stacey relayed what they had found in the container. "That's awesome. Thank you."

Micalah turned as Angel disconnected the call.

"What is it?" Micalah asked.

"The girls have been rescued, and Flagler has a team in place to pick up whoever comes to meet the container when it arrives in the US."

"That's great. With the information provided by Pigott, catching Barnes shouldn't be a problem either. I'll call you with an update when I get back in the US."

"I'll take good care of her," she said softly. Since Micalah's arrival, she hadn't really had the opportunity to talk privately with Ellie. She didn't need to hear Ellie say Micalah was a good friend. She could see it in Micalah's face and her actions.

Micalah nodded. "Thank you for not making me say it."

She smiled. "Have a safe trip."

She headed back to Ellie's office. It was time for her nightly briefing, and she couldn't wait for a few seconds alone with Ellie.

* * *

Ellie closed the door behind Angel. She had sent Chloe home hours ago. The embassy employees were happy to be able to return to their homes throughout the city.

She willingly fell into Angel's arms and relaxed as they tightened around her. She inhaled the scent that had become a part of her over the last couple of weeks. She wasn't sure where they were going to go after this. No doubt Angel would be sent on a new mission soon.

"Can you stay until Micalah sends word that she's found Barnes?"

"I plan to stay until everyone involved is caught. Even the mysterious Lars."

"And then maybe a little longer?"

"I can."

She pulled back so she could look into Angel's eyes. "Seriously. You'll stay for a while?"

"Vince thinks my team should remain in place for a few more weeks to make sure everyone involved is in the hands of authorities. He wants to make sure you and your staff are safe."

"That's great. Though it will be hard for me to concentrate while you're here."

Angel smiled. "If you can make it until my team leaves, then I'll be on my own time. All restrictions will be removed, and touching will be allowed. Welcomed even."

"You're staying after your team leaves?" Ellie gushed.

"Vince has agreed that I need a couple weeks of vacation."

"He has?"

"He thinks a nice sandy location would be good."

"I know the perfect place."

Bella Books, Inc.

Women. Books. Even Better Together.

P.O. Box 10543
Tallahassee, FL 32302

Phone: 800-729-4992
www.bellabooks.com

CPSIA information can be obtained
at www.ICGtesting.com
Printed in the USA
LVHW042013141219
640521LV00001B/1/P